PAMELA DARLING

one hidden truth

authorHOUSE®

AuthorHouse™
1663 Liberty Drive
Bloomington, IN 47403
www.authorhouse.com
Phone: 1-800-839-8640

Published by AuthorHouse   12/10/2012

ISBN: 978-1-4772-5034-1 (sc)
ISBN: 978-1-4772-5035-8 (e)

acknowledgements

To my dearest Husband Bob, who's never-ending patience and encouragement has been my greatest asset. Also for the many cups of coffee!

To my lovely daughter Suzanne who has shown support and love throughout all I attempt to do.

To the Creative Writing Group who had to suffer my initial attempts to write. And latterly to Caroline and Jo to whom I owe eternal thanks for their continued friendship, support and critiques.

prologue

North England 1901

CAREFUL NOT TO SLIP on the wet cobblestones, Lizzy pulled the hood of her rough black cloak over her head as protection from the incessant soft drizzle.

Low hanging smoky grey clouds separated slightly, as daylight broke through, turning night into day

A sharp gust of wind ripped open her cloak as she entered an alley that divided the back yards of two rows of terraced cottages. Clutching at her cloak with cold-nipped fingers her haste to reach her destination quickened her step.

Another few minutes and she stood outside the back gate of number twenty-seven North Street. Turning the rusty wrought-iron ring handle to lift the latch and putting her shoulder to the gate to give an extra push, it squeakily swung open to reveal a very small concrete yard with a coalbunker occupying one third of the space. She rapped her knuckle on the deep green door in front of her and waited. The window upstairs opened and she looked up.

"The time has come Mrs. McCullen" she called out softly.

The window closed and within seconds the door was opened for her to enter.

Mrs. McCullen, a short woman with little character in her face, pulled Lizzy into the scullery, like a spider catching a fly.

"How long since the birth?" she demanded.

"It's only four hours. Both mother and baby were distraught by the birth and the doctor has not long gone."

"Boy or girl?"

"A boy. Quite a small baby."

"Has he cried for a feed yet?"

"No. He was sleeping when I left."

"Good. Just wait while I get dressed.

The two women hurried through the rain to York House in silence. They encountered no one on the way.

Once in the house Lizzy went back upstairs to her mistress and Mrs. McCullen waited in the tastefully decorated front parlour. Sitting in a small chintz-nursing chair, she mused on the next few months. How fortunate that it should be a boy. It was not as if she could replace the yearning she felt for her lost son, but she would have the satisfaction of breast-feeding the young bairn. Thanks to Doctor McDonald, this was her fourth assignment. He trusted her stoic determination to keep a secret at all costs together with her ability to be a capable wet-nurse.

Biting on her bottom lip, she recalled the separation from her last charge. This baby could not have been more aptly timed and would be balm to the constant wound she carried with her. She knew with certainty the pain would return when the time to hand him over into the sole care of the adoptive mother came. A faint smile touched her lips. She considered herself blessed that she would have the privilege of rearing another child and for that she was grateful.

Wrapped tightly in a white crotchet blanket, Mr. Dalgleish placed the baby into her arms. She averted her eyes from his. It was not often a man would be seen with tear brimmed eyes.

He spoke with difficulty, as if he had a lump in his throat.

"Immediately you arrive at your destination, you are to give the leather wallet wrapped inside the plaid coverlet to the parents. Do you understand?"

"Of course Mr. Dalgleish; you can trust me implicitly."

He carried the small portmanteau filled with necessities for her onward journey and handed it to the driver.

Holding Mrs. McCullen's elbow in his hand he wished her good speed and helped her to climb into the carriage closing the door behind her wanting to keep the cold air away from the baby.

His face showed fresh and prominent frown lines. The driver tipped his hat in response to Mr. Dalgleish's instructions to make haste to his destination, promising that he would be richly rewarded upon his return.

Within minutes, the early morning mist enveloped the horse and carriage as it sped on its way.

Resting his forehead in his right hand he groaned out loud.

"Forgive me Ellen, my sweet dear Ellen. Please God I do not live to rue this day."

chapter 1

Ellen

Northumberland 1901

ELLEN CAST HER TIRED blue eyes towards the small bundle lying by her side. Hitching her soft woollen crochet shawl higher on her shoulders to keep warm, she leant against the feather pillows and closed her eyes. Her mouth moved very slightly as if offering a silent prayer, whilst her chest rose and fell rapidly; her breathing laboured. Abruptly she twisted her weakened body and reached out to pull the blanket gently away from the baby's face to reveal his blotchy red skin, long soft eyelashes resting nearly to his cheeks, his tiny mouth moist from the movement of his tongue and a small knuckle under his chin. With her forefinger, she stroked the fine downy hair that covered his head. With a furrowed brow, the baby stirred and part opened his eyes. Ellen drew her fingertip along the side of his face taking in the warmth and softness of his skin, until she reached the tiny fingers made into a fist that unfurled and gripped her finger.

"God bless you little one," she whispered.

Amazed at the strength in his little fingers she uncurled them gently and took her finger away, "and may He always protect you from the one who has so harmed me and brought shame to his family."

Ellen cautiously turned onto her side in the hope of avoiding the sharp stabbing pain that had plagued her for the past hour. As she turned a flood of hot, sticky blood gushed from her inside. She gasped. Her sharp piercing cry filled the house, as an excruciating pain seared through every fibre of her being. She was plunged into the depths of purgatory.

❧❧❧❧❧❧❧

Low voices, and the sound of drapes being drawn across the windows, welcomed Ellen back into consciousness. The smell and sound of sparks spluttering from the hot coals burning in the fireplace, and the warmth in the air, gave her the courage to move each finger independently under the bedclothes. She was alive! She gained the confidence to run the palms of her hands gently over her body, stroking soft warm skin where the baby had been. Her heart skipped a beat. The baby. Her heart beat faster and her head throbbed. His baby… my bastard baby. Her mind struggled to remember her baby's eyelashes … his grip. Her body felt feverishly hot. She listened. No hushed voices. Reluctant to open her eyes, she stayed still, wishing to float back into unconsciousness. Her mouth was parched and she moaned slightly. She moved a little, the pain kicked in. She gasped.

"Mistress Ellen, are you awake?"

Ellen barely nodded her head. Her voice was hoarse.

"Is that you Lizzy?"

"Yes mistress. God be praised you are back with us. We have all been so worried."

Lizzy fussed with the bed covers, tears trickling onto her cheeks.

"Oh Miss Ellen, you have been so ill. Two days we have prayed for you to live. Your parents have left your side only to take turns to sleep. Your father has been beside himself with grief. I must call him to let him know you are back with us."

She rushed to the heavy door onto the landing, excitedly calling down the stairs.

"Mr Dalgleish … Mr Dalgleish … Miss Ellen is awake."

She hurried back to Ellen, a broad smile emphasising the roundness of her face and deepening the fine creases around her light blue eyes. Smoothing her white starched apron over a rather rotund stomach, she very quietly told Ellen.

"Your Ma and Pa … so great has been their distress Miss Ellen … they have sent Robert to relatives in the South of England and John to your uncle Richard in Scotland to avoid any distractions.

Tears slowly escaped and trickled onto Ellen's pale cheeks, down her neck and into the pillow that supported her head. She drew the sleeve of her nightdress across her misty eyes and turned towards the empty space where her son had lain. She clasped the hand of her trusted friend.

"Oh Lizzy he was so small," she murmured.

Hearing footsteps outside her room, she swallowed back further tears and breathed in deeply.

Catherine Dalgleish cautiously entered the warm, dimly lit room and seemed to glide across the room towards her daughter.

"Ellen my dear child … my sweet, sweet child."

She dabbed at her eyes with a lace edged handkerchief, took hold of Ellen's hand and searched the pale, tired face that looked up at her.

"Are you warm enough child? Lizzy build the fire up a little more."

Anxiously she waited for Ellen to speak.

From the doorway, Robert Dalgleish observed his wife's attempt to empathise with their daughter, but as usual, she lacked the warmth he would expect a mother to have for her daughter. When did she become this way he thought. Was it only since Ellen had blossomed into a young woman? He felt sickened by his thought that it could be jealousy. He comforted himself with the knowledge she was the same with him. Did she ever love me he wondered?

He recalled a time when she had confided in him that it was her parents' belief that a woman did not have to love a man to be a faithful wife and lover. Is that exactly how she has been with me? I cannot fault her, as a wife and lover, so why then are we not happy.

He walked to the other side of the bed, bent over and kissed his daughter's cheek. Tasting salt upon his lips, he caressed a lock of the tousled chestnut coloured hair that had fallen upon her forehead. He smiled affectionately at her.

"I know it's painful at the moment, but you will get better."

He paused and looked across at Catherine.

"If your mother would like to spend time with you when the weather improves, you could both take a long vacation to America. You could spend your eighteenth birthday with your cousins. What do you say to that?"

Catherine clapped her hands in glee.

"Ellen, how wonderful, we will enjoy ourselves so much. Your Papa is so kind and thoughtful. You must do everything Doctor Carr recommends to fully recover and then we can go shopping and plan our trip ... you will love New York" she gushed.

With great difficulty, Ellen attempted to sit up while Lizzy plumped the pillows to give her more support. Gratefully accepting the glass of water handed to her by her father, she took small sips to give time for thought.

Jumbled, hurt, and tormented thoughts crowded into her head. I suppose this is what they want me to do. To go away ... forget what has happened ... my baby and I will be dismissed from their minds! Upon our return Mama will enthusiastically tell all her friends what a wonderful vacation it was ... act all sentimental because we have the perfect relationship and then proceed to get back to her normal social life in the knowledge that no shame will lay at the family's door and no questions asked.

Catherine stood waiting for her daughter's acceptance of the plan; although etched upon her porcelain doll-like face were the signs of impatience. Taking Ellen's hand in hers, she looked beseechingly into her daughter's listless eyes.

"I'm only doing what I think will be best for you my dear."

Ellen smiled weakly and complacently nodded in agreement. In a last feeble attempt to change her mother's mind, she asked.

"I know you are Mama, but what about Robert and John?"

Her parents shared a conspiratorial look and Catherine light-heartedly continued.

"No problem, your brothers can stay with Uncle Jack and Aunt Millie. Your Papa will be busy with his work, but he is going to start training them very soon. It is time for them to be fully acquainted with how the family business works."

Nodding in assent Robert Dalgleish reassured Ellen that this was true.

"They've got to learn to be responsible men. Working will give them a purpose and keep them out of mischief. I have been far too lenient and your Mama has pampered them for longer than is healthy for boys of their ages." Almost as an after-thought he added "Working amongst the Dockers for a while will give them good grounding for the future."

Catherine stared agog. "No … Robert … I thought they would work in the offices. It will be horrible for them," she protested strongly.

"I'm not arguing my dear. They need lessons in life, most especially Robert, and that is what I intend will happen."

He kissed Ellen on the forehead before walking from the room whilst his wife threw him a disdainful look and turned her head away from him.

Once on their own Catherine pursed her lips and shook her head.

"There are times when I despair of your father ever understanding your brothers. Do not worry I will talk with him when he is in a better mood … all will be well Ellen. You need plenty of rest. Soon we will return home and be out of this place, you will be back in your familiar surroundings, and this awful time will be eradicated forever. Just you wait and see."

"Do you think so Mama? It will only be a holiday if we go to New York? I'm not being sent away am I?"

Hardly able to keep her eyes open she struggled to hear her mother's voice as sleep reclaimed her body and mind.

chapter 2

Kate and Bill - One Year Later

THE INFANT'S GURGLES AND squeals of delight greeted Bill Smith when he returned home from his final Saturday morning's gruelling work at the Tyneside Docks. Tired, together with mixed emotions, he threw his well-worn overcoat and cloth cap over the newel post at the bottom of the stairs. He used the toecap of his right dusty boot and pushed on the heel of his left boot until his foot had worked itself free. Seated on the second tread he tugged the other boot off and then tossed both under the stairwell.

He remained on the stairs, elbows on his knees, staring at a hole in his sock. Deep in thought about the enormity of the changes ahead, he suddenly became overwhelmed with worry. He had always seen himself as an ordinary working man, with no high expectations from life. To bring home a weekly pay packet was sufficient for Bill Smith. Hard work and an honest day's work for an honest day's wage was his philosophy. Thankfully, his wife harboured ambitions for him. It was she who encouraged and supported all his endeavours whether it was making a cradle for the baby or doing a good days work in the shipyard.

Remembering that fateful moment when he had walked into

the office of his employer Mr Dalgleish, for whom he had enormous respect, he could still feel how ill at ease he was. It was most unusual to be called to the office. Mr Dalgleish motioned for him to sit down on the chair in front of his desk, which again was unusual. His first thought was every man's greatest fear. Unemployment. A cloud of resentment settled upon his shoulders as he waited for the unfair dreaded words. He willed himself to listen properly as the man's words gradually infiltrated his mind. Were they words of praise that reached his ears? The boss was telling him that his foremanship and manner with the men was a commendable asset. A new job was on offer; supervising the building of Simon's Town Dock and with it came a home and an excellent wage.

Mr Dalgleish understood it was a big decision to make; even so, he wanted an answer within the next few days.

Dazed and full of questions, such as how could good fortune of this kind have come his way, he spent the remainder of the day in shock. North Shields was his birthplace and the thought of living thousands of miles away sent shivers down his spine. Full of tremulous excitement he willed himself not to run home that evening. Kate would be proud of him, he knew that much, but he was unable to imagine how she would react. It would have to be the right thing for both of them of that he was certain.

It was not often that Bill rendered his wife speechless. He almost laughed as she stood waiting, her mouth in an O shape, for him to tell her it was a ruse. Realising nothing more was to follow, her immediate response of "We can't … what about my sisters?" Then, little by little, she found reasons for why it could be good to go. They talked into the early hours without reaching a definite decision. Curled into each other like spoons, they waited for sleep to come. Bill hoped that Kate would make the decision for them by morning. Bill was not known for his willingness to be decisive although a kinder man would be hard to find. Whereas Kate made decisions, once deliberated on, with absolute conviction.

Now here he was the passage papers in his hands. They were to board the next Union Castle Vessel that sailed in to the Cape of Good Hope. Three more days and they would be off. Sheer disbelief descended over him, his heartbeat quickened causing him to breath in deeply several times to keep calm. He stood up and with the palms of his hands smoothed his thick dark hair off his face. Three strides took him to the doorway of a small dingy back room. He listened to the happy voices of Kate and John and was inwardly able to relax before entering.

Both mother and child welcomed him with big smiles. His son's was a toothless one with dribble running down his chin, his wife's face animated, with the pleasure she gained at the sight of him. Returning their smiles, he came fully into the room. Kate jumped up, John in her arms and thrust the child into his.

"Here you take him for a moment while I get your dinner out of the oven."

She kissed him fully on his lips enjoying the feel of his neatly trimmed moustache on her mouth.

"Ooh I love you Bill Smith," she said gleefully before she turned to leave the room.

"Wait a moment Kate, take a look at this."

Bill pulled her back by the arm and placed the Passage papers in her hand.

"Oh my it's really happening." Kate's voice squealed completely out of character for her.

"Ay it is, and it's too late to change our minds."

Throwing John into the air, and repeating the words to his son, he caught the little lad in his large firm hands and laughed at the child's obvious excitement that he was going to play games with him.

"Now Bill don't over-excite him or he'll never settle down for his afternoon sleep. I promised Mrs. McCullen I would keep his routine."

With a mock grimace on his face and throwing the delighted child back in the air he guffawed.

"Oh my goodness, we mustn't break Mrs. McCullen's routine must we John?"

"You'll make him as daft as you Bill Smith."

With her nose in the air she went into the scullery, returning within minutes with a large over-filled plate of potatoes, meat swimming in thick gravy, and dumplings. She placed it on the ready prepared table for him.

"Be fair Bill, she probably had a point and she always meant well. Now give him here and I'll put him down for an hour. Everyone will want to see him later and I don't want him grisly and bad-tempered."

Stubbornly John hung on to his father's collar, while Kate urged him to let go. Bill laughed and physically prized the tiny fingers from his shirt.

"There little fella you go with your Mama while your Da has his dinner."

Frowning Kate gave him a stern look.

"Bill you must stop this Da thing. You're making it harder for him to get used to Mama and Papa."

"I know, I know. Sorry. I might find it easier once we're away from here. I feel a right ass if my mates are about."

Nodding Kate left him to his dinner. She knew it was out of Bill's comfort zone although she was having no problem with it at all. Secretly she found it rather agreeable.

Kate looked at the mantel clock. She pushed away a stray hair that was irritating her, and now left a flour smudge on her forehead. She had worked in haste to finish the baking before John woke up. Already Kate was missing the reliability of Mrs. McCullen's assistance with the care of the toddler. She was worried he would wake and become demanding before her chores were finished. Mrs. McCullen might have been dominating and sometimes frustrating, but she did have her good points. Kate had been looking forward to this day when she could finally be free to have the sole care of John. She recalled the tears in Mrs. McCullen's eyes as she had kissed him goodbye. She had genuinely loved the baby and Kate's compassion for the woman was obvious. Kate understood the pain of separation. She shuddered at the thought it.

Come on, she told herself, get a move on, the family will be here before I know where I am, and me not even tidied up yet.

Removing another baking tray of sausage rolls from the oven, and well pleased with the results, she rubbed the flour from her hands onto her apron. The family relied on a good spread when they came for tea or supper and she always lived up to their expectations. Small beads of perspiration stood out on her forehead and her armpits had become moist. The room hot from the range seemed overbearing. She supposed from her conversations with other women that it was possible her change, as they called it, had arrived. Whatever, she was most uncomfortable with it. She cleared the scullery of pots and pans and then hurriedly had a quick strip wash.

With a clean dress on, her hair brushed into a loose bun in the nape of her neck, a little lipstick applied to her full lips, she quickly returned to her familiar cool and controlled image. By the time she took John from his cot, she was calm and ready to give him her full attention. Smiling down at him, his podgy arms excitedly flaying, a wide smile on his face, he happily waited for Kate to lift him. She playfully clapped her hands "Who's a good boy then". Kate glowed with happiness.

※※※※※※※※

Kate's three younger sisters were the first to arrive around six o'clock that evening. The thrill of seeing their sister showed in their wide sparkling eyes and smiles. Holding her arms wide to embrace each of them in turn, they exchanged kisses. She had been like a mother to them since the eldest turned thirteen and the other two only eight and nine years old. Both parents had died from consumption leaving Kate and her sisters to fend for themselves. She and Amelia were working in the laundry at the time, the two younger girls, Jane and Violet, were still of school age, and Kate insisted they should have the same benefits as she and Amelia, and ensured they continued to go to school. She kept house and cooked dinner each evening when she finished work while Amelia darned and mended the little clothing they had. As far as Kate was concerned, the reward was to keep the family together and daily prayer had improved her resolve to keep her promise.

Now nearly twenty years on they all had their own families. Kate was the only one not able to have a child of her own and this had been a great sadness to them all.

"No men?" Kate enquired curiously.

"Don't worry they'll be along later with the offspring. We insisted we have a clear hour with you and John if this is to be our last visit, before you leave us," Amelia piped up trying to keep a cheerful note to her voice, when indeed she was feeling the opposite. It was unbearable to consider that Kate would not be a ten-minute walk away after next week.

Their rapid chatter came to a halt. Rudely interrupted by a loud wail, all heads turned towards John, exactly as he intended. He had quickly learned that this sound commanded immediate and pleasant attention, particularly from women; something his tiny mind could not imagine would ever stop working. His three aunties responded accordingly and with delighted smiles and eager arms to hold him, proved his theory correct. He was in his element.

Looking on, Kate tutted at her sisters although the smile on her face gave no indication of disapproval whatsoever. She was more than grateful for the wonderful blessing of having such an adorable child in her care. Without any warning, the thought that this might be the last time she would witness such a scene brought a lump to her throat. What would life be like without her sisters? Unable to bear the thought she busied herself, made a pot of tea, blinked back the threat of a teardrop and turned her attention to the fact that Bill was still not home.

Her hope that he and his brothers would refrain from spending time in the local was beginning to wane. Her sisters could depend on their husbands. She hid her disappointment in Bill extremely well.

※※※※※※※※

It was eight o'clock before he and his three older brothers and their wives fell through the front door. Putting on a brave smile Kate greeted them into her home with as much cordiality as she could muster up. Her cheeks had coloured with shame, knowing that the neighbours would have heard their raucous laughter, and would be talking about them. She bitterly disapproved of this type of behaviour and could feel the anger well up inside her. Bill had let her down again! She had seen drink turn Bill's brothers and their friends into absolute ruffians at times and she could not, and would not, accept it from Bill. Being the perfect hostess, she tolerated the bitter smell of beer on their breath and the affectionate, but coarse jokes they were cracking. She offered the freshly baked bread and sausage rolls to her guests in the hope it would soak some of the drink up. They ate with gusto, complimenting her on being the best of cooks, and as much as she tried to stay angry, she found it near on impossible as they sincerely talked about how much they were going to miss their little brother, Kate and the baby. Bill grinned ruefully at her, across the tops of their heads from the other side of the room, hoping that she would understand how very difficult it was for him to refuse the extra few beers without upsetting his brothers. He was not oblivious to the restraint she had needed to exercise over her feelings of frustration. He knew the difference between her naturally wide smile and the tight smile they had received when she first greeted them.

Closing the front door quietly behind her sisters, Kate leaned her back against it and listened to the noise coming from the front room. She was tired. Wearily she climbed the stairs to check on John, who amazingly stayed asleep throughout the evening despite the rumpus downstairs. John stirred slightly as she pulled the blankets up around his shoulders and kissed his forehead. At least life won't change that much for this little chap, she thought, as she closed the door on him. Everything in life is new for him and he will be away from all the soot and grime of this place. Her mood lightened as she pictured their new home with a garden where John could play and the air would be clean; yes, all would be well once they settled in Simon's Town.

※ ※ ※ ※ ※ ※ ※ ※

When Bill closed the front door on his brothers, it was well after midnight. His head ached from drinking and smoking and he was looking forward to his bed. With a heavy step, he climbed the stairs.

He guessed Kate had gone to bed some time ago. He had a hazy memory of her saying goodnight and was not surprised to see the bedroom door closed. For the sake of a quiet life, he would sleep in the room Mrs. McCullen had just vacated. Life for Bill had been quite different since the arrival of John, especially when it came to those times when he so wanted to make love to Kate. She had pushed him away saying not while there was someone else in the house.

He crept into the other bedroom hoping their intimacy would return once they reached South Africa and had a home to themselves once again.

chapter 3

Kate

2 Wharf Street,
Simon's Town
South Africa
21st February 1906

My Dearest Amelia,

It does so comfort me to receive your letters, which I read over and over. Knowing about life in North Shields, and to know that my three sisters and their families are healthy is such a comfort. The employment situation there sounds awful. Thank the Good Lord that your men are still getting work.

My life here continues much as it has from the time that we first arrived nearly four years ago. I still find the heat quite exhausting at times and appreciate living so close to the water, where at least gentle breezes from the ocean act as a fan. I still wrinkle my nose up when they bring in the catch of tuna fish. It is such a strong smell. Much stronger than the fish we bring in at home. However, tuna makes a good healthy meal and is very tasty.

Never did I believe I could miss a dull, cold, drizzly day in North Shields, and yet I find myself yearning to be back with you and huddled *around the range, the kettle boiling and the drop scones ready to come out of the oven. It seems such an age since we shared laughter and long chats. There, now I am feeling melancholy, I must move on to other things dear sister before my salty tears drop and smudge my writing.*

You will be glad to hear that Bill has deservedly earned the respect of all his fellow workers. There never was a man as intent as my Bill for getting a job done well and on time. He has a way with other men. They put everything they have into getting the job done to his specifications. He very rarely has to dive these days and although that eases the worry for me, I do believe he misses the adventure of going down. The changes are many at the dock, and it is far busier than we had ever imagined when we first came here I realise I have omitted to tell you that one of his closest friends died whilst on a dive last week, and I am certain he is harbouring feelings of guilt as he has been extra quiet these last few days. To be honest if he had still been on the diving team it could well have been he that met his end. I cannot bear to contemplate such a thing so I am going to leave it at that.

It is exciting to watch the steamers come into dock with their crew and deckhands. They are so capable and strong, carrying out their duties, providing a welcome sight for us women. You may laugh Amelia, but there is very little other distraction. Our own men tease us, but it is a conversation piece that entertains us and is harmless.

There is a great deal more work for the local men, mainly in the storehouses, which means many of the families have benefitted from the expansion. As I have said in previous letters, many of the workers are Malays. They are fond of singing their own characteristic songs and can be heard singing at some part of the day, every day of the week. I find the sounds rather pleasant and have grown used to it now. The Malay cricketers beat the Royal Navy team last week, which for the Navy is unthinkable, so you can see they are making their mark.

Bill and his gang still have much construction work to carry out and he is expecting more work will come his way once the present contract comes to an end, so in answer to your question we will not be coming home for months, possibly years. Bill has settled far more than I have. He enjoys the climate and the people, and sees this country as his home now. I appreciate the beauty of the place, and it is a very pleasant way of life, but it can never be home for me. We are happy enough, but I miss England and my dear family.

Now I am becoming melancholy again. How different it would be if you could be here with us.

Our community is growing fast. When we first arrived, John was one of the only children and now he is one of thirty! Of course, most of the women are younger and all happily nest making. Like myself, most of them have adapted to this way of life and overall we enjoy each other's company. We have one spoke in the wheel, and that is Mary O'Leary. I mentioned her previously to you. Do you remember? She is loud and has some arrogant ways. She truly lowers the tone of the place with her 'goings on'. Honestly, she has three young sons, who she allows to run riot, and often if you please without any clothes on! Can you believe that? There is a rumour that she is once again pregnant so there will be yet another O'Leary. That will be four within five years. I cannot really blame the children for their behaviour with such a mother. I was told that she often accompanies her husband to the clubhouse and can drink as much as any man. She amuses the men, and of course, they encourage her to sing, if that is what you can call it, together with her fancy dancing. Bill says very little to me when he has seen her there, but then he knows I find it distasteful. Apparently, she has suggested that the women have a clubhouse where they can enjoy a night out. I cannot imagine why women would want such a place to go to can you.

Now let me tell you about John. In the past few months, he has grown rapidly and is tall for his age. His eyes are bluer than ever, and it looks as if he has a halo where the sun has bleached his deep chestnut hair. He has a kind and happy nature and still captures the heart of every woman here with the flutter of eyelashes and his appealing smile. He really is a tinker. When Bill is at home, he constantly wants to copy everything he does. His curiosity is sometimes very testing, but he learns quickly and Bill enjoys teaching him how to do woodwork, together with other practical skills. As you can imagine Bill is convinced John will follow his example and work in the docks. For my part, I want to see John go a lot further and am pleased to let you know that I have been able to get him into St. Joseph's School. The money will be *well spent and is exactly what it was meant for. Bill says it won't make a man of him, but I am adamant this is as it should be when it comes to education; I insist we keep our promise.*

We have a new house girl, her name is Latifa, and John absolutely adores her and she him. If Bill is at work, he follows her around like a puppy. She is a good girl and does her work well. She does not know her exact age, but at a guess, I would say sixteen. She sees her family every Saturday afternoon. Some of the families here only give their servants one afternoon a month to be with their families but I think that is mean and cruel. The girls are very young, some as young as thirteen. Latifa is the eldest child of six and her mother is expecting her seventh any day now. Her family, like so many black people, are poor, and yet they always have smiling eyes and mouths. It is good to send her home with cakes for her brothers and sisters. I know this is a big treat for them and it seems such a small thing to do.

We are tanned from the sun now. I know it does my skin no favours. Bill and I are looking older because of it. I rub olive oil into my skin to keep it supple, which is the best I can do. I read somewhere that all sorts of skin preparations are now sold in the big Department Store in Newcastle. How I yearn for one of our trips to Newcastle Amelia. We did so enjoy them did we not? Have you been there recently?

Only yesterday, I heard a rumour via one of the new families who arrived a week ago, that Mr Dalgleish is selling the Tyneside Shipyard. Do you know if this is true? Since coming here, he rarely communicates with Bill directly, although the payments never fail to reach the bank account for John's upkeep. I have kept my word and forwarded several photographs of John to the address provided and unless I hear, to the contrary I will continue to do so once each year. I am still undecided about how and if we should tell our darling John that we adopted him. It is a dilemma for us you know. Without the inheritance, there would be no need for any such worry. I go along with the saying that silence is golden.

This afternoon I am entertaining the wives of our Foremen in the English style garden we have worked on over the past year. It is not easy ground and only certain plants will grow well at the foot of the mountains, but I am happy with the result. From the veranda, I can watch John play on the swing and the climbing frame that Bill made and surrounded with a good amount of sand to make it safer should he fall. Luckily, it has not blocked my view of the lawn, which is surrounded by an abundance of flowers and bushes. Beyond our boundary fencing, we have a superb panorama of the bluest sea that sparkles and glitters in the distance. I wish you could see it Amelia I know you would fall in love with it as I have done.

I am worried to hear from my friend Martha that there is supposedly a young woman in the town with smallpox. Fortunately, she is in quarantine, but should there be an outbreak of the disease we could well face an epidemic. With all the comings and goings in the dock, disease spreads quickly and easily. Nothing could be worse especially in this heat. We will pray that God is watching over us and protect us from it. I am sure one of the women will have further news by the time we start the garden party, they usually do. The men will join us when they get back from the club, hungry and in high spirits. I no longer have high expectations of Bill. Once a drinker always a drinker. I suppose I should be thankful that he does not lose control of his senses as some of them do. I will say this Amelia, I will do my damndest to keep John away from the demon drink if it is the last thing that I do!

I wonder how long it will be before this letter reaches you my dear sister. I wait with longing and eager anticipation for your letters. To have news from home is so precious. Your last letter to me only took six weeks to arrive. I will ask the lamplighter to take this letter to the Post Office for me, and hopefully, it will be on its way to you very soon. He is more than happy to earn an extra penny.

I must end this letter. John is waiting for his lunch and there is much to do before my guests arrive. On the other hand, I am loathe putting my pen down because I so often seal the envelope then remember I have forgotten to include something I had intended to write about.

Can you believe it; I have just thought; I meant to tell you that John has a very cute girlfriend, for whom he declares undying love! Her name is Alice and she is his constant companion now. It is fun for me to have a little girl around the house and I enjoy taking the two of them to the beach. She, like John, is an only child. I smile as I watch them. John is so attentive to her, a proper little gentleman. This is fine while they are both only five years old, I am not so sure if I will feel the same in ten years' time!

I really must go.

With fondest love always from your sister,
Kate

chapter 4

John

Simon's Town — South Africa 1919

IMAGINING A COUNTRY HIS parents called home was beyond his comprehension. He had heard stories about North Shields throughout his life and that is all they had ever been; stories. England sounded cold and hostile. When they arrived there in February, it was likely to be icy cold. There could even be snow. The whole idea of ice, snow and bitter cold was inconceivable.

He stood outside the only home he had lived in since the age of one, on the sun-bleached wooden veranda. He gazed reflectively at the garden he had played in as a young child, and where he had watched his mother put years of loving work into, creating what she called her English garden. A gust of wind swept through those lovingly planted shrubs as if to test their endurance to survive a little violence from time to time, and just as quickly quietened and returned to a breeze. He eyed the three large battered cabin trunks, stamped up with Southampton, England, standing close by the steps to the veranda. A desire to destroy them by kicking them until they were unrecognisable pulsed furiously through his tall lean body. Abruptly leaping over the veranda, and to escape his chaotic emotions, John made off for the harbour.

Memories of the night before refused to leave his mind. Ranting, he had angrily accused his parents of cruelty; that they did not care about his feelings otherwise, they would stay in Simon's Town. He hated recalling the hurt look in their eyes when he told them he hated them. Tears sprung to his eyes. Brushing them away he refused to feel guilty why should he. Unasked questions continued relentlessly to fill his head. Why had they not told him a lot earlier that they would like to go back to England? Unconvinced that the reasons they gave for their decision were genuine, he kicked violently at loose stones as though they were the problem.

He had not noticed that Papa was unwell, and Mama was always worrying about her sisters. So what was different?

He unbuttoned his light linen shirt and exposed his manly chest to the soft warm balmy breeze in the hope it would cool him slightly. The thought that this wonderful way of life was soon not to be his any longer was unbelievable. He walked without purpose until his breathing calmed. He slowed his pace and looked across to the ocean. The view quickened the blood in his veins and the muscles in his body relaxed. He might have no choice about leaving this place right now, but no one could stop him coming back when he reached twenty-one. Yes, he would return and that would shock them.

This decision made he turned into the familiar well-trodden leafy pathway, his solace throughout his adolescence. Protecting his head from low reaching tree branches, he continued on his way with certainty. All I have to do is sort my mind out, and who better to do that with than Alice, he thought.

Emerging from the shady path into the mid-day sun, John cupped his hand over his eyes until he could re-adjust his vision. Shimmering reflections of the sun bounced off the water's surface and the powder blue sky merged, leaving no sign of the two being separate. John sat on the sparse dry grass, his arms hugging his shins and his eyes obsessively observing the scene to retain it as an indelible imprint in his head. A single tear rolled down his young face. Not to have this place to run to ever again… I hate England … I hate the whole world … I hate Ma and Pa.

🦋🦋🦋🦋🦋🦋🦋🦋

His thirst awakened him to his surroundings. With no disturbances, he had remained motionless for more than an hour. Having considered his situation repeatedly, he concluded he would have to ask questions. Please or offend, he thought, I should be told the truth.

He lit a cigarette, exhaled deeply, and made his way to see Alice. Alice is genuine, a real diamond. I'm going to miss her, I'm already missing her just thinking it. She's been my best girl friend. She always understands. I wonder how she feels about me going away. Will she miss me? He hastened his step. His temples throbbed and his heart beat fast. Only Alice could help him to go because he would ask her to wait for him to come back.

His mood lightened and he threw the cigarette butt down, grinding it deep into the ground.

🦋🦋🦋🦋🦋🦋🦋🦋

Alice snuggled into his smooth chest, noticing some fine hairs had begun to grow and teasingly stroked them. "I love you Johnny. "She murmured.

Hidden by the tall plant life around them they caressed and kissed in the way only virgins can.

Fully aroused John burrowed his face into her fine silky brown hair. "I love you too Alice and I can't bear the thought of not seeing you until I am old enough to return."

"Will you come back Johnny? It's a long way to travel."

"Alice I promise you I will be back. I want you to wait for me. Will you do that for me?"

Kissing her ears and then her neck with soft moist lips, he felt her body mould into his. His hand crept under her skirt. Alice stiffened. "No" she whispered.

Gazing into her warm brown eyes and caressing her face and lips with the lightest touch of his finger, he whispered "I adore you Alice, you know that don't you?"

She nodded, taking his hand and kissing it ardently. "I'm going to miss you so much ... you will come back when you can, won't you? ... We could write," she murmured.

"Of course we can ... but you will meet and fall in love with another. Then you will forget me my dearest Alice."

"No, never" Alice protested passionately. "I have always loved you, since I was a little girl ... I idolised you from the beginning."

Tenderly he kissed her lips. "I hate the thought of going away as much as you do Alice. It will be a long time before I can forgive my parents for this."

"Oh don't say that Johnny ... there is nothing for them to stay for now. While your Papa was working, he had a reason to be here. And you said yourself that he has been under the weather since his last injury. You should try and understand them a little more." She ran her fingers through his thick wavy hair and turned his face toward hers. "I'm hoping my parents will want to leave soon. How good would that be? Can you imagine it, both of us in England; it would be as though nothing had separated us."

John leaned on one elbow and kissed her nose. "It's not just that Alice ... it's something else ... I haven't got my head round it yet ... but I've discovered something that I wish I never had."

Her large eyes opened wider. "What?"

"You promise to tell no one Alice?"

"Of course, you know you can trust me"

"I was being particularly awkward last night when I was told to help with some packing ... and ... I accidently knocked against a pile of papers that spilled to the floor. I kicked them with my toe causing them to separate ... went down on my knees to pick them up ... and ...and ... found my Birth Certificate was among them. Of course, I looked at it and for the first time saw my name in full ... and then read that I was born in Morpeth and not North Shields. It didn't have my mother's name on it ... instead it had someone called Ellen Dalgleish."

Alice waited in silence for him to continue, but took hold of his hand to show she cared.

"I was awful Alice. I demanded to know what it meant. My Mama stood with her hands over her mouth and Papa told me to calm down. I was beside myself with anger Alice … I wouldn't listen … then … I could hardly believe my ears … Papa was shouting at me to stop it … he was furious with me … he has never shouted like that at me in my life … he said they would explain when I calmed down."

Putting her arm around his shoulder Alice said softly "Poor you. What happened then?"

Their eyes met in mutual disquiet. "They told me they had adopted me, when I was only two days old." John's voice faltered "Alice I never knew … I never guessed … I can only say I feel stripped of everything I ever believed about myself. My family isn't really my family. I feel empty."

Alice laid her head on his shoulder not knowing how to help him.

"Did your Papa tell you how it all came about? Did he have any information about your natural mother?"

"I felt so sick; I told them I didn't want to hear anything else. Alice, I was in shock … I said I hated them … that I wished I'd never been born … I was infuriated that my Mama was crying … oh Alice I pushed her off me and walked out."

Attuned to the other they responded to the delicate situation they shared by lying close to each other like babes in the woods. The warm breeze fluttered through the tall grasses, and leaves on the trees. The silence, interrupted by songs of birds in the distance, was all they were conscious of around them. As if in a dreamlike state, they caressed and stroked each other's soft smooth young flesh with new sensations entering parts of their bodies they had never dreamed existed. They breathed short excited breaths, desiring more; yearning for the passion they felt, to be consummated. He penetrated her pulsating, eager and willing softness, and without instruction, they moved in perfect harmony, enjoying mutual joy and gratification.

Their bodies locked together, and hearts beating as one, their heightened hunger lessened. A sense of peace and contentment entered into their satiated newly discovered bodies.

After many whispered soft endearments and promises of marriage and true love forever, John carefully moved away from her. His movements were slow and tender "I will be back for you Alice, you know I will."

"I wish I could come with you." She sighed forlornly. "You must try and talk to your parents more … let them explain so that you can understand."

"Maybe." John lit a cigarette and inhaled deeply. "Whatever is said it won't change anything now will it? No one else knows about it, except you now of course, and … well what the hell let's just forget about it."

"If that's what you want Johnny, but remember I care and if you change your mind …." Saddened by the thought that her offer was no longer possible after today she finished "you could always write about it in your letters to me." She smiled weakly, her eyes brimming with tears.

"I guess I could, but I've already decided to forget about it. If a woman somewhere did not want to keep the baby she gave birth to then all I have to say is, I would prefer the story stays unknown. Can you imagine doing such a thing Alice? How can any woman give away her own child? No I would never want to know about her," he said defiantly.

Meekly Alice agreed, although she secretly hoped he would think about it more when he recovered from the shock.

They delayed their parting for as long as was possible, holding on tightly to each other as they stood watching the ocean. When they let go they agreed both should walk away, neither watching the other disappear. Alice turned to wave, hoping John would do the same. Tears streamed down her cheeks. John had his back to her as he strode doggedly on his way. She never knew he also cried.

chapter 5

The Journey Back to England

ANOTHER SWELL, ANOTHER BREAKER, covered the ship's decks as it surged through the angry ocean. Heaving and wrenching John groaned from the pain of an empty stomach and strained muscles. He staggered unsteadily to the edge of the port side, gulping at the salty air, his lips and face dry from the salt in the gale force wind. Rubbing both his arms roughly against the cold wind that whipped into his damp clothing and through to his bones, he looked into the grey, turning to black, clouds that surrounded the ship. Not a glimpse of light could be seen through their denseness causing him to tremble.

He leaned against the ship's rail and closed his eyes. This was awful. The agony of his stretched throat, stomach muscles and painful ribs completely consumed his thoughts. He prayed for this dreadful affliction to pass and wondered how much more he could bear before he could join his parents in their cabin to see how they were faring. Feeling ill, they had retired two days previously. Startled out of his thoughts he felt himself blown further along the rail by the force of an extra-large wave pounding against the ship's side. Freezing seawater drenched him through. Pushing his hair off his face, he turned blindly staggering to the stairs leading down to the main deck. The heavy entrance door resisted his strength to open; he forced his weight against it, and pushed repeatedly until it yielded, whereupon he lurched forward into the large seating area where the warmth and odour of passengers crowded together and the stench of rancid vomit filled the room.

Trying to compose himself, he covered his nose and mouth with his hands to alleviate his gagging. He gradually steadied his stumbling gait until once again the sea pounded the ship and promptly propelled him into the nearest empty chair. Abashed, he apologised profusely to the young man sitting to his left for his abrupt and ungainly landing.

"No worries – just glad we're still living" the man jested. The effort of his humour brought about a racking cough that violently shook his body. He covered his mouth with the palms of his hands and spluttered.

"At least we can move about, not like the poor sods below confined to their cabins," he continued.

Wearily John nodded as he settled into his seat, realising he had almost forgotten the agonies his parents were going through. The new wave of sickness he felt was not seasickness, but guilt. He could have managed to get to the cabin. He knew how distressed they were when he left them. Instead, he had continued with his hostile behaviour. Petulance was so childish. He immediately resolved to go down and apologise as soon as he felt stronger.

As he looked around, he noticed it was mostly young people of a similar age to himself and presumed they also had parents suffering from seasickness.

Little Molly O'Leary was hugging her youngest baby brother, while her twin sisters slept with their heads leaning against each other, thumbs in their mouths, at the hem of her dress. He felt a momentary pang of pity for her. At least he had no worry about dependent siblings.

He tried to remember how many siblings she had, at least six to his knowledge. He wished he had listened more carefully to his mother's ruminations. Molly had been a pupil at the free school;

that much he did know, so their paths had rarely crossed. Unable to suppress a grin, he thought of the pleasure her mother had given the other women when she spoke of Molly's mother's capers. He had never understood their disdain. She sounded good fun from what he had heard. His father had intimated that the more the other women scorned her the more outrageous her behaviour became. It occurred to John that Mr and Mrs. O'Leary were quite infamous in their own way, but then he supposed all families had their little idiosyncrasies'.

Again, the ship pitched ferociously, hurling those on the port side to the floor. Doors slammed and banged. Tables and chairs crashed onto their sides flinging loose objects in all directions. From where he sat John could see that, somehow, Molly had saved the children from being crushed. She was whimpering with pain as she begged a large man who had fallen onto her arm, to try to move off her. John automatically staggered to her aid. The man was unconscious, his head bleeding profusely. Without further thought, John dragged the man's body off Molly's arm, causing her more pain. With the man laid to one side, he was relieved that her cries of anguish abated.

Kneeling by her side, he noted the angle of her arm and his stomach turned. Beads of sweat glistened on her brow and her face had a greyish tinge. Lifting her shoulders, he cradled her head in his arms and whispered, "Are you alright?"

With effort, she nodded slightly and fretfully murmured, "the baby ... where is the baby?"

Amazed to see that the baby was indeed fine he assured her not to worry. The twins, both badly shaken, had the baby cradled between them in their laps. He smiled kindly "Well done girls ... good catch." They grinned with shy delight.

He looked back at Molly. "He is fine, but your arm is in an awkward position. I think you will need the doctor."

Still supporting her shoulders, he attempted to make her more comfortable. Molly shook her head. "No ... leave it ...I'll manage," she said trying to pull herself out of his hold. She immediately drew back gasping and biting her lip to stop screaming as a stabbing pain shoot through her.

John scanned the chaos around him in the hope he might see someone who could give Molly some help. All he saw was children and adults alike trying to comfort each other. Members of the crew were doing their best to bring help and calm. They managed to seat those who were unharmed and called instructions to others where it was required.

The knot in John's stomach tightened and his head was pounding. Under his breath, he cursed the damned weather and the misery it was creating for the crew and passengers. As a boy, he had listened with eager anticipation to many a seaman's stories of adventures at sea, of storms and wrecks, but he could not recall admissions of seasickness, bedlam and terror. He fought back his rising panic wondering what was in front of all of them.

Molly whimpered, her pain obviously heightened by the uncomfortable position she was lying in. Feeling impotent John turned his attention back to her.

"Stay still Molly, someone will be here soon."

His voice was calm and controlled belying the true state of his body, except for the fact that his arm was trembling from the weight of her head and shoulders. With care, he tried to ease himself into a different position to let his other arm take some of the weight. Molly stoically tried to hide the intense pain she was experiencing while John questioned how he would have behaved in her situation. His admiration of her courage increased ten-fold.

Shouting out orders above the confusion the Captain's First Hand stepped gingerly over and through those still lying on the floor. It was difficult to believe that so deep a voice could be housed in the tall thin man with slightly greying hair as his voice boomed out.

"The doctor is doing his best to get round to everybody. Is there any one that I can help?"

Looking directly at John and Molly he dropped to his knees and lowered his voice.

"Poor lass, let's see what is going on here."

Giving John a knowing wink, he spoke in a reassuring tone to Molly.

"Just a little sharp pull and I can get this arm sorted. Can I do this for you sweetheart?"

With a nod of her head, and no more ado, he expertly yanked her arm. A loud snap, and a scream that would sicken the strongest of men, and he had the arm back in its normal position. Concerned and perturbed John kissed her cheek, wiping away her tears and murmuring small words of comfort, in an attempt to let her know she was not alone.

The Captain's First Hand rose to his feet, slapped John on the back and moved on to inspect the man who had fallen onto Molly.

He motioned for another crew member, instructed him to get the man lifted and taken to the sick bay before he bled to death, then continued on his way.

The twin's deep blue eyes silently appealed for some answers as their sister remained so still and quiet. Much like Molly's, John thought, their tiny white faces seemed too small to house such large eyes, With as much re-assurance as he could muster into his voice, he told the twins that Molly was only resting and would soon be as good as new. The baby, obviously hungry, was becoming fractious and difficult for the twins to manage. John realised he felt as anxious as they did; he had no idea about babies. He prayed Molly would soon recover and take control of the baby.

It was a puzzle to him that Molly was in this situation. He felt uneasy. Where were her older brothers and more especially where was Molly's mother? He knew his Mama labelled her "an unsuitable mother" and he was now inclined to agree. It was unfair for a young girl to have charge of three young children. He decided some mothers had a lot to answer to where their children were concerned. It was hard to accept that thinking this way reminded him that he also was the child of an unsuitable mother. He closed his eyes and massaged the lids. Tired, tense and aching he craved a clean comfortable bed to rest his weary body.

Molly made a movement and distracted him from his thoughts. Looking into her eyes, he welcomed her back with a smile. She returned a faint smile before her eyes darted to where the twins sat, still trying their hardest to quieten their baby brother, but with little success. She quickly sat up, and to ease the dizziness she felt she massaged the temples of her face with her fingers until it lessened.

Extricating herself from John's arms, her eyes lowered, she apologised for causing him so much trouble. John, mesmerised by the length of her eyelashes assured her it had been no trouble and with his help, she rose from the floor and into a chair. She took the baby, wincing in pain as she lifted him from the twins, and as if by magic produced a bottle of milk from her shabby cotton bag. The baby's sobs subsided as Molly encouraged him to suck the teat. Identifying the teat with comfort the baby latched on to it with glee.

Back at her feet, the twins rummaged through the bag until they found a small bag of biscuits. Flabbergasted, John watched them settle down as though nothing had disturbed them.

"Are you alright Molly?" he enquired.

"I'll be fine now, thank you once again for your help …. Mm… I'm sorry I don't know your name?"

"It's John. John Smith" and with a strange mixture of reluctance and relief he took his leave of them, walking unsteadily through the on-going turmoil. Before he reached the exit door he paused to take a last look to where Molly was seated, then kicked the debris away from under his feet and pushed hard against the door. The cold, damp air felt good on his face.

The lashing rain had abated slightly and to his relief his stomach felt less upset. Clutching at the handrails, he climbed the stairs to the upper deck and watched the dark turbulent ocean. More certain than ever that his parents' decision to return to England was a mistake he felt his anger return. Without this trip, his birth certificate would have remained concealed. He wished he could erase the picture of the moment he discovered it and read Birth Certificate for John Dalgleish Smith - Mother - Ellen Dalgleish. Why had he found it? As hard as he might try to convince himself that he was the true son of Bill and Kate Smith a small voice in the back of his head whispered you are a bastard child John Smith.

chapter 6

Later on the Same Day

SWAYING BACK AND FORTH, John struggled along the corridor leading to his parents' cabin. He faced the door with trepidation before opening it. Peering round the door, and catching the panic within his mother's eyes, an immediate sense of foreboding entered his soul. Moving to his father's bunk he fell to his knees and placed his hand on his father's burning forehead; his face was gaunt and his eyes restless. Taking hold of his father's hands, he held them to own face.

"Papa … oh Papa …what's wrong?"

He felt his animosity loosen its hold and like an abscess lanced, his hurt and pain drained away. A rush of warmth and love flowed in his veins for the man he had known as his father. The father who had devoted his life to caring for him.

His father's voice was weak and hoarse as he attempted to answer.

"I'm so thirsty son … and my gut feels on fire …like a red hot poker in there …" he joked before he cried out from another vicious attack of pain. Writhing he curled himself into a ball, and let out a deep sigh as the pain lessened. "I'm dying son."

"No" John choked on the word. "No, I will get the doctor to come down here and he will give you something to make you well. I refuse to let you die. Not like this … you want to see North Shields again don't you? You have to be there to show me around Papa." He stifled his tears.

The nod was barely there "I would love to get there John, but it's not going to happen." Again, the pain creased him and the veins in his hands protruded in his clenched calloused hands.

The muffled cries from his mother cut through the concern he had for his father. An irrational feeling of anger welled up and in his anguish he sniped at her, "Why is the doctor not here? You should have called the doctor."

Kate shot him a reproachful look and sobbed into her handkerchief.

"I did. He came yesterday and gave me this medicine." She held the bottle out for John to see. "But your Papa said it was no good and only wanted water … he refused to take it … I called for the doctor again this morning … but the cabin boy was ill … and … I was too frightened to leave the cabin." She looked up at him red eyed.

"Aw Mama, I'm sorry." Seeing how thin and drawn she had become since they began their voyage made him feel miserable. It pained him to know he had not been there when she needed him.

He rang the bell to alert the cabin boy. Seconds passed by and he rang again. Impatiently, he repeatedly rang the bell until he wearied himself, accepting there was no cabin boy to respond.

In great mental pain, he watched his father pull his knees into his chest to relieve the agony he was suffering. He doubted his father realised he was whimpering with the pain, such humiliation in ordinary circumstances.

"Don't ever let them see you shed a tear boy" were the words he would say to John whenever he showed signs of upset.

Without further thought John took two large strides to the door and told his mother, he would be back with the doctor. Ignoring her plea not to leave them he ran as fast as his feet and the rolling ship would allow as he made his way to the medical room. Red faced and panting he flew down the next two flights of stairs, halting abruptly when faced by a tired and dishevelled looking nurse holding her hands palms up. "Slow down, slow down. What's wrong?"

Gasping for breath he spluttered "My father, he needs help, he needs the doctor urgently … I think he is dying."

"What's the cabin number? I will give the doctor a message as soon as he comes out from the treatment room."

"He's got to come now," John, pleaded loudly. "Don't you understand he is going to die if he doesn't come now?"

Noticing John's clenched white knuckles the nurse said calmly, a hand on his arm. "The doctor will be with you very soon; now go back and stay with your father until he gets there. You can be of more help to him if you are with him."

With a wobble in his voice, John relented. "He will be as quick as he can won't he?"

With a warm smile, the nurse nodded. "He will, just a short while I promise." Then she turned and went back into the treatment room.

John sped back to the cabin, muttering under his breath all the way "Please God, keep him safe … don't let him die. I've never asked you for anything, please don't let me down."

Another upsurge of foreboding overcame him. The door was ajar. Slowing his pace he listened carefully, it was silent. A cold chill ran down his spine as he pushed the door open to see his mother rocking his father in her arms, her silent tears trickling down her face and onto his. He felt frozen to the spot as grief filled every fibre of his being. He gradually slid down the door and cried noiselessly into his hands.

The doctor arrived ten minutes later to witness this scene. Shaking his head sadly, he offered them his sympathy and said he would make the necessary arrangements for a burial at sea.

Neither John nor Kate said anything.

chapter 7

John and Molly O'Leary - 1921

A LARGE EXPANSE OF swirling smog hung over the River Tyne, blotting out the sunset. It was a still and chilly evening, but it had not deterred John and Molly from their regular Sunday walk. Their friendship had grown slowly but surely in the last weeks on the ship. She had shown such tender empathy for him when his father died creating a bond between them that may never have come about in any other circumstance.

With John's arm around Molly's shoulders, they ambled in a companionable silence. John pondered his future. He had a fascination for the sea, except that since the experience of crossing the oceans he liked it far better when he was on dry land. Ideas of exporting and importing goods from one country to another excited him. He was hoping to explore the possibility of apprenticeship with a Shipping Company. The river now buzzed with ships docking there from India, Africa and China offering many opportunities for work. He nurtured a secret notion that he would walk into the Dalgleish Shipping Yard for an interview and somehow there would be recognition of him. He knew it was a fantasy, but for the first time he hoped for help.

To gain a place within the Dalgleish business and become a valued protégé filled his secret longing for acceptance.

Wild imaginings crowded his waking hours although he made no attempt to make them a reality by going to the Company. His obsessive thoughts served to blank memories of his Father's death, whilst he could then imagine he still had a father somewhere, even if unknown to him. He was confused. Life felt chaotic. He fiercely dismissed any suggestions from Kate that he was puzzled, possibly curious about a family he should have had a place in. Why did they give him up for adoption? Had he not had a happy life with Mama and Papa? It had never crossed his mind that they were not his true parents. He loved them. Except, since he found out, his feelings fluctuated from love to hate within seconds. These emotions seemed bizarre and frightening, so much so he feared sharing these thoughts with anyone, even Molly, his greatest confidante.

He had grown tired of Kate's urging him to consider banking, the law or else to fulfil his artistic talents and train to be an architect. The education he had received more than satisfied the entrance criteria for any of these careers, but none of them excited him. He also felt frustrated that she refused to disguise her disapproval of Molly. He continually ignored her criticisms of Molly and her family, stating she was not good enough for him. He thought this was ridiculous and adamantly refused to let her come between them. He now called her Kate rather than Mama. He knew it upset her, that she was grieving, and that his stubbornness added to her distress and yet still he held fast to his antagonistic behaviour.

He appreciated that Kate had his welfare at heart, and yet it sometimes rankled that she wished to dictate to him what she held to be right and wrong. She expected, almost demanded, that he agree with her opinions. The more she did this the more he resented her.

He harboured thoughts of moving to the south of England. Here in the north was misery and poverty. Women and children suffered the humiliation of scratching around for food and clothing, while their husbands and fathers were on strike and refusing to return to the mines unless the government kept their promise to subsidise the coal industry. In John's eyes, although he admired the men for their bravery to fight their cause and had a good deal of sympathy for their plight, he hated seeing the women struggle against all odds. None of this felt comfortable and he no longer saw a future for himself here in the North.

His uncles had kindly suggested they spend time together to establish some kind of connection with him and to keep his father's memory alive, only John found after several visits, that he had no affinity with them and knew he wanted more out of life than they had settled for. His lack of interest in further visits had gained Kate's support, and he detected some relief. She made no secret of the fact that she wanted more for him and had always ensured he had the best possible education. She would be disappointed if he forgot that privilege and did not pursue a gratifying and rewarding career, and he did not want to let her down.

Molly caressed the hand that lay firmly on her shoulder.

"Is everything alright John?" she queried.

John bit his bottom lip and surrendered his wanderings for the time being and smiled into her smooth innocent face, her deep blue eyes seeming larger than ever as they gazed exclusively into his.

"Sorry ... I was lost in thought," he explained.

His frown convinced Molly that he was perplexed about something.

"Is it something to do with us?" She asked tentatively.

John affectionately pulled her closer to him. "Most definitely not. You are my little angel. No, I was contemplating whether I honestly want to stay here in the North. I find it depressing and hopeless. The more I think about it the more I deduce I would be happier away from here."

Molly gulped down a deep breath. "Are you going back to Simon's Town?"

"No way" he said quickly. "I don't intend to board a ship for a very long time, if ever." He emphasized the word ever to prove how decisive he was. "No ... I was thinking of somewhere like ... London."

"Oh John, how exciting. You are so clever you are sure to do well there. Everybody says London is the place to be. You might even find a job that appeals to you."

"I might ... although I have no idea how I should go about it. I could rent a room and familiarise myself with the city. I can't lose anything can I?"

"Of course not."

"Would you miss me? Miss our Sunday walks?" He jested.

Stopping still and facing him Molly looked in earnest at his smiling face.

"Oh John, of course I would, very much so, but your career is important ... and I think you should do anything you can to further it." To press her point she continued, "Whatever, I will stand by you, you know I will."

With her face tilted up, a look of adoration for him in her eyes, and her full plump lips slightly parted, John felt startled by his strength of feelings for her. It staggered him. His pulse quickened as he lowered his face, took her hands in his and kissed her slowly, their lips expressing the ardour they shared for each other.

Their lips parted and Molly lowered her eyes with embarrassment, a deep flush covering her cheeks.

John lifted her chin with his forefinger, kissed her gently on the end of her nose.

"You are a funny girl, but you're my funny girl ... when I have found a job and am earning good money ... Molly ... will you marry me?"

Molly answered instantly in a quiet voice. "Yes ... if you still want to when that time comes ... but I think you will meet someone beautiful and sophisticated in London ... someone educated and in the same class as you ... someone who could entertain your friends and never let you down."

Taking her hand in his John laughed and began to run pulling her with him as he went.

"I'll not want anyone but you Molly, and until you promise you will marry me I'll not stop running."

They ran until she begged him to stop. "Promise first" he panted.

"I promise," she giggled feeling her feet leave the ground as he twisted her round.

"I love you for who you are Molly O'Leary and don't you forget it." He whispered in her ear.

Molly smiled up at him. "I know, but there is nearly five years until I am twenty-one and a lot can happen in that time."

John tutted "You are far too sensible for your age. Take my word for it ... we will get married. I can wait, and in the meantime, I will strive to achieve the best job to prove I can offer you and our children everything you will ever need. So the question is can you wait for me to do that?"

Chuckling mischievously, she turned away from him and began to walk.

"Just five years John Smith or I will have to marry another."

Catching up with her John said playfully.

"Do not fear, I will have a wedding booked and a gold band on your left hand my girl ... twenty-one and you are mine ... and don't you forget it."

It was quite dark, the smog thicker and the foghorns from the ships sounding off every few minutes, when John remembered the time of the ferry to get Molly back home. "Come on Molly, run ... the boat leaves in four minutes ...!

Then, they ran like children with soft contented grins on their faces. They now had a dream.

John's hope that Alice would answer his letter no longer felt important. He would deal with that when she contacted him ... and he could escape from the North.

chapter 8

Molly

Four Years Later

MOLLY'S ARM FELL TO her side as the last carriage of the train disappeared into the bright sunlight. An overwhelming sinking feeling went through her as once again she faced at least another month before John's next visit. The weeks in between visits felt endless and empty, although she never gave any indication of this to John. Her letters were buoyant and full of amusing accounts of her everyday life as a shop-girl in her Uncle Charles' ironmongers. Together with her on-going role as surrogate mother to her four youngest siblings, she had remained steadfast in her capacity to support John with love and encouragement. She had instinctively known when he had needed to talk about his worries. Without her keen perception over these difficult years he would have remained bottled up, of this she was certain. Entrenched in his work and learning all he could about how the Press worked she had been his backbone

She stood alone on the platform. Reluctant to leave she stared down at the three small, but perfectly cut diamonds set in a thick band of gold on the third finger of her left hand. The sun's rays played with the facets of the stones, encouraging brilliant and vibrant colours to glitter for their owner. A soft smile lightened up Molly's pale waifish looking face and her enormous blue eyes glistened and sparkled with delight. She raised her hand to her lips and kissed the ring before taking a deep breath and walking slowly away from the railway station.

From the seat on the bus to Tynemouth Village, she vacantly observed the passing luscious green countryside in an effort not to consider too deeply Kate's first ever invitation to come for afternoon tea. Even thinking about it brought a nauseous churning in her stomach. John, so thrilled that his mother had at last accepted Molly was to be her future daughter-in-law, he had made Molly promise to write and tell him all about it in her next letter. He reminded her very lovingly that she was his fiancée and that meant she was part of his family now. If that was so, she wondered why she could feel her confidence now slowly ebbing away. Without him by her side, she felt very small and powerless. As she stepped off the bus, opposite Percy Square, Molly wished fervently that she and Kate would become friends after this afternoon. She walked across the road with as much confidence as she could muster, to number six, noticing that it was a very modest house in comparison with the others in the square. Seeing it jogged her memory. She recalled John telling her, that he had had to laugh at his mother's comment when she first moved here, "that at least she was able to live in the more elegant end of the village."

Molly had no opportunity to knock on the fine black front door; it was held wide open by Kate's sister Amelia. Her face glowed with obvious happy anticipation of their visitor. Molly's anxiety lessened as she felt the warmth of this woman and readily returned the welcoming smile. The two sisters, now widows, had combined their assets to buy the house between them. Molly wondered if it was such a good thing, two women running a home. She imagined there would need to be a very comfortable relationship to cope with every day conflict.

"Come on in." Amelia exclaimed waving her hands towards the

far end of the hall. "We're in the back parlour where it is cooler." Closing the door behind Molly, she shuffled in front of her. "You must be tired out after all your travelling today, and yet you still look fresh and pretty as a picture in that blue dress."

Molly followed the dumpy figure and thought how likeable Amelia was.

"Molly's here Kate," she cried out as they approached the parlour door.

"Well show the girl in then Amelia"

With the help of a walking stick, Kate raised her angular frame from the armchair.

"Excuse me for not coming to the door Molly, but I have had a particularly bad day with this old body of mine."

"Oh you really shouldn't have disturbed yourself Mrs. Smith. It must pain you each time you get up from your chair," said Molly sympathetically.

"Well it's not easy," Kate sighed "but on the other hand it's not good for me to be sitting around for long periods of time. She sat back down and indicated Molly to seat herself on the cottage style couch opposite.

"I sometimes wonder if it was foolish to come back to England … so many things were more pleasant. How different life would be if we had stayed in Simon's Town. John never wanted to leave, but it is too late now for regrets. You must miss it too Molly … the weather suited me far more there, and we had such a lot of pleasant families around us."

She paused, while she carefully put her next sentence together. Slowly she added

"and you and I may still have our loved ones with us. How is your father managing without your mother Molly?"

The directness of her question caused Molly to feel a little shaky.

"He is very lonely without her, but he has begun to socialise again thank you."

She held back telling Kate that he was in fact a womanizer and forgot his troubles whilst in the company of women friends at his local social club.

Kate nodded.

"Good … I know only too well how hard it is to be without the one you love … I'm not sure I will ever get over my Bill dying in the way he did."

Molly felt uneasy and sat quietly wondering how to respond to a woman with whom she had hardly spoken to before today, when Amelia came to her aid.

"I guess the three of us have had similar feelings, but we deal with the passing of our loved ones in different ways. Today we should be celebrating that we shall soon become family and what a joy that will be."

Amelia bustled around the room and put the finishing touches to a small round table laid up with a fresh white linen tablecloth and the best china tea set.

"Come and sit here Molly and I will sit opposite" she turned to Kate.

"I will fetch the tea and cakes while you get to the table.

Amelia happily carried out the task with her constant chatter as she moved back and forwards into the room. Finally finished she took a seat at the table and beamed like an excited child ready for a tea party.

Molly appreciated Amelia's easy manner and was surprised to find she was far more relaxed than she had imagined she could be. So much so that she found herself laughing freely at some of Amelia's amusing anecdotes.

Half an hour passed before Kate interrupted Amelia and jokingly scolded her for gaining all the attention.

"I think you should give Molly a chance to get a word in so she can tell us all about her plans for the wedding, don't you?"

"Yes of course she must. I promise to keep quiet from now on Kate. I'm so sorry, please forgive me Molly, I'm such as chatterbox."

Amelia giggled in a slightly abashed way and helped herself to another cake.

"So" said Kate piercing Molly's comfortable state of mind, "what exactly has that son of mine got you into?"

"What do you mean?" Molly stammered.

"I have a great love for my son, but I do know that he can have over high expectations of others. Is he expecting your Father to foot the bill of this wedding? I would hate to think it was too much for him."

There was a silence as Molly gazed awkwardly into her lap.

"John is taking care of the finances Mrs. Smith."

Molly wondered miserably why this question was raised after John had reassured her that Kate knew of his plans.

"Well, now John is going up in the world, and has established himself with The Times, I guess he can afford it … and of course I will also contribute."

Kate looked smugly at Amelia when her sister raised her eyebrows while still saying.

"You will make a very pretty bride my dear and of course your sisters will be bridesmaids?"

Halfway between a bite into her scone Molly was aghast.

"No, as I am certain John has told you, we are to have a very small and quiet wedding. Then we are having a wedding breakfast in Miss Charlotte's Dinner and Tea Rooms in South Shields. It's how we want it to be."

She and John had decided this very early on to avoid awkward differences between the two families, both of them very conscious that Molly's father and brothers would be overwhelmed by too formal an occasion.

"Yes he did … but I imagined you would still want all the trimmings Molly, that's what every girl wants isn't it?"

Smiling Molly shook her head.

"Not this girl … I am quite content with the plans we have made … I love John and it will be wonderful to be his wife."

Clapping her hands Amelia smiled back.

"and John is a very lucky man to have found a girl who can understand what marriage is really about … you will make a lovely bride and groom."

Sitting back in her chair Kate gave Molly a quizzical look.

"You do know John will be expected to socialise with clients who could be upper class and have different values to yours, and as his wife he will need you by his side to entertain and attend many functions. I know John … he will expect you to be the ideal hostess and wife … even if you should have children. But then again, knowing John the way I do, he will assume that you will hire a nanny so that you can be free to be with him."

Molly spoke softly.

"We may have some ups and downs, but John has said all along that he wants a wife and children, and that although he will have a career, his family will always come first."

"And I'm sure he means it. But you're both young and don't realise the pressures that you will face. A man's job always comes first. He owes that alliance to his employer and it will be the same for John. Even now, he chooses to work for a national newspaper, rather than a local one, which means you two are separated for weeks on end. Would he love you if you wanted him to come back from London and find a position as a local reporter?"

Molly shook her head in protest.

"I'm sure he would, but I wouldn't want him to give up the marvellous opportunity he has been offered by the Telegraph. I will eventually join him in London once we are married and there will be no more separations."

"Oh Molly, you are a good girl. So generous. I only say these things because I care and want you to be prepared."

Kate reached out as if in affection and patted Molly's flushed cheekbone with a thin cold hand

Molly looked into Kate's eyes and removed the cold hand from her face, which had sent a chill down her spine, and with a smile on her lips but not in her eyes, she heard the chill in her own voice.

"I'm sure you are right Mrs. Smith and I appreciate your concern, but John and I are committed to each other. We will overcome the adversities I know we will."

Kate condescendingly nodded, a thin smile fixed on her lips.

"You are both young and I know how much you mean to each

other, so I will not mention this again. I felt it only proper that I bring these things to your notice. John often has his head in the clouds and does not think things through rationally. He has probably given no thought to the difference in your education and family background and the strain he will put you through to keep up with him. But, as you say Molly, you will overcome those things."

Molly toyed with the half-eaten cake on her plate. Not wishing to meet Kate's eyes, she kept her lids lowered and said quietly,

"Have you spoken to John about these things?"

Kate laughed aloud.

"Of course, but men never listen to a mother's advice.

"We women have to stick together and subtly help a man to find the answers. He has to believe all decisions come from him. Have you not learned that yet Molly?"

"I guess not." Molly raised her eyes to meet Kate's "but I'm certain I can learn if I want to."

"Another cup of tea?"

Amelia said flourishing the teapot in front of Molly.

"I've never heard such nonsense Kate; my Percy always made his own decisions. I only had to ask for his help and he was always willing to listen."

"Oh, Amelia, you'd romanticise anything." Kate scoffed. "And of course, Percy wasn't exactly in the most prestigious position was he?"

"Maybe not, but he was a gentleman. He lost his life saving the others in that mineshaft. Not anyone would go back like he did." Retaliated Amelia.

"Amelia, we aren't here to talk about Percy."

"No, well then let Molly tell us what sort of wedding she wants and stop being such a pessimist."

Molly taken aback by Amelia's ability to assert herself inwardly took note of Kate's apparent nonchalance. It was as if nothing touched her. Was she like this with John she wondered?

After a short silence, Kate cleared her throat before inviting Molly to please call her Kate now they had acquainted themselves. They would soon be family, Mrs. Smith sounded too formal, and it would possibly be unnatural for Molly to address her as Mama.

Molly accepted the attempt to be friendlier with her usual generosity although her wariness was cemented.

The clock on the mantelpiece struck four. Molly rose to her feet.

"I really have to make a move. Thank you for the tea Kate, my bus for the Quayside ferry will be along very soon and I must be on it to be back in South Shields in time to prepare tea."

"You shouldn't have to be looking after the family at your age. You have done it for so long. I'm surprised your father didn't remarry so your brothers and sister could have a mother again." Kate muttered.

"You did it for long enough with us," Amelia reminded her. "Where would we have been without you?"

"That's different, we had neither parent." Kate said stubbornly.

"I really must go," said Molly not wishing the conversation to become hostile. "I'll see myself to the door."

"You will do no such thing."

Amelia was up and bustling towards her. Putting her arm around Molly's waist, she said.

"You will come and see us again. Next time John comes home perhaps we could all have dinner together." Turning towards Kate, she said, "You would like that wouldn't you Kate?"

Kate nodded "That would be very pleasant."

Molly smiled and walked to the front door with Amelia who affectionately squeezed her hand.

"Take no notice of Kate. She'll come around eventually."

"You are so sweet Amelia, thank you."

Molly placed a quick peck on Amelia's chubby cheek and headed towards the bus stop some fifty yards from the Square.

She hardly noticed the journey back to South Shields. Thoughts of how life would be with John in the future spun chaotically out of control. Kate could be right she thought. How would she fare when she was in London? She was a country girl and knew nothing about city life. It was difficult to hear John's reassurance in her head. She would talk about it in her next letter to him.

chapter 9

John - London 1927

THE KEYS OF THE Remington struck the paper furiously as John's fingers flew across the keyboard, a cigarette stuck to his bottom lip, ash scattered around his desk and chair. A waste-paper basket overflowing with crumpled previous attempts at the article was an indication of many false starts.

Yanking the paper from the typewriter, he read his report for the tenth time. "Wheels of Industry Grind to a Halt – Docks Lie Idle" – "Royal Navy Called in to be Temporary Dockers." He decided the Headers gave his story power. He was satisfied. He lit another cigarette from the one he released from his lip, leaned back in his chair and crossed his legs upon the desk. Throwing the finished article down with an act of competency it landed neatly on the floor, while at the same time his eyes roved around the office. Some of his colleagues were still banging away at their typewriters, while others had taken up a similar stance to his. The room, shrouded with cigarette smoke and curling itself around the occupants made it difficult to see clearly, although it was clear how hard the reporters laboured for hours to produce an article of the standard expected by the Telegraph Newspaper. Reporters not making the grade did not survive long.

John rubbed away at the stubble on his chin. How long would it be before the Print Works also downed tools? He could see it coming, not something he had envisaged when he first entered the trade. It was thought to be secure, the safest trade to enter. Now here he was, the baby due any day and faced with his worst nightmare, his and Molly's security at risk. The pregnancy had not been easy and Molly had endured weeks at a time in bed, on the doctor's advice, so he had fiercely protected her from the gravity of the situation.

A sudden wave of tiredness swept through his body. He massaged the area above his eyebrows to relieve the pressure and then squinted at the clock on the far wall of the office. It had gone midnight. John groaned inwardly, another night of being absent from home. Thank God, Aunt Amelia had prolonged her stay and offered to remain with them until after the birth.

Scraping his chair away from his desk, be grabbed his briefcase off the floor and rose to his feet. "Night boys, I'm off" he called out. He derived a lot of amusement from calling them boys, knowing he was the youngest of them, and they humoured him.

"Night Johnnie boy" some replied, while others motioned with their hands that they had heard him, but were too busy to stop.

Throwing the final draft into the Editor's 'in-basket' he grinned as he got the thumbs up from his boss.

"I've got to go boss."

"Yeah, Yeah. Go and see if your missus has made a father of you yet."

"But don't forget; get your arse back in here by noon, latest."

"Will do. Thanks boss."

John ran down the two flights of stairs and breathed in the cold night air.

The full moon glowed onto the empty streets of London giving enough light to walk easily and safely. Long fast strides very soon brought him to Hyde Park Corner, looking bare and empty without its regular speakers and protesters that gathered here daily with their placards and banners. The quiet of the early morning, and the frosty mist gave no indication of the enormous grief and struggle borne by the unemployed workers who fought tenaciously over the shameful wage reductions offered by industry. Lloyd George and the liberals were now struggling to keep their promises to create jobs, and the disillusioned workers constantly expressed their anger towards them by picketing in this area.

John crossed the road and walked with more spring in his step. Remembering that he was fortunate in contrast to the presently unemployed, he headed along the side streets eager to reach home. Ten minutes later, his rapid breathing caused him to stop temporarily at the bottom of the steps leading to the front door. Seeing a crack of artificial light through the drawn curtain drapes his heart quickened with anticipation. His hand trembled as he fumbled with his key trying to find the lock, and with a deep breath, he slowly opened the door, careful to close it quietly. He strained his ears thinking he would hear voices, but all was silent. Climbing the stairs two at a time, he tiptoed across the tiny landing to the bedroom. With trepidation, he opened the door and peeped in. Molly was sleeping soundly and Amelia deep in slumber on the bedside chair had Molly's hand in hers. Creeping further into the room John looked fondly at his Aunt and wife. They had become close friends and loved each other dearly much to John's pleasure. A slight sound in what appeared to be in the corner of the room caught his attention. The top drawer, from the chest of drawers, was safely sitting on the nursing chair. Feeling somewhat giddy from what felt like a double somersault happening in his heart, and his clenched stomach restricting his breathing, the sound of a baby's snuffling reached his ears. Tentatively he approached the drawer and looked down. A pink satin bow lay on top of the little bundle wrapped in a white shawl. Smiling with delight, he shook his head in disbelief and gazed lovingly upon the face of his tiny daughter. "Hello Helen" he whispered "welcome to the world."

✄ ✄ ✄ ✄ ✄ ✄ ✄

Forcing his eyes to open, his chin upon his chest, he moved his neck from one side to the other to loosen up. Massaging his neck, he rested his head against the back of the chair. It took a few seconds for his mind to engage with his waking world. He struggled momentarily wondering why he was fully dressed and sleeping in his favourite armchair. The sound of clinking crockery from the scullery alerted him and jolted him into the present. Of course, the baby! Molly!

Confused and dazed he jumped to his feet and made straight for the bedroom. He stopped by the door and savoured the picture in front of him. Molly, looking flushed and happy, her eyes delightedly fixed upon her baby daughter, kept her nestled to her breast as if she found it the most natural thing in the world to do. Raising her eyes to the sound of John's entrance, she smiled broadly and murmured "Oh John look she is perfect."

"She's not only perfect she is beautiful" John replied sincerely as he knelt by the side of the bed and kissed her waiting lips. With his forefinger, he stroked the dark hair at the nape of the baby's head.

"I can't believe she's really here. When I woke, I thought I had dreamed about the pink ribbon baby. What a clever way of letting me know Molly." He took hold of her hand "and you Molly, how was it for you?"

Not waiting for an answer, he saw with concern that tears had welled up in her eyes. "Oh sweetheart, I'm sorry I wasn't here."

Shaking her head in protest, Molly brushed the flowing tears from her cheeks and laid her head back on the pillow.

"I'm just very tired, take no notice of me. All that matters is that you are here now. She squeezed his hand. "I love you."

The baby paused from her sucking and moved her tiny head away from the breast.

"I think she wants a cuddle from her Da," Molly said, as she removed the baby and held her out to John.

Gingerly, he took her. Molly giggled with joy.

"Hold her close to you. You won't hurt her you know."

He smiled sheepishly and felt the warm tiny body close to his chest. She smelled sweet from Molly's milk. He gazed at her tiny hands and feet and the miniscule nails. A strange, never experienced before feeling, washed over him. He kissed her forehead, overwhelmed by the love he had for her. He looked at Molly who watched him with admiration. "She is gorgeous Molly."

A light tap on the door, and in came a beaming Amelia, a breakfast tray laid up for two in her hands.

"Time for breakfast you two. I will have baby while you both eat. John, jump into bed with her and keep her company," she lovingly commanded

John hugged his aunt.

"I love you. Thank you for being here. I don't have to go to work until late today so time with my clever, beautiful wife will be wonderful."

Without a moment's hesitation he was by Molly's side.

Amelia had an even larger beam on her face as she took the baby and left them alone. She could not have loved them more if they had been her own children.

The new father ate with gusto while Molly nibbled at some toast. With the teapot drained, they leaned against the pillows; John with his arm around Molly's shoulders kissed her cheek.

"You're very hot," he said with a concerned note in his voice. "When will the midwife be back to check on you?"

"Mmm, I think she said some time during the afternoon" Molly replied sleepily, her eyes closed.

"You must be very tired my darling and it is only six o'clock now, so why not get some more sleep before Helen needs feeding again?"

Opening her eyes wide, Molly grinned.

"Oh, so she really is a Helen then?"

"Certainly is" he laughed kissing her on the lips, "but only if you still agree," he added more seriously.

"It's a lovely name, so she will be Helen Mary, Katherine Smith. That way she has got both our mothers' names and then when we have a son he can have our fathers' names with his."

John cuddled up close to her "Mm sounds right … but I love having a daughter." His voice faded out and within seconds, they were sleeping.

A few hours and John was awake. Shaking Molly's shoulder gently he caressed her neck with his lips.

"I'm going to go into work a bit earlier, and hopefully I can be back before the midwife comes." He slipped out of bed quietly.

He heard her drowsy "alright" and watched as she promptly went back to sleep.

John felt nervous about leaving her. She was still very hot and her cheeks remained flushed. He hesitated before leaving the room, he knew little about the workings of women, and it scared him to see her this way. Molly's normal complexion was pale, sometimes a little too pale, but if she was no different when he returned he promised himself he would pay for the doctor to make a visit.

Amelia calmed his unease and shooed him on his way, telling him not to worry and that she would keep a vigilant eye on Molly and the baby.

⁂⁂⁂⁂⁂⁂⁂

John, overwhelmed by the congratulations, and good feelings from his work colleagues was happier than he believed possible. The Editor had produced a bottle of whisky for the men to share, much to their surprise, which caused a great deal of banter about why was John so extra special.

The light-hearted chat continued throughout the morning albeit they worked diligently, and yet John constantly watched the clock. He wanted to be back with Molly and he found his concentration wandering from time to time.

Willing the hands to move on to the twelve and one he lit one cigarette after another in an effort to stay focused on his work. The thought of not having been with her at the birth made him wince inside. She never made life difficult for him. Never had. He knew he could not say that for himself towards her. His job had always come first.

Twelve o'clock, another hour and he could go. He looked at the clock yet once again. He wished he could find it easy to ask for an extra hour, but it was not his way. He classed himself as a conscientious worker no matter what.

He heard his name called and turned to see the Editor beckoning him to come to his office. Involuntarily he shivered. Puzzled by his reactions to this day he moved quickly and saw the telephone receiver lying on the Editor's desk. The Editor inclined a nod in its direction and left John alone to take the call.

Amelia's voice sounded somewhat edgy. "You need to come home John … as quickly as is possible."

His mind in turmoil, his senses swimming frantically he heard his voice echoing inside his head. "Why?"

"Are you still there John? Please leave work and come home … Molly is ill."

His heart beating double fast, he replaced the telephone receiver on the cradle. Opening the door with a feeling of numbness, he told the Editor apprehensively that there was a problem at home and would have to leave.

He felt an arm around his shoulder, and heard words of reassurance, intended to create calm, and felt himself pushed gently towards the stairs.

❧❧❧❧❧❧❧❧

As if an automatic switch had taken over, he made the journey home without seeing or hearing anything on the way.

Amelia stood at the front door, her eyes red and puffy. Taking his hand, she led him up the stairs where the doctor stood by Molly's still body.

A muted roaring sound in his ears obscured the doctor's words. A sudden rush of nausea swept over him. He rubbed his cold, moist hands along the sides of his trousers. As a kind of helpless swoon came over him, an intense silent scream pulsed through his veins.

He sank into the armchair next to the bed, his eyes heavy with tears. He could not look. His fist took on a life of its own as it pummelled the arm of the chair. Tears streamed down his face. Rising from the chair, he staggered out of the room, ran down the stairs and slammed the front door behind him.

Without further thought he walked, and walked until he reached the park. Collapsing onto a bench he stared ahead, his eyes glazed, seeing nothing but the lake.

He felt his heart break. He needed to love and be loved and once again, his God had let him down.

chapter 10

Kate

UNUSED TO THE TELEPHONE Kate warily answered the insistent shrill ringing noise. Lifting the receiver, she shuddered at the scratchy vague noises coming through. It was a struggle to hear the tiny voice. "Hello … hello." She waited. She spoke loudly into the speaker. "Is that you Amelia?

She shook the receiver in frustration. Awful instrument she thought scornfully. Suddenly the crackling subsided and Amelia's voice became distinctive.

"Amelia? Slow down and speak clearly. I can hardly hear you." She paused, "Are you crying or have you caught a cold?"

The colour in her face faded as the enormity of Amelia's words came through.

"I don't understand … why has John left the house … you need him with you … what is wrong with the boy?"

Again, the intrusive crackle. With enormous difficulty, she tried to make out the gist of Amelia's message.

"So the baby is alright"

She covered her other ear hoping that Amelia's voice would be more distinct. The crackle did not subside and Kate's frustration grew.

"So how ill is Molly?"

"Dead … Are you saying dead?" She exclaimed in an incredulous tone.

What little colour was left in her face drained away completely. A whisper escaped from her hand-covered mouth.

"Oh no … John, my poor John".

Stunned and shocked she breathed deeply in an effort to think clearly. Amelia's muffled sobs continued during the silent pause as she waited for Kate's response.

Kate knew without doubt what she had to do. What she always did. What others expected from her. What she expected of herself. Someone had to take control of the situation and who better than she. Loudly and clearly, her thoughts became words.

"Now listen Amelia. Can you hear me? You have to be brave and calm for when John gets back, because he will come back, once he calms down. He will need you more than ever now. Clearly, I will pay all expenses for the necessary arrangements so you have nothing to worry about in that respect. Can you do that Amelia?"

Amelia's trembling yes reached her ears.

"Tell John to telephone me as soon as he can so I can talk to him. We have to arrange for the child's welfare as a matter of urgency. That is all-important now. We must find a wet-nurse for her. In the meantime I will pray for you, John and the little one."

The line crackled badly.

"What is that Amelia?"

She angrily banged the receiver against her walking stick.

"Calm down. The doctor will know of a nurse, he will take care of that for you. As soon as it is possible, you can bring the baby here. … I know Amelia, but I am sure John will want that. We will speak later."

Putting the telephone receiver back on the cradle, Kate took another deep breath and with a shaky hand wiped the tears away from her cheeks.

Shocked and bewildered she made her way to the parlour in a

stupor and sat down. Another child left without a mother. Life was unfair, cruel. She leaned her aching head back letting the exhaustion she felt have its way.

Her bones seemed to ache more than ever when she eventually made her way to the kitchen. She sighed "what next?"

Waiting for the kettle on the range to boil she sat at the table, head in hands and realised there was only one possible answer. She and Amelia would have to raise the child to the best of their abilities. John would want to keep his daughter, of course he would, and he would not be able to do that without her help.

With a heavy heart, she thought of Mr Dalgleish. She shuddered as she imagined the baby abandoned by his natural family. Never, she vowed, would that happen in the Smith family.

chapter 11

Helen - 1930

THE WHITE WOODEN FRONT gate swung rhythmically. Waist length, deep chestnut coloured tresses, bounced against the back of her small delicate body. The wide white satin ribbon that secured her hair to prevent it from falling onto her face bobbed precariously as she brushed away the strands that had escaped its clasp. She leaned over the gate, looking both ways. What special wonder would he bring? She gave a happy giggle in eager anticipation of seeing her Da.

Hearing a window open she swung round and grinned. She knew it would be Auntie Am.

"No sign of him yet?"

Helen shook her head vigorously, causing the ribbon to slip further into her hair.

"Do you want your cardigan on? The breeze is a bit chilly."

"No, don't want it."

Nothing could drag her away from her gate. Steadfastly and stubbornly she hung on, swinging back and forth until she heard the window close. Twisting round to satisfy her curiosity that Auntie Am had given up the fight, she happily waited on the gate. A rumble passed through her tummy. As much as she would love to run indoors and ask for a raw carrot to quell her hunger, the thought of missing him turn the corner was unbearable. She pictured the roast dinner and gravy that Auntie Am was so good at cooking, and her hunger increased. Pleadingly, her words came out in a singsong voice.

"Hurry up Da … hurry up Da, please hurry up Da."

Excitement and anticipation bubbled up in her again, as she imagined what new present he would bring. Never for a moment was there any doubt in her mind that there would be no present. Helen loved all her dolls and teddies, but he had promised something different this time. She hugged the hope of a pram for her dollies or a tricycle. Auntie Am would let her ride it on the pavement if she asked nicely. Grandma might be a bit tetchy, but Helen had learned that to give a really big smile and a hug was the way to Grandma's heart.

Lost in daydreaming, her foot slipped and she scraped her knee against the wooden gate. Distressed, she rubbed the graze, holding back the tears that threatened to fall. Glancing at her shoe, she saw with dismay there was a scuff. Furiously she tried to clean it with her spit. Aunt Am did that with her handkerchief when there was a smudge on her face and it always worked. Then the sound of happy whistling caught her ear; her head shot up and she peered over the gate. With growing excitement she called "Da" and without further heed to her Grandma's instructions not to leave the front garden she ran as fast as her tiny legs could go. The smile on her face grew wider as he ran towards her and with complete confidence; she threw herself into his outstretched arms trusting implicitly he would catch her. John swung her round several times, before carefully lowering her to the ground. Taking hold of her tiny hand, he laughed with joy as she skipped happily alongside. She adored her Da.

John attempted to whistle again, but found his eyes welling with tears. This tiny edition of his Molly. The eyes that sparkled along with a smile so wide, it filled her face. Molly lived on in Helen so how could she be forgotten. He smiled down at her, greatly amused by her obvious curiosity to know what was in the big bag he carried. His own eagerness to see her surprised look put a skip in his step and his love for his daughter was almost more than he could bear.

Auntie Am waved from the gate, and as always welcomed him with arms outstretched ready to hug him. John bent down to receive her greeting; he was now far too tall for his aunt's hugs so released Helen's hand to make it easier for both of them. Helen, impatient to have her Da back tugged at his arm, so fearful he would forget she was there. Her Grandma often told her that sometimes she has to wait her turn, so she did, but this was her Da and she wanted him to be there for her alone. To lessen her anxiety she skipped around them with alacrity.

From the window, Kate observed the scene and felt a stab of envy. Her sister's ability to express her love in such an open way left her wanting. Unable to recall the last time John had looked to her for comfort caused Kate heartache.

In response to John's glance towards her, she put a false fixed smile upon her lips. He waved his hand and smiled as he freed himself from Amelia's hug. The tiredness around his eyes made her worry. Was all this travel, back and forwards from London, taking its toll on him? How long would it be before he could see Helen again after today? She moved away from the window as the three of them walked to the front door. She leaned heavily on her walking stick struggling with the pain in her back and legs before attempting to walk across the room to greet John. Compassionately he gently held her before a final squeeze of affection. Involuntarily she winced and stiffened. With a sincere apology, he dropped his arms as if she had rejected him.

"How are you Mama?

"I'm as well as ever."

Wishing desperately she could explain the tenderness in her body, so he could understand her reaction, she turned slightly away from him. "And you? Before he was able to answer, she added with sarcasm.

"You are obviously very well; I can smell you are nicely inebriated. What public house did you stop in?"

"Aw come on Mama. I only had one pint. I had to see Bertie before coming here; because"… he turned to Helen "I had to collect a very special something for my little girl."

Helen's eyes widened as he slowly opened the brown bag and as if by magic produced a tiny fluffy tabby kitten.

She shrieked with delight. "For me Da?"

"Yes for you. You must be gentle and take good care of him though. Do you promise you will Helen?

Solemnly she nodded her head.

"And you must not let him scratch Grandma's furniture."

"I promise." Helen held out her small hands impatient for John to hand her the kitten.

"What's his name Da?"

"He hasn't got one yet. What would you like to call him?"

"Fluffy. I want to call him Fluffy. Oh look Grandma isn't he lovely?"

"Lovely" Agreed Kate and smiled at her granddaughter's obvious delight.

"You had better show him where the backyard is. He will have to know where to go for his toilet."

She sent a scathing look across to John as Helen happily left the room with her kitten.

"Do you never think John? A child of four years old is not able to be responsible for a pet. You have put more work upon your Aunt Amelia and me."

Amelia stepped in.

"Oh Kate, it will be fine. I can manage, and look how happy he has made Helen."

That's as maybe, but John you must start to think about others and the consequences of your actions."

"I know, I know. Sorry Kate. However, you are glad to see me aren't you?"

His familiar boyish mischievous smile melted her hostility immediately. He kissed her cheek.

"Maybe I should marry a good woman to help me with Helen, but admit it Mama, you would miss her so much."

His eyes pleaded with her.

"You know I would and it is not a good idea to marry for that reason alone."

Smiling she wagged her finger at him.

"However it would be good if you could remember that we get no younger John."

She let out an exaggerated sigh.

"Enough of this let us all enjoy our Sunday dinner. We have your favourite beef roast, with rice pudding to follow."

John swallowed hard. Different thoughts dashed through his mind. Kate's constant expectations of him, was very trying. Should he consider taking Helen away from here, he could employ some help? What sort of life could he offer her if he let her travel with him? Knowing his next assignment was to work from New York and visits would be impossible, brought a lump to his throat.

His habitual drinking was increasing. If he had Helen with him, would it make a difference? She might fill the emptiness he felt.

Conscious that Kate expected some appreciation he leapt back into action.

"Wonderful. I'm famished. I'll go wash my hands and tell Helen to come back in. You haven't forgotten that I have to be away by five today Kate? Sorry it's such a short visit this time."

Kate shook her head showing her resignation.

"If it's what it takes to get on, you have to do it.

John observed the lunch time ritual of Kate's home. Helen was reminded to go to the bathroom. Wash her hands. Sit at the table properly. No elbows please. No talking. An almost forgotten memory about his father came to mind. He recalled his voice; his laugh, the smell of fresh beer on his breath and his defiant words. "Leave the lad alone for goodness sake woman."

Drawing a sharp breath he realised his body was tense; his head filled with memories of raised voices and angry words.

Helen obeyed without question. So like her mother he thought, at the same time reminding himself, that it had done him no harm, and that children have to learn to be socially accepted.

He took comfort from the fact that his daughter was fortunate and had Amelia to bring fun and laughter into her life.

Molly had never said a bad word about Kate, and although he always suspected something unpleasant had occurred between them he had chosen to pretend he had no sense of the atmosphere that arose when Kate was in their company.

An overwhelming sense of guilt and sadness washed over him. Ashamed, he berated himself. He had proved to be an ineffective husband and here he was, a pathetic father figure for his daughter. At the time of Molly's death he agreed with Kate's plans; he had no option but to accept her offer to raise Helen. He had not considered then that he was as good as giving her away.

Glancing across at Kate and Amelia, he smiled. Both gave Helen their undivided attention when she politely asked for more gravy. Suddenly it was as if he was the stranger. These were the only two women he had in his present life. He was indebted to them forever for their generosity towards his daughter. Indeed, if he was honest, Molly's death had provided them with a purpose to live through widowhood.

Gazing at the petite little girl facing him he gulped in air with his food and spluttered madly trying to regain control of his oesophagus. Only Helen was his true family, his only known blood relative.

Amelia, obviously fearful, jumped to her feet and pummelled his back until he recovered. He waved her away and with a hoarse voice told her he would survive, whilst Kate admonished him for gulping down his food.

Consumed by a desperate and urgent need to reclaim his daughter he bit his lip to hold back the words. He wanted to announce here and now that he was taking her home with him.

He became aware of Helen's large anxious eyes watching him. To put her at ease he smiled and gave a playful wink. Her face lit up. How easily I could ruin her young life with selfish behaviour he reflected. She proudly placed her knife and fork onto her empty plate.

"I'm finished. Thank you for a lovely dinner Grandma".

"I'm glad you enjoyed it" Kate replied. "Just a few minutes and you can have your rice pudding. You are a very good girl."

Amelia clapped her hands in approval.

"She certainly is. And a very pretty girl too."

John, sensitive to the love these three shared, cringed inwardly as he imagined separating them. He could not do it. On the other hand, separation from him, he believed, would not be so unbearable for them. He convinced himself that he was the outsider now, and he doubted they would miss him that much.

Later, he hugged Helen a little more tightly than was normal; silently praying that she would understand his reasoning when she was older. He let go of her and with a false cheerfulness, wished her goodbye.

With long strides, he turned the corner at the end of the Square, once more returning for the last time, Helen and Aunt Amelia's enthusiastic waves.

With a deep breath he made a vow that when he came back to North Shields he would have made a success of his career. He refused to be a disappointment to Kate or Helen. It was the best he could do.

chapter 12

John - May 1931

"WHAT THE HELL?"

John rolled over onto his stomach and hid his face into the pillow. The pain felt worse. He tossed his body on to its side.

"Alright, alright" he shouted out to whoever was banging on his door. He sat on the side of the bed and put his aching, tousled head into his hands. If only the room would stay still. With no saliva his mouth felt parched and his tongue twice its size. A wave of nausea entered his gut and he made a beeline to the bathroom. The banging on the door seemed in time with the banging in his head.

"Go away" he shouted out angrily.

"Mr Smith it is six o'clock. Have you forgotten that you requested I did not stop knocking until you answered your door? So open the door Mr Smith."

A groan, verging on a growl, gushed out while he spewed into the toilet pan. Oh God ... so he had. He forced a muffled response.

"Thanks Harry. You can go now."

"No Mr Smith, you said you had to open the door before I go away."

John stared blearily into the mirror. His red puffy eyes squinted back at him. He did not look good. He splashed cold water onto his face and mopping it with a towel staggered to the door. A gap of five inches fulfilled the agreement as far as Harry was concerned. The door was open!

"You look dreadful Mr .Smith. Do you want me to get you something?"

"What do you suggest Harry? A hair of the dog?"

"A pint of milk might be more agreeable Mr Smith. I'll get you something."

He turned on his heel and disappeared down the hallway.

John went back to the bathroom and sluiced himself with cold water, had a shave and cleaned his teeth. By the time Harry returned he was dressed and groomed.

Harry handed him a jug of milk saying he hoped he would soon feel better.

John grinned sheepishly.

"Thanks Harry. I appreciate it... I'll see if I can bring you something back from this official opening I'm reporting on today."

"Well just don't let anyone know how to get as high as that building is." Joked Harry

"Try not to. It has a lot more floors than the Iron Building and beats the Chrysler. Even I couldn't get that high." John returned good-humouredly.

Laughing Harry turned on his heel "See you this evening Mr Smith" and then headed off down the hall.

John thanked his lucky stars that he had made friends with the staff at this small hotel. They all liked him. They were knowledgeable, and discreet, about how he managed to get hold of decent alcohol. He lit a cigarette and put his bits together.

He meandered through the park. The trees were in full bud and the fragrance of dew in the grass filled his nostrils. Taking deep gulps of air to expand his lungs energised and brought him back to life. Quickening his pace he marvelled at the brilliance of the lake for this early hour in the morning. His mind wandered back to his favourite view of the sea in Simons Town, would he ever see that again he wondered and a light nostalgia washed over him. What became of

Alice … he regretted she had not replied to his letters; it would have been nice to stay in touch. He imagined she was probably a wife and mother of several children by now.

He wished his head would stop aching. Mornings were no fun since he had taken to drinking so late into the night with his pals. He was getting drunker at the clandestine establishments in this city more than he ever did in the public houses in England.

If only his head would stop aching. He was unable to appreciate the beauty of the park whilst hung-over like this. He shrugged his shoulders; he liked a drink or two, so what. Calling out a cheery good morning to an elderly man walking his dog lifted his spirits. He liked the people of New York. Everybody was far friendlier here.

He could see Kate's disapproving look in his mind's eye. He grinned. Fancy talking to people he did not know! At least he had the satisfaction of not having to answer to a parent. Life was so much better.

〰〰〰〰〰〰〰

The group of reporters jostled with each other in an effort to gain a favoured position. John was not backward in using his aggressive stance at times like this. His intention was to get a good story and photograph, the best headline, and to ensure he got answers to prepared questions.

His editor, a true taskmaster, had given his backing to this posting. John appreciated the encouragement and support of the man, and now intended to prove that his estimation of him was worthwhile. Some colleagues back home had lost their jobs, and employment was little better here. To keep on top of things and be the best was the only way forward. He shoved an older and smaller man out of his way, forcing his way to the front. A tall, thickset figure stood in front of him.

"Come on George, make way for a pal"

A bearded face turned around.

"God didn't expect to see you today. You must be feeling dreadful."

"Not at all," John lied. "Always up with the lark, that's me. Have I missed anything?"

"No. Usual stuff. Just things being put into place"

John caught sight of a slender, attractive auburn haired woman, walking around in the foyer of the building.

"She looks like someone worth knowing" he said in a conspiratory tone.

"Out of your league, young John. More my type I would say" George retorted.

"You're a married man with children George. Behave yourself and give the likes of me a chance."

Alongside the older men he worked with John enjoyed a little banter.

"You don't know what I'm saving you from. Stay single and carefree if you've any sense."

John laughed. "Whatever you say George, but a little fun here and there is rather nice."

The crowd was dense after the official opening, and yet John was still able to identify her. She moved around quietly with elegance and grace. The smile that hovered on her lips looked slightly mischievous. Her hair waved closely to her head fell into loose waves that bounced upon her shoulders. He felt a slight shudder. Something about her hair reminded him of Helen. He swallowed the remains of the pink lemonade in his glass and made a concerted effort to take his eyes off her. Walking across to the drinks table he made contact with his old buddy, Joseph, from a rival newspaper. He asked casually.

How long you been in Manhattan now?

"Long enough" was his usual growled response.

"Well then you would know where to take a woman if you wanted to wine and dine her … and you know … mmm … finish the evening with a little intrigue, wouldn't you?"

"Maybe. Who exactly are you trying to impress John? I've seen your roving eye today. It wouldn't be the rather lovely redhead would it?" His tone was caustic.

"Can't say it's not, but on the other hand, I haven't been introduced, so she has no idea that I'm in the room. Treat my question as purely hypothetical for the moment."

"Well I'll tell you something for nothing." Joseph sneered. "You stand as much chance with that gal as I do getting invited to the Whitehouse."

John raised his eyebrows quizzically.

"As far as I know, Miss Victoria Delaney shows little interest in men. She's usually in the company of her uncle, the high powered Mr James Delaney, and her male cousins."

"What, the pioneers behind this building?"

"Yep. A very wealthy family. The girl is an adopted daughter so I gather. The family brought her back from England. When Mrs. Delaney died word went round that the girl suffered some kind of illness and I think I'm right in saying this is one of her first public appearances."

John shook his head in disbelief.

"You'd never know. She looks pretty confident to me."

Joseph turned to catch sight of the girl "I agree. As I said, it was a rumour." He shrugged "Difficult to say, the Delaneys like to keep a tight lid on their personal affairs."

"How do I get her to notice me my friend?"

"I have no idea John." He growled. "The only thing you might have in common with her is dear old England, but I wouldn't hold my breath if I was you."

John nodded thoughtfully and after some more casual talk wandered in and out of the crowd, keeping his ear open for extra information to make his article more interesting.

At no time did he become so engrossed in his conversations that he lost sight of Victoria Delaney.

Victoria

So easy to be happy, no more crying now she murmured.

The buzz and excitement was intoxicating. Rubbing shoulders

with characters she would never have met if it were not for Uncle James. Her role as hostess for him at this gathering made her feel real and alive. No longer hiding behind her guardian angel Aunt Ellen for protection from the outside world she was now brave enough to show her face.

Surprisingly, Victoria found she could easily engage in a little banter and small talk with a group of reporters before moving on to socialise with some politicians and their wives. It was hard not to give a backward glance at the tall, over-vibrant young man who had joined them and dominated the conversation. The fascination she felt puzzled her and made her draw in her breath. Although the way he had gazed at her with open admiration, embarrassed her, she had boldly returned his gaze before moving on, her heart beating fast and her cheeks hot and flushed.

Unnerved, her eyes frantically searched the room until she spied him. She breathed a sigh of relief. Uncle James was there. Immediately she began to relax. The thought of his not being there for her sent shivers along her spine. Keeping her eyes fixed upon him she told herself how much easier it was to be calm, even happy when he was close by.

She headed in his direction thinking one day … one day… I **will** walk across the threshold with confidence. No more fear. His words echoed in her mind. "Hold your head high, become part of society, put away childish fears, come, live life, love life. You are safe, I won't leave you."

A smile came to her lips and she happily joined her cousins and the young group of people with them.

James Delaney convinced he had seen a spark in his niece was taken aback. Never had he seen her face this beautifully flushed, the over-bright sparkle in her eyes or the way she nervously twisted a strand of loosened hair. He watched her as she walked away from his group a little later aware of how becoming she had grown. Of course, she would attract the attentions of men. He had promised his wife to protect their niece from any unsuitable suitors and he would.

James' eyes flitted back and forward from his niece to the young man. Though the young reporter stood with his back to him it was obvious from his casual stance, his head and shoulder movements that he had Victoria captivated with whatever he was saying to her. He could see her eyes and lips were smiling as if she was highly amused by him.

James surprised, by the strength of his protective feelings kept a zealous eye on her. He had kept a constant watch over her since his wife had died, protecting her from vulnerable situations, and yet at the same time encouraging her to have faith in her own abilities. He wanted her to take her place in society. Had he not cajoled and manipulated her to be at this very function so she could meet those outside of the family? He realised the feeling he had was jealousy to see that an unknown person could elicit such a response when it had taken him months. He tried to convince himself that he was delighted for her; was it not the very thing he hoped for her. Situations such as this could increase her confidence and social etiquette so she no longer had to look to him for her every need.

This very realisation caused James' heart to sink and his grief welled up within him. Since Ellen's death, his niece had been a powerful diversion for him.

Struggling to retrieve his sense of decorum he turned sharply and walked purposely towards a group of colleagues. This was not the time or place for painful reflections.

Shortly afterwards he looked in her direction and smiled encouragingly in acknowledgement of her glance and was gratified to see the fleeting look of relief in her eyes. Had she feared his disapproval?

Deftly he manoeuvred himself through the crowd until he reached William his eldest son. He spoke quietly as he passed him by.

"See if you can find out who Ria's admirer is. I suppose it is possible that Irvine might know, he's hanging about in some unsuitable places these days."

He greeted the rest of the company where his son Irvine was happily doing the entertaining and decided to enjoy the boy's obvious talent at capturing his audience. Irvine never failed him; he turned to his father with a charming smile.

"Exciting time's father, what would we do without your foresight? I suspect this building will impress many generations to come. It's amazing."

Heads nodded with enthusiasm and applause. James delighted in the animated conversation, interlaced with laughter and jovial humour.

James Delaney and partners had achieved both a financial reward and the satisfaction of providing their fellowmen with positive optimism that this age of discontent and financial deprivation would soon pass. James was certain that this injection of positive thinking was in the public interest and the project had thrilled him more than any other.

Keeping a vigilant eye on his niece, he courteously accepted congratulations and praise from those around him, answered their questions where appropriate and maintained a cool demeanour, and yet inside he continued to struggle with conflicting emotions.

He welcomed Ria's approach by stepping towards her and putting his arm around her waist. She had a beaming smile on her face.

"Oh Uncle James, hasn't it been an amazing day?"

"It most certainly has, and you have captured a great many hearts. You are a natural born hostess Ria."

"I'm not quite sure where I get it from then" she grinned. "Mother was quiet and withdrawn and my Father … well let's just say I don't think I get it from him."

"Do you suppose I will ever get to meet him?"

"Not if I have anything to do with it."

The words fell from her mouth as if she had no control over what she was saying. She found it unbelievable that she had brought her Father into the conversation. Her mind had closed down on him so long ago she was aghast at the slip.

James pulled her closer to him.

"Don't go getting upset. Put it out of your mind and enjoy the little time we have left here. I observed you seem to have had some agreeable time with the Reporters today. Do you think we will get some decent reviews?"

Ria's cheeks flushed.

"Oh some of them were being a touch playful, but yes how could anyone not be impressed by such a building?"

"You could prove to be a trustworthy press secretary for me Ria. You are friendly and yet efficient. That is an admirable combination in this line of business. You could try it and it will be another skill. Not many women enter industry but I can see a future for you if you want it."

"Mm ... perhaps. I'm not sure whether I've got it in me."

"There's no rush. We will talk another time. In the meantime run along and find some people of your own age. You need to have fun."

Ria slipped back into the throng with a new energy. She felt bubbly. With slight hesitation she looked around, if she could seem to bump into him by chance it would not appear forward. Before she could put her plan into action she gleefully watched the very person making a beeline for her. Uncle James did say she needed to have fun.

Well maybe she would.

chapter 13

John — One Week Later

"THERE'S GOING TO BE a raid."
John's head shot round. Hastily swigging down the last drop of whisky and wiping his mouth with the back of his hand, a cold sweat came over him as the mayhem began. It was imperative he escape the premises before the police raid. He could plead some excuse, such as he was there researching the sale of illegal alcohol, but he was doubtful whether that would work.

Barely breathing he kept his head down. Surprised by his capacity to be caught up in the pandemonium and yet remain acutely aware of everything that was going on instilled a greater confidence in his ability to stay detached. The music, lowered to a reasonable level and within minutes there was not a trace of alcohol. Groups of men and women reclined nonchantly around tables now magically set out with soft drinks. The smoke from their cigarettes spiralled above their heads adding to the haze that hung like an ominous cloud over and around them. Weaving in and out of the tables, he spotted several famous faces, one of whom was with someone he recognised immediately. It was the son of James Delaney. Fleetingly their eyes met. Marvelling at his boldness to stay put he moved on.

John continued to keep his head down as he pushed himself into the crowded vestibule. Shit, he could hear raised voices from outside. He shoved his shoulder and elbow against those on his right hand side. "Come on" he hissed and once again rammed his body forward. He felt himself lurch towards the exit, another few paces, and he could squeeze through the door. The area was packed. They halted. Any further movement was impossible. "What the hell are they doing?" The panic that reached his ears was from his own raised voice.

"Move, you bloody idiots, move."

A man's voice bellowed from the front of the crowd.

"It's you who needs to move buddy. Go the other way. They're outside waiting for us."

John's pulse raised another notch; he could feel it throb in his temple. Unable to move either way, he felt stuck. There were more people behind him than in front.

Forcing his body round in one quick gyration, he faced the opposite way.

"What are you all waiting for, you heard the man, move yourselves."

Shocked by the aggression in his voice, the urge to push and shove became stronger. He had to find his way out of this place; arrest was not an option. He hardly recognised himself as he bellowed out.

"I said move."

The crowd obediently turned around upon his command and moved en masse, like lemmings, automatically heading for the next nearest exit.

At least he had them moving. His heart pounded and beads of sweat broke out on his forehead. The place was now hot and airless, and he needed fresh air. Overwhelmed by the fear of no escape he stared wildly about him, there had to be another way.

Feeling his sleeve roughly tugged, a frantic glance told him it was Delaney. Without question, he found himself dragged to one side as the crowd hurried on past, very glad to fill his space.

"Follow me"

In a stupor John kept pace, trusting Delaney knew more than himself. Anguished, he silently vowed, if he got out of this mess, it would be the last time he would do anything unlawful. Determinedly, he jostled with the crowd to keep up; there were now three people between him and Delaney. Ramming his body into the narrow space, he ignored the raised protest of the crowd around him. His alcohol levels, giving him false courage, lead him to antagonise anyone who got in his way. His only thought was to escape the nightmare.

At last, they reached a fire exit door. Delaney struggled with the handle, putting his shoulder against the door to help force it open. It did not budge... John added the weight of his shoulder and together they shoved. The lock gave way and the door flew open exposing them to an unlit walkway and six burly police officers waiting for them.

It was more than obvious to John these men were not fools and were hardened to the likes of him. His false courage caved in. There was nowhere to go. He watched Delaney and together they conceded defeat.

The police van was full. It was noisy. Everybody claimed to be innocent of any misdoing. John and two other men smelt foul from their own vomit and lowered their heads in humiliation as insults and jeers came from their companions.

When Delaney landed in the first police van, he called out to John.

"Say nothing. Just hang on in there."

John, dragged by two of the police and pushed roughly into the second van knew he was in for one of the worst experiences of his life.

The Police counter, manned by two officious officers, was bedlam. Taking pleasure in reading the crowd their rights, they then had them ushered to the cells by other self-important fellow-officers.

John remained with his head in his hands for several hours wondering what would happen next. He should be at the office in two hours.

Would Joseph come up with the bail? He would be in his debt forever if he did. He had considered asking Harry, but decided it would be foolhardy to involve the hotel staff. The quieter he could keep this the better. The possibility was that he could soon be on his way back to England with his tail between his legs. He groaned inwardly and cursed his own stupidity.

A loud voice penetrated his thoughts.

"John Smith, you're out. Get yourself together man, before we change our minds. Come on, come on."

Bewildered John got to his feet. The officer ran his truncheon along the bars of the cell mocking John as he did so.

"John Smith – what sort of a name is that? Typically English, or is it a cover up? We might have to check you out yet."

The cell door was unlocked and flung to one side.

"Move man"

The officer slammed the door behind him and almost caught the back of John's legs. The officer pushed him in front and walked him to the outer office.

"And don't let us see you back here again or else. Now get out of here."

Looking around him John could see no sign of Joseph. Approaching the counter he asked the officer who had bailed him out of custody. With a surly glance and a lot of huffing, the Officer checked his list.

"Says here it was Mr James Delaney, I presume you know him."

He added sarcastically,

"Calls it giving everyone a second chance, especially them from England. Does that answer your question Mr Smith?"

Nonplussed, John nodded, and thankfully headed for the exit. His mind was racing with unanswered questions, and yet at the same time he was too tired to think deeply about them. He raced across to the park and hurried back to the hotel. With a bit of luck he could clean up and still arrive at the office before his start time.

Mounting the stairs two at a time he reached his room panting and exhausted. Relief welled up in him as he almost fell against the door and jiggled the key in the lock. The key clicked into place and the door swung open. Once inside, he leaned heavily against it and closed his eyes, hardly able to believe he was free. His head thumped uncontrollably from yet another headache.

Wearily he stripped off his clothes where he stood and looked at the pile in disgust, deciding to bin them on his way to the office. The thought of requesting a laundry wash nauseated him.

Removing the sweat and filth of his ordeal with thick soapsuds, he massaged his body, watching the hot water taking it down the plughole and even further, down to the sewers where he knew it belonged. He let the water from the shower head continue to run over his hair and face for a long time, reluctant to emerge from its comforting warmth.

The Police Officer's disdainful comments about his name plagued him. Shaking his head, he wondered why. It had never bothered him before. For some unknown reason his name and the night's events merged like the scum that flowed around the shower and into the drain. With a jolt, he turned the water off. This was not the time to ruminate he had to get ready for work.

As was routine Harry knocked on the door. With a towel around his waist, John opened the door slightly and asked Harry for a hot drink and toast.

"No point starting the day with an empty stomach" he joked.

Harry answered with his usual discretion "None at all Sir" and at the same time handed him a hand-written parchment envelope.

"Hand-delivered about ten minutes ago Sir."

John bit on his bottom lip as he took the envelope and Harry hurried back down the corridor.

He opened it slowly and pulled the quality parchment paper out carefully. He tremulously unfolded the letter and read.

Fifth Avenue
New York

Mr John Smith,
I understand you and my son Irvine have something in common after last night.

I would be much obliged if you would accept an invitation to join me this evening for dinner at 8 p.m.
I look forward to seeing you then.

Yours sincerely,
James Delaney

John pondered the contents, wondering quite what James Delaney meant by in common. Was it the club, the alcohol or spending the night behind bars? Apprehensive about the invitation from James Delaney, he rubbed his chin roughly, conjuring up the scene in the liquor establishment. The image of Irvine Delaney, James Delaney's son, so confidently slouched at that table and not seeming perturbed by the disturbance came to mind. Did he think he would disclose the fact that his son was there. Did he think he was someone who didn't know how to keep certain things close to his chest? Did the Delaneys see him as a threat? His stomach tensed into a knot. He would have to prove he was trustworthy. It was in his interest as much as theirs to keep the episode quiet.

He walked to the table under his window, put his pen and ink to work.

Dear Mr Delaney,

I am happy to accept your kind invitation, and look forward to seeing you this evening.

Yours sincerely,

John Smith

Asking someone to deliver his letter by express, he handed the letter in to the reception desk as he left the hotel and headed towards the office.

chapter 14

Victoria — Fifth Avenue

AGITATED BY HER UNCLE James' announcement that there was an extra three guests for dinner, Ria nibbled the inside of her mouth and bottom lip. Inwardly dismayed that he had sprung this upon her she attempted to suppress feelings of panic. Having believed implicitly that he was the one person who truly understood her anxiety, tears filled her eyes. She had not felt this vulnerable for a long time. The catering was not a problem; it had far more to do with her state of mind. She had learned that if she planned everything down to the very last detail, she could cope, and was rewarded with praise and approval.

He had dismissed her worries and told her he had every faith in her ability to manage. His normal habit was to persuade and encourage her until she conceded to agree, and yet today he appeared oblivious to her distress.

True he had reassured her it was good practice; that an extra three persons at the table would make very little difference to the usual four or five she catered for, and kissed her forehead softly before leaving her.

Glancing towards the framed photograph of Ellen Delaney on

the piano, she craved the woman's serenity and confidence. The tender eyes and warm smile reached out to her. There was something precious and fragile in the face. The sleek thick dark waved hair brought a memory of the soft fragrance that always surrounded her. The unexpectedness of it took her by surprise and with her hand cupped against her mouth, her eyes brimming, a wave of grief swept through her. The loss of her aunt was as painful as that of her mother. Memories of their long talks by the firelight, the laughter, the tears, the hugs, flooded in. The strongest memory by far was Ellen's conviction that no matter what befell you in life, all would be well; that you had to flow with the tide and trust in God. It was she who had given Ria the will to live after her mother died, and with the benefit of time, she had proved that it was possible to laugh again. Ria knew it was for selfish reasons that she wished Aunt Ellen had lived longer. She had come so close to walking out of the house without Ellen alongside. She had constantly instilled courage for her to put one foot in front of the other and feel free from her fears.

She brushed a teardrop from her cheek. She had men in her life, but not the love of another woman. She often meditated on Ellen's words of wisdom, but recently even they seemed to have evaporated. She felt bereft and abandoned.

Physically shaking herself away from these morbid thoughts, she wondered if, by travelling to another country where she was unknown, she could re-invent herself. Both her mother and Aunt Ellen had talked of her likeness to her paternal grandmother, who apparently was a fearless lady. Much to her family's consternation, she had travelled unescorted, without her husband, on many occasions. Ria had long harboured a desire to be strong and independent like her grandmother. The whole concept of travel excited her.

She shivered. Common-sense told her she first had to overcome the phobia that had for so long held her prisoner within the house. She had escaped from her father with the help of Aunt Ellen, and Uncle James was doing his best in her absence. A surge to resolve her predicament provided her with new energy. She would do it and soon.

She headed for the kitchen to let Gracie know that there would be eight for dinner tonight.

Meanwhile, situated at the far end of the house, James sat at the large mahogany desk in his office. The early morning sun filtered through the part open window, throwing shadows around the room. A gentle breeze moved the brocade drapes back and forth. With eyes closed, he summoned Ellen's spirit into the room. Desperate for her to be here he felt some comfort; it was as if she was soothing his furrowed brow. He remained still, locked in his imaginary embrace of her. He lost all sense of time before reluctantly releasing her.

Staring at a small highly polished, ornately carved mahogany box, James felt his curiosity grow. This was Ellen's private box. Always amused by her need to store away small mementoes, he wondered now what she would say about his curiosity. He could imagine her placid smile, and assuring him, she loved to have one secret box. His mind floated back over time; remembering funny little incidents like an impulsive hug or kiss at the most unexpected moments. Often she puzzled him by withdrawing from some family occasion claiming she had a headache. He never pushed for explanations.

William and Irvine were her greatest delight but when they were out of sight, she remained agitated until they were reunited; and the extreme anxiety she suffered when either of them was ill. No amount of reassurance lessened her worry or could prise her away from their bedside. She was gentle and compliant, happy to oblige in her wifely duties except when her boys were in any way distressed, and then she was defiant.

He recognised the tense relationship between her mother and two brothers and within a short time of their marriage, she rarely mentioned them. Her father wrote to her occasionally, and did visit on several occasions although these also came to a halt.

A woman more loving and warm would be hard to find. Rarely did she utter a bad word or make judgements about others. Although intrigued by her quiet and dismissive way when he offered to take her to England, he still held his counsel.

When her mother did visit, he found her a rather self-centred woman, who lacked sincere warmth. It was a different story with her father. Ellen was relaxed in his company and he showed a caring attitude toward her. There had been no contact in years. He shook his head sadly.

James swallowed hard. His reluctance to look inside the box grew with every passing second. He lit a cigar deep in thought. He had to look again. He had discovered the box a few days after Ellen's death and had carelessly flicked through its contents. Ill at ease, he had guiltily returned it to its rightful home, out of sight.

Determined to end his illogical thought, he emptied the contents of the box onto his desk, letting a few minutes elapse before choosing to study the four miniature gold framed photographs. Studying them closely he decided they must be the same child. A plump, bright eyed baby, possibly six to nine months old, then another aged about four years standing in the middle of a slight dark haired, moustached man and a rather severe looking woman, her dark hair brushed into a loose bun in the nape of neck. They were all smiling for the camera. In the background, he could see what was possibly their home; the ground they stood upon looked dry and dusty. A schoolboy, a satchel over his arm and a lazy smile on his lips, filled one of the other frames. As James searched the photograph, he thought the boy was standing on high ground with the sea in the background. The last one was of a tall well-built young man, his hair blown by the wind and the same lazy smile that sat comfortably on his face. In the background was a large building, possibly a school and yet again he could just detect the sea.

James continued to stare at all four pictures. Slowly, he turned to look at the back of them and as he expected Ellen's small neat handwriting giving a date and the name John on each one.

He then carefully unfolded a letter and read the few still clearly written lines.

My Darling Ellen

Do not fret. The child is well. His parents have named him John, and they have taken him to South Africa. I will not mention this again and you must destroy this letter. You have nothing to fear. Enjoy your life in America. You can have children with James and be happy.

I enclose a photograph.

I will love you always

Your devoted Father.

James turned the letter over; it was undated. Without moving for many minutes, he deliberated the conversation with his son. What had William told him? The words echoed in his head. His name is John Smith. Born 1901. He works for The Times and was born in the north of England. Well educated in South Africa, and returned to England in 1921. Widowed a few years ago, so bad luck for a young man, and is working here on a temporary basis. Just an ordinary kind of guy with ambition to get on in life.

James put his head in his hands. Could this really be a coincidence? Is it possible that this ordinary kind of guy is the half-brother of his and Ellen's sons?

He pushed his chair back and stood gazing out of the window. With slow deliberate movements, he tore the faded notepaper into tiny pieces and let them drop into the wastepaper bin.

chapter 15

The Delaney Boys

FIFTEEN MINUTES TO KILL gave him too much time for thinking. John had strolled slowly along to Fifth Avenue so as not to arrive at the Delaney household too early. He had misjudged his timing.

He had successfully kept busy since he arrived in New York and managed to block out Molly's death and all that went with it. One slow stroll and grief swept over him in a way that he had not experienced since those early weeks.

His thoughts took him to places he had fought hard to keep at bay, with work and alcohol. He pined for Molly's warm soft flesh within his arms, her gentle kisses on his forehead, and the playful way she ran her tongue around his ears and neck. He physically ached for her. An inward sigh seeped into his every limb.

Molly, why was life so cruel?

He checked the numbers of the houses, he was nearly there; his head throbbed as sad thoughts gathered momentum.

Why us? … Why so short a time together? … Can you see me? I work hard, and do what I know you would want me to. … What a mess I am without you Molly.

He saw he was just one block away from his destination and his stomach turned.

Even as I go along a sidewalk I'm craving for whisky ... I hate who I have become ... and you would too. .. I'm a disgrace. ... I've let you down Molly.

The lump in John's throat made it difficult to swallow. He so had to get a grip on himself before he presented himself to his host. His step faltered, as the craving for alcohol took a hold on him. Turning abruptly, his head down, he retraced his footsteps to a Speakeasy close by.

Ria pushed open another window to let in the cool air. She thought it was surprisingly warm for May, or, she conjectured was it her struggle for composure? The thought of meeting Irvine's two new girl friends, he often talked about friends but rarely brought them to the house, was thrilling.

Apparently, he had also met a charming Englishman who was a journalist. Her heart skipped a beat, suppose it was that fascinating reporter from last week. Imagining it set up flutters in her stomach. She would be tongue tied and embarrassed. Breathing deeply she admonished her silly thoughts and remembered Uncle James, surely he would instil the confidence she needed. As long as he was with them, she would be fine.

The clock in the hall struck eight o'clock and James entered the sitting room. His spontaneous smile flashed across to Ria before he nodded a hello to William and his fiancée Geraldine.

"I do hope Irvine is not going to do his usual trick and arrive thirty minutes late."

William shrugged his shoulders, and took Geraldine's hand in his.

"I never know what Irvine might do Father, but I do hope he isn't running late because I'm famished. What have we got for dinner this evening Ria?"

Ria grinned mischievously. "I'm not telling you, except to say that it's something you like a lot, one of your favourites."

"Great, that means it's either steak or pheasant. Am I right?"

"Could be" Ria beamed as she left the room to answer the front door bell.

Two very becoming young blonde-haired women smiled broadly at Ria as she invited them in.

"You must be Moira and Margaret. Irvine told me to be prepared to meet two beautiful women, but I didn't expect you to be twins!"

"Didn't he warn you? He really is a rascal." They both laughed infectiously. Ria warmed to them immediately, they must be about my own age she mused. Showing them into the sitting room, she made the introductions.

James sat benignly in his armchair, enjoying the young people's conversation and trying hard not to let his annoyance with Irvine's absence slip into his tone of voice.

"And exactly where did you meet Irvine" he asked when there was a lull.

"I think the first time we met was in Club 21?"

The sisters collaborated before agreeing, both quite obviously in awe of James.

Both girls turned towards the door and smiled broadly.

Irvine looked in, grinned, and then looked directly over to James.

"Good evening father."

Looking behind him to indicate he had someone with him he gave a nod for his guest to follow him.

"And, look who I found making his way here, our other guest John. Come on in John. Let me introduce you to everyone."

Determined to remember names, as was his basic skill, John concentrated and repeated the names upon introduction. The twins, and Geraldine, he realised were the only people he had not seen in his travels. He quickly noted Ria's flushed cheeks, and felt somewhat flattered that he caused this reaction in her. Cautiously, he smiled and immediately turned his attention back to Irvine whilst Ria called them into the dining room.

James sat at the head of the table and expertly carved the pheasant, while Ria explained what was in each of the tureens. He absorbed their light-hearted banter and casual conversation as he offered each of them their plate. He was quietly pleased with his idea. How else was Ria going to meet people of her own age?

He observed John and Ria's playful chatter that mingled nicely in with Irvine and the two girls' flirty ways. He secretly wondered how the twins would be if they were separated from each other. He kept a discerning eye on William and Geraldine, exclusively locked in serious debate about the state of the dollar. He worried slightly about their lack of rapport with their peers. It perturbed him that his sons often displayed signs of conflict, both unable to show charity to the other. His late wife could often encourage them to compromise, consider the opinions of others and if need be, to agree to disagree. She had a genuine skill that he had envied. Now a lone parent, it exasperated him that the boys delighted in their rivalry. He sat up with a start when he realised he constantly fretted about them and it was tiring him.

"Is something wrong Uncle James" Ria's concerned voice cut through the chatter.

"No, not at all my dear. Just feeling my age I guess."

"Feeling left out Father?" Irvine enquired with a small snigger. "We don't do it deliberately, honest."

"I'm sure you don't son. Remind me; tell me where you met Moira and Margaret they thought it was at Club 21?

Irvine averted his eyes.

"Him, yes I think it was."

Keeping his eyes fixed on Irvine, James cleared his throat.

"We must have a chat later, and you say you met John in First Avenue? Seems you both like to frequent the same places."

"Aw come on Father, we're not the only ones."

"No I don't doubt that, but as John knows, and I am not excluding you, it's not so funny when the place gets raided. Would you agree John?"

John felt the blood drain from his head. Here was the man who got him out of trouble and Irvine was spilling the beans about where they met tonight.

He muttered quietly "No it's not Sir."

He prayed for someone to break the silence. The food he had just consumed felt heavy in his stomach.

He frowned slightly and glanced up at James.

"I've been doing a lot of thinking today. As much as I love being in New York I have asked my Editor if there is any chance of being transferred back to England"

He paused, thinking I've done it now; I really will have to ask for a transfer and then added.

"You've been very good to me Sir and I appreciate it."

Not expecting to be handed the solution to his problem so promptly, this seemed to be the ideal answer. James smiled contentedly.

"I think you are a very sensible and clever journalist John, I'm sure you have a brilliant career waiting for you back in England."

"Thank you sir. I will probably be here for a while yet at least until a suitable opening occurs."

"Well until you leave here, you might like to stay in touch. I'm sure Ria and Irvine would welcome your company."

Ria's face lit up.

"I will be happy to be friends, even if it will be short term. What part of England are you from John?"

James listened expectantly.

"I was born in Northumberland, but spent my first twenty years in South Africa. I wasn't happy about returning to England, it is so cold and damp, and I still yearn to go back to Simon's Town, back to where I was known, back to my friends."

"So why not go back there?" William chipped in.

"I might, but I have family responsibilities, and I want to further my career before I decide."

"Have you brothers and sisters John?" Ria asked as she handed him his coffee.

"No I was the only child."

No mention of adoption thought James. It could be mere coincidence. My hypothesis was highly improbable.

Embarrassed by the attention he was receiving John tried to distract them.

"And how about you Victoria, I think I heard that you have lived in England.

He gratefully recalled the conversation between himself and George.

"Where do you originate from? Have you brothers and sisters?"

"Please call me Ria. All my friends call me Ria."

She rubbed at her nose as though it itched.

"No John I have no brothers and sisters. I think of William and Irvine as my brothers, although they are my cousins really. Durham is my hometown, so not so far from your birthplace John. Strange that isn't it? I came to live here when I was seventeen and as long as Uncle James wants me, I will stay here. Someday, I might want to travel, perhaps I could go to South Africa!"

She flashed a wide smile at James.

"That would be an adventure my dear. You and John will have to talk about South Africa."

James admired Ria's spirit. It was good to hear she and John had something in common, but it did not alter the fact that he had decided, it would be best for him and his sons if John was kept in the dark about his suspicions.

Ellen's secret went with her when she left this world.

He turned his attention to William and Irvine surprised by his spontaneous resolve to adjust to his loss of Ellen. His announcement was unplanned and impetuous.

"I'm seriously thinking of taking a trip abroad myself. I would like to seek out some of your mother's relatives. Your grandparents have not responded to my letters so I am at a loss to know whether they are still alive."

"Can I trust you both to keep an eye on my business affairs while I'm away?"

Taken aback the two young men looked at each other with raised eyebrows. William spoke quickly.

"You know you can trust me. Is Irvine responsible enough?"

He shook his head.

"I don't know."

"I most certainly am," protested Irvine. "Give me the chance Father and I will prove it."

He stared coldly at William.

"You're not the only one who can be successful. I happen to have some very valuable contacts."

"Yes don't I just know it, but Al Capone is not exactly the sort of contact we want."

"Grow up" snapped Irvine.

"Father doesn't get the likes of me and John out of bother for no good reason. It is in his interest to have certain contacts in these difficult times. It's lucrative and that's not an exaggeration."

He glanced over at James.

"I am as able as William and I will prove it father."

James raised his hand to stop the bickering. He did not want any more talk about Speakeasys in front of his guests.

"I know you can both do it. I would not have suggested it if I did not think so. What you will need to do is learn how to work together. You more than proved your skills with the Wall Street crisis William. Now I'm challenging the two of you to become a team. Can you do that?"

He studied the two young men in front of him. He revelled in the satisfaction of having sons.

Ellen had always lavished unconditional love upon them. At the time, he had found it unnecessary, but now he could see the long-term benefits.

His lifetime vision for a family empire, was no secret, it could become a reality if the boys accepted this new responsibility with confidence. In his eyes, it required passion and complete involvement in business to succeed.

He remembered sadly how detached he had felt from his father's shipping business and how upon the demise of his father, he still had no interest or wish to be involved. He had accepted his financial legacy and let the business dissolve with no sense of disloyalty to his father. His mother's look of disappointment when he had vehemently refused to relinquish his love of architecture in favour of a shipping industry stayed etched upon his memory for all time. If his older brother had not tragically died at the young age of eighteen the situation would never have arisen. James had no expectations to live up to. Exclusion was familiar to him. He had never been included in the little intimate chats his father and brother would enter into, no matter how often he argued that he was old enough to do so. If the truth be known, he had never completely recovered from this hurt.

William's voice cut through his thoughts.

"Thanks for your confidence in us Father. Of course, we can do it. We're both grown men for goodness sake."

He gave his brother an apologetic lop-sided grin

"I'm game if you are Irvine"

Irvine offered William his hand

"Put it there bruv" and then over-heartedly slapped his brother's back as he attempted to embrace a rather embarrassed William.

"We'll do just fine us two. I can see Delaney & Co becoming Delaney & Sons before the year's end"

James offered his glass up and the three of them drank a toast to the future, oblivious to the other five in the room acting as the perfect audience, silent until the finale. They brought attention to themselves with a burst of applause. The Delaney men laughed in unison and toasted their guests.

A stab of jealousy startled John enthused by this show of family unity. He flashed a wide smile at Ria in an attempt to steady himself. She quickly smiled back as if quelling some anxiety of her own. He wondered whether she shared the same aloneness.

Would she travel with James? The thought of meeting up with her in England excited him. In the meantime, he intended to see as much of her as was possible before he returned home.

chapter 16

John and Ria

JOHN STOLE A FURTIVE glance at Ria's profile. A pearl droplet decorated her tiny earlobe and her long sweeping eyelashes curled gently upon her lower lashes. Her neck was long and slender and the subtle perfume she wore lingered on her skin, lightly wafting his way each time she moved. He caressed her hand, which lay comfortably in his. She turned her head and smiled.

The seats were comfortable in the Movie House and around them, an aura of intimacy exuded from other young couples cuddled up and lost in their own private worlds. Thinking her smile was a signal of acceptance for them to enter the intimacy he clasped her fingers gently and lightly stroked the inside of her palm.

Something about her provoked a feeling of tenderness. No woman had evoked this in him since Molly, which alarmed him somewhat because he did not want commitment at this time in his life. He lifted her hand to his lips and kissed her fingers determined that he could enjoy her company without embarking on a serious courtship. He knew he was capable of coercing her into a false sense of security with loving endearments. It came easy to John. He was not slow in coming forward when a woman succumbed to his smooth talk. Ria snuggled in closer to him. He doubted she would appreciate this side of him. She was clearly different, naive, and even shy. He might have to tread carefully and be extra loving.

Tonight was an opportunity to test out whether their relationship could work. Their impending parting due to his return to England was drawing near. He was booked for the next passenger/freight ship leaving New York Harbour.

Tonight was important. He wanted to celebrate, amazingly without alcohol he realised. New York had proved to be more interesting and enjoyable than he had envisaged. There was no doubt that his time here had been successful both as a journalist and with friendships. As a popular and well-liked member of the newspaper team, he was returning to England with far more confidence. He had an ability to seek out stories that caught the readers' imaginations and his bold headlines had become second nature to him now. He sometimes marvelled at his own exuberance and instinct to ferret out the truth. He was eager to focus on the poverty and unemployment situation back in England. His interest in politics and social issues had developed. He wanted to challenge what he perceived to be injustices to the working class.

He had recognised over the past months that unearthing the human plight behind a situation procured far more readers.

The background music to the movie indicated a romantic and happy ending, which brought a smile to John's lips. He had chosen the right film for Ria. He noticed the tear that ran along her cheek and onto her mouth. She wiped her cheek with the back of her hand and sighed. "Oh what a lovely end. I do love a happy ending."

Joining the crowd, they, like all the other couples, jostled good-naturedly to exit the building. John slipped his arm around Ria's tiny waist and felt the softness of her hip movement against his hand. "Shall we go for coffee now?" he suggested with mock seduction. She nodded good-humouredly and allowed him to pull her closer to him.

The streets around Times Square bustled with people as John and Ria slipped into the nearest coffee bar that had a vacant table by the window. They slid onto the bench seat and Ria took her lightweight wrap from her shoulders. She giggled. "I feel like a naughty child. You know – the one who takes the last cake?"

Acting hurt John kept a straight face. "I was hoping you might feel more like the cat that got the cream."

Ria looked puzzled.

Replacing his hurt look with a smile John said jokingly.

"Like, have you, or have you not, made a real catch? This is I John Smith, loveable bachelor, sweeping you, the most attractive gal around here, off your feet. When did you last have such a delightful date?" John winked to put her at ease and kissed her on the cheek.

Grinning, Ria shook her head in mock despair. "I'll never get used to your sense of humour."

"You will, I promise you will." John pulled her hands into his. "I want to get to know all about you and what makes you laugh."

Lingering for as long as possible over their coffees, they agreed it would be good to walk back to Fifth Avenue via the park. It was quite a distance to the park, not something he believed Ria would normally undertake when wearing high heels. Opening the door for her, he told her lightly that he wanted to keep her out and never take her home.

"Until you get bored with me." Ria punched his arm playfully.

When they arrived at the park they strolled quietly hand in hand appreciating the warmth of the late evening air, oblivious of other couples who wandered the park in a similar way until a sudden strong wind blew up, whipping and buffeting their clothes against their bodies.

Everyone began to look for cover. Laughingly they raced towards the shelter of a large spreading tree that John fervently hoped they could keep solely to themselves. Panting they leaned against the trunk of the tree.

"You look gorgeous," John, blurted out. "You should run and laugh more often it brings you to life."

Looking up into his face Ria smiled "It's you who brings me to life. You are such fun to be with."

Protected and safe they watched torrential rain pelt and bounce off the ground around them, cooling the air enough for Ria to pull her wrap more firmly around her shoulders.

John hugged Ria in close to him and kissed her softly, his heart beating faster. She closed her eyes tentatively and returned his kiss. Unprepared for the impact of his kiss, a surge of emotion rushed to her head and a sliver of excitement ran along her spine. She meltingly succumbed to the smell of his skin against her face and to the warmth of his arms.

Encouraged, John teased her mouth open with his tongue, and pushed himself hard against her.

Ria's eyes opened wide. Feeling the strength of his passion, her panic began to rise. She struggled to release her lips from his, pushing for all her worth against his chest for him to free her.

Shaking her head fitfully, tears flowing, she pushed even harder at his chest and broke away from his embrace.

"No John" she sobbed.

John dropped his arms and took a step back. A surge of anger pulsed through his veins. Bewildered and frustrated he stared at her his lips pursed, unable to speak.

Calming down he registered her obvious distress and was jolted back to the last time he had caused tears. He remembered Alice who as a young virgin had cried when she asked him to promise to come back for her. It was easy to promise, not so easy to make it happen. He had written once, received no answer and Alice was forgotten.

Had he learnt nothing about women? On the other hand, what had he done now that was so distressing?

John tried to keep the hopelessness out of his voice.

"Why not, don't you like me?"

Shaking her head wildly she brushed away the tears.

He lifted his hands and framed her face.

"What's wrong Ria?"

She hung her head like a small child caught doing something naughty and half stammered.

"I'm sorry John if I gave you a false impression … I really want to be friends with you … but you have to understand … it can't go any further than that."

"But I don't understand Ria. We could be so good together." His eyes pleaded with hers. "Is it my lack of social standing? Maybe you think I'm not financially secure enough for you … Is that it? Or is it more likely "he said accusingly, "that I wouldn't be acceptable to James Delaney?"

Ria brushed away her tears. "Please John don't. It's none of those things."

"I don't believe you Ria" His arms dropped down by his side again. He realised that he'd never quite felt for any girl what he was starting to feel for Ria. He was enchanted with her.

Ria returned his pleading look and took his face in her hands. "John listen to me … it's not you, it's me."

John shook his head impatiently. "I don't understand Ria."

After a long pause she faltered, her head hung low.

"Do you promise not to say a word to anyone if I tell you something… something I have told only one other? I care a lot about you John … and I will understand if you decide not to stay in touch with me."

Stirred by her humble demeanour John nuzzled his head into her fragrant smelling hair and murmured "of course," his words almost drowned out by the torrential rain.

She raised her head, "really John I mean it, you must swear you will never tell another soul."

Clasping his face in her hands, she pleaded "promise?"

He nodded acquiescently his eyes fixed on hers. A sense of calm descended on him nothing she could say would change the powerful affection he felt for her.

Ria took her hands away from his face. "Will you hold me, while I try to explain?"

Once again, he nodded. She slowly turned her back to him, took his arms and placed them around her waist, her own hands pressed against his. John strained to hear her quiet hesitant voice.

"I was a little girl, when … somebody did some very bad things to me."

A prolonged pause pursued as she gathered the strength to go on.

"I learned things no little girl should know about … I ached to tell my mother … she was ill so often, I .. I was afraid to worry her. He often told me it would be wicked to tell her … if I did, it could kill her. I suppose I learned I could detach myself, my mind, to protect me from feeling anything … whenever he called me … " she held her breath and then gasped "I made believe it wasn't me … that I could become numb by … I can't explain … I just did it."

She pulled his arms tighter into her.

"I now feel unable to control the instant detachment … I … can you understand I can't have a relationship with a man, any man? It is as if my mind takes over as it did with him … I am no good to you John. I'm damaged goods, soiled and dirty."

Taking a deep breath, her voice trembled "There John now you can see it has nothing to do with you."

John's throat tightened, together with his grip on her. Gently nuzzling her neck, he frantically searched his mind to say something that could be comforting to her. Her confession was beyond his understanding.

They stood locked in their silence, listening to the rain.

Sometime later, he gently turned her around, embraced her and kissed her tearstained face.

"Thank you Ria. You are so brave. I love you for your honesty. I have never been as courageous as you have. I am trying to take it all in."

Once again, he lightly kissed her face.

I've never known anything like it … and of course you are worried about our becoming lovers, but it doesn't stop us from staying friends does it?"

"You still want me to be your friend?"

"Of course I do, more than ever now. How dare someone ruin the life of such a lovely person? I could kill him for you, honest I could."

Ria detected anger in his voice and reacted fearfully.

"I wouldn't want you to do that. Believe me John, he isn't worth it."

Is he still alive?"

"I don't know. I haven't seen him in many years and I've buried that part of my life."

She saw John bristle.

Pleading, she pulled at his arm.

"Please John I don't want to talk about it anymore. It's stopped raining and I'd like to go home now."

Her face was pale and drawn and his heart went out to her.

"Of course."

He looked around them and became aware that the park was looking very shabby. "It's about time someone did something about this park. Look at the litter" he exclaimed as if seeing it for the first time. He was suddenly angry and kicked at the rubbish by their feet. It was upsetting to see this great park neglected and abused by the very people who wanted it.

"I must investigate who manages the park," he grumbled.

Ria smiled weakly. "You do that John."

They walked hand in hand, both lost in thought, until they reached the Delaney house.

"I won't ask you in tonight John. I would rather go straight to bed."

She glimpsed a look of anxiety in his face.

"I still have another four days before we leave so could we meet for one more time to say goodbye?"

"I will say au revoir, never goodbye" John joked. The thought of never seeing her again, made his heart miss a beat and sent waves of melancholy through him.

Ria smiled and put her arms around him with a warm hug.

"You are a kind and dear man." She kissed his cheek. "Goodnight John."

He detected a little catch in her voice and wanted to hold her close. A rush of questions came into his mind. The urge to receive answers caused him to hold her away from him.

"Sleep well Ria. Goodnight."

He turned on his heel and walked away quickly before he could say anything he would regret.

Ria watched him until he turned the corner and then quietly closed the front door and headed straight for her bedroom.

A few minutes later, there was a tap on her bedroom door.

"Is everything alright Ria?" James called out.

"Everything is absolutely fine" she called back cheerfully.

She buried her face in her pillow and let it soak up her tears.

✂✂✂✂✂✂✂✂

Breathing hard from his fast walk back to the hotel John thanked Charlie for handing him an envelope before returning to his room. The neat handwriting well known to John brought a smile to his face. It could not have arrived at a better time. He needed to feel a connection with home at this time. His confusion had not diminished. Ria's story had upset him, far more than he would have believed.

He unearthed a bottle from its hiding place and poured a large drink. He gulped down half of it and let out a large sigh. He slit open the envelope, removed the lightweight writing paper and lay back on his bed. He read no more than My Dear John before closing his eyes and drifting into oblivion.

chapter 17

Tynemouth Village

THERE WAS SALT IN the air, and a bite in the September breeze. Ria having forgotten how raw the seasons could be in the north of England pulled her coat closer to her body and shivered.

She stood in front of the black front door, looking around before knocking. She took delight in the late flowering hybrid roses that grew in the centre of the square beckoning any passer-by to admire both their beauty and delicate fragrance. She decided there was something rather pleasant about Tynemouth Village. With the memory of John's furrowed brow and tear-filled eyes when they said goodbye, she knocked firmly on the door.

The door opened slowly. Two pale faces greeted her. A tall, thin, grey haired woman, and a slight young child with long chestnut coloured hair pulled back into two tightly plaited ropes, that reached her waist, looked at her with curious eyes. Ria gasped silently at the sorrow she recognised in their eyes and moved toward them with compassion. She held her hand out to the woman who then raised a frail twisted hand and feebly placed it into Ria's.

"I am John's friend, Victoria Delaney, and you must be John's mother?"

Kate nodded. Her dull grief ridden eyes instantly took in Ria's elegance and grace. Obviously, a woman of class she decided. Strange, she thought, John had hardly made mention of this fine young woman, at least not by name, in his letters to her.

Two tugs on her coat diverted Ria's attention from Kate to Helen. The little girl announced in a clear sweet voice "and I am Helen."

"Hello Helen. What a pretty name you have."

Helen, with her up-turned face, looked at her grandmother and said gleefully "That's what you say isn't it grandma?"

The transformation on Kate's drawn face, when she bestowed a smile on Helen gave Ria an entirely new impression. She no longer seemed an elderly woman, more a loving mother.

"Well, now you know, it really is true. Please come in Victoria. As you will see our living accommodation is small, probably very different to what you are used to."

"Not at all" Ria said stepping over the threshold and into the sunlit filled front lounge. "What a beautifully light room" she exclaimed.

Kate warmed to her visitor. She is like a breath of light and fresh air she thought.

"We have a pretty garden too" Helen chipped in. "I can show you if you want to see. Aunty Am worked in it every day, and that is why it grows so well. She used to say she was closer to God in her garden than anywhere else in the world didn't she Grandma?"

The two adults looked at Helen with affection, both appreciating the ability of the young to be unafraid of the truth. Helen lowered her head and cast her sad eyes up to Kate "although we do miss her so much don't we Grandma?"

"We do indeed, but she has left us her wonderful garden to look at every day hasn't she?"

"Come and see 'Toria." Helen pulled at Ria's arm and urged her to follow. Kate nodded her agreement, and Ria, amused by the child's inability to pronounce her name correctly, followed the animated little girl into the garden.

❧❧❧❧❧❧❧❧

The two women sat companionably in opposite armchairs, while Helen slept peacefully on the couch with Fluffy curled at her feet.

"She always has her afternoon sleep at about this time," Kate explained.

Ria nodded and mused silently. And how about you Kate? Do you take advantage of this time to have a sleep because I see you are exhausted. I saw a similar look in my own mother's eyes when she was unwell. I so often let her think I needed to sleep in the knowledge that she could rest.

Kate was pleasantly surprised at her own ease with this unknown young woman. Her usual wariness and lack of trust in strangers was lowered which made her far more approachable and friendly. Amelia had constantly told her that others experienced her as hostile and she would implore her to be more open to others whereas Kate believed that offering her prayers to God should be enough. In her opinion, confiding in others would bring nothing but trouble.

Noticing that Kate's breathing was shallow, Ria leaned towards her

"Are you feeling unwell Mrs. Smith?"

A whisper of a smile played on Kate's lips. This young woman was certainly observant. The worry of a constant heavy ache in her chest would not go away no matter how much hot water she sipped.

"Mm I am a little breathless sometimes, but it is nothing to worry about thank you."

Ria wondered if she should bring her visit to an end.

"Would you prefer I take my leave of you and let you rest?"

"No my dear I am enjoying your company. You cannot leave until Helen is awake and can say goodbye to you. She becomes extremely upset if people appear to disappear."

"Oh I would hate for her to feel I did not want to say goodbye to her. Did she feel Amelia disappeared? It must have been very difficult for you over the past weeks with a young child in your care."

"Yes, it has not been easy."

"Was Amelia your only sister?"

"No, I still have two sisters. They live in Scotland, so I do not see them although we keep in touch by letter. It seems all my relationships are based on letters," she added sadly.

"Hopefully that will change when John arrives back in England" comforted Ria.

"Possibly. It depends on his work situation of course. I would not want him to think he has to be here when I have lots of help from my church friends.

Kate rubbed her forehead and said in a tired voice.

"It's Helen I worry about. It is nine months since John visited. She hardly knows him or he her comes to that. Amelia was so much stronger and could take her out to play. My sister had such a loving way about her with the patience of a saint and nothing was ever too much for her"

Horrified that tears were close her voice trembled.

"Oh my dear, please forgive me. I don't know what has come over me."

Compassion for John's mother filled Ria's heart.

"What came over you was sadness and grief. It is a long time since I lost my mother and I lost a very special aunt some time ago, and I still feel overcome by the pain every now and again. I think it is most natural."

"You are very kind Victoria," Kate said wiping her eyes with her handkerchief.

"My close friends call me Ria. Please feel free to do the same. I promised John I would call on you, and I must say it is a privilege to meet you and Helen. He is very lucky to have such a caring mother and beautiful daughter to come home to. If it is not too much of an imposition I would very much like to visit again."

Feeling an early affection for Ria, Kate smiled.

"It would be very nice to see you again and I look forward to the next time. Where are you staying?"

"Not too far from here. I am travelling with my Uncle James and we are staying with friends in Morpeth. We are trying to track down my grandparents, although to be honest I have no recollection of them. Uncle James was married to their daughter, and he has had no word from them since he wrote to tell them of her death. He is concerned that they may no longer be alive. It will be a shame if that is the case because I have hoped to meet them."

Kate visibly straightened up. "If they have lived in this area all of their life I might know of them" she offered.

"Oh ... I hadn't given that a thought," Ria said thoughtfully. "Well their name was Dalgleish. Robert and Catherine Dalgleish. My grandfather was a ship owner and apparently a much respected employer."

Nonplussed Kate felt the blood run away from her head. This was not possible. After all these years, someone from the Dalgleish family was here in her home. She sank back into the armchair. What was she to do?

"Oh Kate, what is wrong" Ria asked with concern. "Are you feeling ill?"

"No, no. Just a silly turn. I'm fine."

Rising to her feet Kate made a concerted effort to get herself back to normal and caressed Ria's arm to reassure her that she was indeed all right.

"Thank you for your concern Ria, but I will be fine. Shall we have some more tea?"

A giggle from Helen and both women turned towards her.

"Can I have a drink please Grandma? I am very thirsty and so is Fluffy." With Fluffy clutched to her, she stood up and carried him out of the room.

"First you must say goodbye to Victoria, she is leaving now," Kate called after her.

Helen put Fluffy onto the floor and ran back to Ria.

"No don't go, stay with us."

Surprised by Kate's change of plan for a further cup of tea, Ria was unsure of the response she should make to the child.

Kate stepped in the breach and said quite firmly, "It's time for our visitor to go, but you must say thank you because she waited until you woke up so she could say goodbye to you."

Looking up with sad eyes Helen did as she was bade.

"Thank you for coming to see us 'Toria."

Together Kate and Helen escorted Ria to the front door.

Kate opened it wide and smiled. "It's been a pleasure to meet you Victoria. Once again thank you for coming to see us. Say goodbye Helen" They both saw Ria open the front gate and waved, waited for her to return the wave and closed the door.

Ria closed the gate behind her, looked over her shoulder saddened by their brief and sharp goodbye only to realise they had already gone inside.

She wondered what she had said or done, to end the visit. She started to walk slowly away from the house feeling worried and unhappy. Once again, she looked over her shoulder and was sure Kate was watching her walk away. Feeling anxious, she was unsure of herself. Would it be better to stay away until John was back in the country? She had intended to offer some help. Helen seemed a sweet child and she might have been able to give Kate some assistance with her.

She shook her head unhappily before breaking into a run. She was convinced John's mother had liked her, but she obviously got it wrong. She slowed down struck by the thought that Kate had somehow detected her secret and was unhappy for John to know her. Her eyes brimmed with tears because she did not blame Kate for protecting her son.

chapter 18

James Delaney

THE NOTICE IN THE local newspaper jumped off the page. Kate's heart missed a beat. She closed her eyes tightly, trying to restrain her shock and disbelief, remaining motionless, unable to comprehend the content, until through half-closed eyes she stared at the page anew.

The implausible words, Robert Dalgleish, flashed back and forward inside her dazed mind. She put her hand to her mouth to stifle the groan that fought to escape. After all this time, it is not possible. First, there was John's friend Victoria Delaney, and now another stranger was asking for information.

With her elbows on her knees, she cupped her chin in her hands stunned. What should she do? She admonished her wild thinking. For goodness sake, Kate Smith, think! Telling herself to remain calm, she read the notice again. This time reading it word for word.

She was positive that Victoria had said her Uncle's name was James; and this was a Mr James Delaney. He was inviting any persons who knew of Robert Dalgleish to meet with him.   Speculatively she folded the newspaper and set it down by her side.

Jumbled thoughts thrashed around inside her head. The promise made to Robert Dalgleish, not to divulge the family secret, was now problematical. She questioned herself. If he was dead, was it a sin to tell? Relentlessly the words, a promise is a promise, thundered through her mind. Memories flooded in, she saw Bill's face, the way he had looked when they discussed adopting John. Had he not said then that to keep such a secret from the child would become a burden to them all? With hindsight, she realised that her longing to have a child, had clouded her thinking. So desperate for a baby all she had wanted was Bill's consent to the agreement before the opportunity was lost forever. Bill had loved her deeply and shared her sadness that they were not blessed with their own baby. It was this knowledge that encouraged her persistence. It had worked, he put aside his doubts, took her in his arms and murmured, "It's not my preferred way, but I pray to God, we never regret it."

Shaking off the past, she contemplated the life she had shared so far with John. She knew categorically that she would not change it, even if she could. She bowed her head in silent prayer.

The memory of Mrs. McCullen, with the wallet, and her small charge, remained as strong now and it was then. The softness of the shawl around his tiny warm body and the smell of baby milk as she handed him over to her were ingrained for life. She would protect him as much now as she would have then.

If as she supposed Victoria Delaney was a grandchild of Robert Dalgleish then she presumed there could be a family tie between she and John. The thought that they might be romantically involved was too awful to imagine. Neither of them deserved destroyed lives. She had to do something before it was too late.

She held on to her walking stick to steady herself and took slow steps into the back parlour to the walnut bureau. Taking a key from behind the mantel clock, she unlocked a small drawer hidden by an outer drawer in the bureau and took out the wallet. She remembered the instructions clearly, but she wanted to read them again for fear her memory had mislead her.

'Bring the boy up as your own. Please choose a Christian name followed by Dalgleish-Smith. He is entitled to have the name and he will receive a modest inheritance when he reaches the age of thirty.

During his childhood, you will receive one hundred guineas each year to go towards his welfare and education.

The money will be added to your husband's pay packet and the inheritance is in safekeeping with a firm of Solicitors by the name of McFadyean & Thynne of Morpeth. This information is solely for Mr William Smith and Mrs. Kathleen Smith. The way in which the boy is told about the adoption is down to how you as parents' deem appropriate.

Mrs. McCullen's reward is with my Solicitors for collection when she leaves your household in exactly one year from today's date. She is known for her ability to be discreet and professional and will impart no information about my family or yours.

Mr Smith will remain as my employee until the boy reaches the age of sixteen. From that time onward, no further constraints will exist.

A Birth Certificate is enclosed to avoid any problems in the place of your abode.'

❧❧❧❧❧❧❧❧

James Delaney looked a fine specimen of a man as he descended the opulent sweeping staircase of the Grand Hotel. He missed his wife Ellen dreadfully at times like this. Her arm linked in his, and her soft voluptuous body alongside him had always felt so proper. However, he did not display any outward signs of loneliness

His mind was full of memories and conflicts. He was feeling dubious about his decision to put a notice in print; on the other hand, it was his last attempt to contact Ellen's parents before leaving the north of England. He felt obliged to do everything possible, to let them know of her death, although Helen had made no request for him to do so, even towards the end of her illness. He was here in memory of his dearest Ellen and for him it was important to do things properly and with respect.

It also felt strange not to have Ria alongside him during these last few days. He had watched her gain confidence in leaps and bounds just recently; and now she had arranged several days out with their friends from Morpeth, which happily for her meant she no longer needed his constant company. He wondered what life would be like without his family around him on a daily basis. I suppose I have to grow old with grace and accept the truth of my circumstances he thought with good humour.

He made his way to the newly decorated lounge and chose to sit at one of the tables by the windows where he was able to see across to the pier and lighthouse and yet keep a keen eye on the entrance doors. There was a gusty wind blowing through the shrubs that grew in the well-manicured lawns at the front of the hotel. He marvelled at their ability to bend and flex to the will of the wind without breaking. A smile hovered on his lips as he realised his own need to withstand a stormy time. Did he have the same flexibility he wondered?

He whiled away the next hour or so reading The Guardian Newspaper. He felt perturbed by a report that staunchly played down Hitler's importance. James felt quite the opposite and believed he was dangerous; the world was in an unhappy state these days. The uncertainty of it all caused a furrow in his forehead.

This was how he looked when Kate had her first sight of him. He looked a worried man. Upon introducing herself to him, he graciously invited her to take a seat.

It was with some hesitancy that a silver-haired woman approached James and Kate. They appeared somewhat conspiratorial to her, their heads bent, studiously reading some papers in front of them. She kept her eyes lowered and put her hand to her brow. Bright sunshine gleamed on the windows momentarily blinding her. Her heart beat fast with apprehension as she stopped in front of them, fingers tightly entwined and knuckles clenched around the handle of her bag. She falteringly gave a light cough to gain their attention.

James turned his head and threw her a questioning look.

"Excuse me sir, my name is Elizabeth Williams" She hesitated slightly. "I was told you are Mr James Delaney?"

James nodded. "That's correct Madam." He felt slightly irritated by her intrusion and there was a hint of impatience in his voice "What can I do for you?"

"Well it was about the notice in the paper sir, but I can come back later if you would prefer."

James looked at Kate who was hastily gathering up the papers from the table and replacing them into her bag.   "I'll leave you to your business Mr Delaney," she said slowly rising from her chair.

"No please stay. Would you have any objections to Miss Williams joining us for a while? It would be a shame to send her away after she's made the effort to come here."

Kate looked warily at the stranger. She did not know of her so there seemed little reason for her to object to her presence. She lowered herself back into her chair and smiled charmingly at both of them. "Of course not."

"Is that agreeable with you Elizabeth?" James asked in a far warmer tone than before.

He patted the chair next to him in response to her acquiescent nod of the head. She removed her coat and sat where he indicated, her blue eyes looking longingly at the teapot.

"I shall order more tea," James said attracting the waiter's attention with a wave of his hand. "Now Miss Williams it is a pleasure to meet you. I presume you know of Mr Robert Dalgleish?"

"I'm usually known as Lizzy Sir, and yes I was employed as his housekeeper until May of last year. Mrs. Dalgleish liked to travel, so it was very often only Mr Dalgleish at home." She stopped suddenly as a new thought came into her head. "Oh I'm sorry, you did want to know about Mr Robert Senior didn't you?"

There was a smile in James eyes. "Yes Lizzy I do. And you... you are Lizzy? Lizzy! The Lizzy that my dear Ellen told me about? She spoke of you with much affection."

With her hand to her mouth, Lizzy stared at him in disbelief. "Do you mean Ellen Dalgleish, his daughter? ... Oh my goodness, is she here with you Sir?"

"If only she was Lizzy. If only she was. Sadly she passed away almost a year ago now."

"No! ... how awful for you Mr Delaney." She caught her breath not knowing what more she could say. She conjured up her last memory of Ellen. It was the day Ellen departed for America, looking so pale and unhappy. Only six weeks after she had given birth as well. The prolonged hug she had bestowed upon Lizzy, as if desperate to feel held in return, only to have the moment broken by her mother urging her to hurry into the carriage without further delay.

With tear filled eyes she wondered if she could have the fortitude to ask if she could see a photograph of Ellen. Nearly thirty years without further contact had passed since that day.

Pouring a cup of tea, Kate then offered it to Lizzy. She wanted to show her sympathy whilst at the same time she was still recoiling from the thoughts that James had earlier put to her. James Delaney appeared a very sincere man, but she could understand how difficult it was for him and that he was worried about his sons' reactions to the fact that their mother had given birth to a child before her marriage to their father. Then there was this aunt of Ria's who was in truth John's real mother. She shuddered inwardly wondering how any of them would react to the consequences of such a disclosure. She snapped out of her thoughts and focused her attention on Lizzy.

"Did you know Mrs. McCullen Lizzy?"

Without hesitation and with amazement in her eyes Lizzy nodded her head. "I only met her once though. Did you know her Madam?"

"I did" Kate answered quietly. "It was me to whom she brought the baby."

The three of them sat in silence as the enormity of their discovery sank in.

James was the first to take hold of the situation. "Tell me do you know the whereabouts of Mr Dalgleish Lizzy?"

"No Sir, but it's believed he could have been lost at sea. He often went out to help the fishermen when the sea was rough and last September he and a friend were last seen going towards the pier. A boat was reported to have been in danger that afternoon and was never recovered."

"And Mrs. Dalgleish?"

"She hadn't lived at the house for a long time Sir. The last time I saw her, she had her cases packed and was to visit her son in Durham, or was it John now I come to think of it?" Lizzy sat pondering and questioning her memory. "No I'm sure it was Robert."

"Does that mean you no longer have contact with the family?"

"Well once Miss Ellen left for America, the household seemed to fall apart. Robert and John both entered the ministry and as I said Mrs. Dalgleish travelled a lot. Sometimes Mr Dalgleish would go with her on the odd occasion. I hope you'll forgive me for saying Sir, but I do believe Mr Dalgleish, although he was always busy with business, was lonely without the family around and that was why he continued to employ me."

A further silence descended upon them. James bit his lip, as he considered his next question.

"One more question Lizzy. The father of Ellen's baby, would you know if this was known to the family?"

"I really don't know Sir. I was not privy to such information. I cannot remember Miss Ellen ever being without a chaperone … of course I did not accompany her when she was out with Mrs. Dalgleish, which was quite a regular occurrence. I must say I found it strange … the whole thing was dealt with quietly and without fuss. No recriminations … and … well such an affluent family. Mr Dalgleish requested that she and I went to live in another area for several months until the baby was born and there were no objections. It was a grand house in Morpeth … number 57 Church Lane … if I remember correctly. We spent a lot of time together going for lovely walks and then needlework in the afternoons. We grew quite close in those few months, but she never ever spoke to me about the baby's father, although I often found her melancholy and would ask if something was troubling her."

Kate listened with interest remembering that the address on the birth certificate had been in Morpeth, but she had never known it was not the family's known address. She leaned forward and gave Lizzy a warm smile.

"I'm sure you were a great solace to Ellen at that time."

"Thank you Madam". Lizzy said with a grateful tone. "And may I ask did everything go well with you and the baby?"

"Yes it did, and he is now a strapping young man with a daughter of his own."

Shaking her head with disbelief Lizzy spoke quietly. "It was all so long ago." She smiled ruefully at James. "I'm sorry I wasn't able to help more, but it's been a privilege to meet you both. Thank you for the tea it was most welcome." She rose from her chair. "I will take my leave of you now and let you continue where you left off."

James rose to his feet, and towering above her wished her goodbye. He and Kate watched her walk away from the hotel, through the window before uttering another word.

"I really don't think anything can be achieved by telling John about your late wife and his relationship to your sons and Ria." Kate sighed.

"I agree with you," James said thoughtfully. "On the other hand I don't want him to be deprived of his inheritance."

"Well as you know, that is exactly how Mr Dalgleish felt. He invested a lot of money into an account for when John reaches thirty. When I give it to him next year I can tell him exactly that, and say there was no further contact from the family, which until today is the truth.

James looked pensive. "I will have to persuade Ria to leave England with me before John returns, I can see no other way to ensure that they don't grow any fonder of each other. It's very sad, but it will save them both a great deal of heartbreak in the long run."

"I'm sure that John will be back within the next few days, so you have to act quickly if this is to work" Kate swallowed hard to keep the tremble from her voice reassuring herself, not for the first time in her life, that she was doing the right thing.

"I will arrange something. It is sad that we had to meet in this way. You obviously love John and his daughter very much. We are both concerned for our families. Let's take comfort in the fact that we have thought carefully about our actions and decisions today."

Kate nodded and took her leave of him.

chapter 19

One Week Later

SO MANY ANGRY UNEMPLOYED men and women carried their placards and banners, in yet another protest march demanding the government find them work. Ria, unable to see above the heads of the crowds, could not identify John amongst the crowd. She climbed the steps leading to a building behind her to afford her a better opportunity to see across the crowd and search him out. She realised it was not going to be easy; neither of them had considered it could be like this. She removed her stylish olive green hat and shook her chestnut hair loose in the hope that he might recognise her better.

A fresh faced young woman climbed the steps smiled and stood beside her. "It's jolly cold isn't it?" She said in a friendly way as she rubbed her hands together and stamped her feet in an attempt to keep warm. Ria nodded, her eyes still fixed on the crowd. Minutes later the girl's face lit up and she scurried down the steps and into the arms of a long faced bearded man.

Ria sighed. She was beginning to feel insecure, as she once again stood alone. She questioned what she should do if they missed each other. Her stomach tightened and she felt nauseous as she realised at no point had she contemplated such a thing until now. Having convinced herself she could do without Uncle James being by her side at all times she weakened and silently pleaded for John to appear immediately. Anxiously casting her eyes across the masses again, she willed him to be there, but after several minutes, she was resigned to his absence. Relapsing into giving herself a hard time for why John might have changed his mind about meeting her, she convinced herself that he had decided not to continue with their relationship. The last vestige of hope seeped away from her.

An urgent desire to flee from her situation took control of her. She descended the steps, her mind clouded and her eyes brimming with tears. Mingling with the crowd, wildly searching the faces of those around, desperate for him to appear, her resolve to stay strong crumbled. Over-wrought, Ria made an impulsive decision to visit her mother's grave.

Escaping the sea of blurred faces, she blindly set off in the direction of the cemetery.

꽃꽃꽃꽃꽃꽃꽃

Panting, her heart pounding, from the long walk, Ria sank to her knees by her mother's gravestone.

'Mary Victoria Dalgleish, nee Archer
Born 19th April 1881 died 19th January 1920.
Beloved wife and mother'

Soundlessly she whispered. "I still can't believe you left me Mama. These last thirteen years have been so hard."

She wiped the tears from her cheeks with the back of her hand and continued to whisper.

"And now Aunt Ellen has joined you … I miss her dreadfully … she was just as you told me Mama … she made me feel safe and loved again … and Uncle James is kind and still keeps me safe. My cousins are like brothers …William and Irvine … and you would really like them Mama."

She stayed still and quiet as if listening for an answer. Minutes ticked by, tears flowed profusely and she shook her head in distress.

"I truly, truly thought I had found a kind man, someone I could love without fear, and who swore he loved me, but today he let me down Mama ... why would he do that ... ? I feel my past will always damage my relationships with men ... did you know that Papa did those things to me Mama?"

Sobs wracked her body.

"No, of course you didn't know ... you would have stopped him, I know you would."

Again she waited as if for an answer, the sobbing gradually subsiding leaving her weakened.

"I will never forgive him ... never, ever.

Back on her feet, she blew a kiss "Goodbye Mama, I don't think I will be passing this way again .... My home is America, where I feel I belong and am part of the Delaney family. It is where I can be happy."

An on-looker saw a beautiful and poised woman walk away from the grave. Although shaken by the sight of the familiar face and unable to believe his eyes, he decided to follow discreetly.

Ria approached the solid wooden door, lifted the wrought iron latch and entered the Cathedral. It appeared empty. She stood still and gazed around. Nothing had changed. The sun on the magnificent stained glass windows shed a myriad of colour into the building while the flames flickered on the tall pillar candles as they always had. The Christ figure on the cross, looked down upon her. Without conscious thought she chose to sit where she and her mother always sat. Memories of her early years and more especially the year prior to her mother's death flooded into her mind. Covering her eyes with the palms of her hands, she tried hard to stem any further tears. She rationalised that the past was unchangeable so why waste tears. She bowed her head and prayed.

"Please Lord Help me. I have tried so hard to forgive him. "

Immobilised Ria remained in the pew unaware that there was someone else present. Time slipped by. In her trance-like state, a slight noise disturbed her. Moving cautiously she gazed over her shoulder. Had someone entered the Cathedral ... her heart missed a beat, fear of seeing her father sent it thumping against her ribs. She rose to her feet but could not see anyone. With her heart in her mouth, she swayed momentarily, necessitating the need to grip the back of the pew in front of her.

Desperately admonishing her foolish thoughts that somehow her father was mystic and knew exactly where she was, as he had when she was a child, did not help. Since returning to England, she had become constantly mindful of the past ... events she had suppressed ... she could no longer deny them.

Angry, that John had tempted her into believing that with time and patience she would forget ... that she could learn to relax and trust men, most particularly him ... caused the anger to well up inside her. He had been so convincing and she had so wanted him to love her. She softened as she remembered their feelings for each other and how strangely exciting she found him. How when he smiled there was a little quirk in the corner of his mouth, and the dimple in his chin that she adored. Then there was that endearing little tuft of hair that refused to lie flat on the crown of his head. Her tense body relaxed. The memory of him felt like a comfortable stole around her shoulders.

When they had said goodbye in New York she had no reason to doubt him and yet today he had not met with her as promised. Why?

Familiar, scathing and deprecating thoughts played havoc with her mind. They were no less painful now than they had ever been John or no John. Listlessly she looked at the Christ figure. Feeling truly abandoned, muffled, almost incoherent words escaped from her mouth "Forgive my thoughts I know they are sinful, but why should I go on. I want to be at peace."

With her head bowed, she gasped. She recognised the two shiny black toecaps from under the cassock. Her head shot up. It was he. She stared at the familiar blue eyes and thick lips and involuntarily stepped back to put more space between them.

"Victoria! How good to see you." His deep voice seemed to boom around the empty cathedral filling every space on its way.

"I thought it was you in the cemetery, it is wonderful to see you again."

Staring as if in a trance, Ria asked quietly, "Is it?"

"Well of course. And look at you ... so beautiful and grown up. Your mother would be proud of you if she was still alive."

"If you say so."

A flicker of consternation crossed his unwrinkled face and the superficial smile left his lips.

"Victoria, you haven't come here to cause trouble I hope?" His voice had taken on a hostile tone as he looked into her unswerving eyes.

"Don't worry; I'm unlikely to change the habit of a lifetime, I know how to keep quiet. The scriptures tell me I should honour my father and my mother, although I am confused about your understanding of them."

Ria's voice had become piercingly quiet as she looked up into his cold blue eyes. "In fact, father, I think I have found the answer to the dilemma of the Virgin Mary. She must have had a father like you."

"Victoria! I forbid you to speak this way ... remember where you are."

Uncharacteristically, Ria retorted without thinking. "Did you remember your God when you crept into my bed?"

With a vice-like grip, his hands on her shoulders, he hissed. "Victoria, I am warning you. I had hoped you had outgrown that vicious tongue of yours. I've told you about it before; no one wants to hear such poisonous words."

He pushed her slightly as he let go of her.

In words almost inaudible, she sniped

"I hate you."

"Victoria! Remember who you are talking to."

She snorted, "As if I could forget. I am leaving. I feel tainted just being here with you."

Trembling she turned on her heel ready to walk away.

"Well remember it was you who came here. I presume it was me you wanted to see. Have I interfered in your life since you elected to live so far away?" He chided her derisively then continued with his tirade.

"I'm sure you enjoy your little chats with your Aunt Ellen. You are so like her you know; she always threatened to tell on me... and what did she do? Nothing! Instead, she upped and went to America... quiet as a dicky bird. Your grandparents stayed silent ... no one had the guts to do anything." He finished sneeringly, "some sister, she didn't even say goodbye. I can just see her now. Making out she was so pure... all prim and proper"

Ria's stomach turned. She felt the assault of his words.

"I'm surprised she isn't with you. Still thinks she is punishing me does she? You can tell her I couldn't give a damn."

Ria's brow furrowed with confusion. What was he suggesting? Had he not heard about his sister's death?

Choking back her grief and frustration, she screeched.

"You tell her yourself and beg her forgiveness, because she's gone where you'll never go. You are pure evil. You deserve to go to hell. "

Sobbing uncontrollably, she picked up a prayer book, lifted her arm and hurled it at him with all her might.

With a thud, he fell to the floor. The blood from his forehead flowed profusely onto the floor.

Terrified Ria sank in shock to the floor, and curled herself into a motionless ball.

His moaning gradually penetrated her mind. Raising her head, she crawled across to him. He reached out and she shuddered at the touch of his hand. Hastily she moved away from him and got to her feet. She stumbled down the aisle and headed towards the door frantic to escape. He called out for help in a frail voice. Even more panicked she grappled with the door, turned and saw him slowly hauling his body in her direction. Ria flung the door open and bolted.

chapter 20

John

THE STATION CLOCK WAS never wrong. With disbelief, he stood staring at his watch, amid the black smoke that belched from the train now pulling away from the platform. It had been a rough sea that caused the delay in the first place but mostly it was his misjudgement of train times and connections. If he had used his sense, he would have refused going for a last drink with his shipmates.

Infuriated by his stupidity John hurried to the station exit and flagged down a taxi. He could well have done without the expense but his optimism that Ria's faith in him not to let her down no matter what, made it seem worth it. Sitting in the car, watching the countryside go by, he made up his mind to buy a motorbike. Now that he was back in England, he decided it would make sense, to enable him to get back and forth, and be independent of the trains and buses. The thought excited him. It was time to make some changes.

Certain that Ria and he could be happy together, he imagined bringing Helen to live with them and forming a content family unit, with the possibility of more children to follow. He had a secure job with future prospects. What more could he want? He had been saving and soon hoped to be in a position to buy a house. A smile hovered on his lips. Ria would be so good for him and Helen. He had a good feeling that even Kate would be receptive to her. How could she not be, Ria was lovely in so many ways. The very thought of her caused his heart to take a leap of intense joy. Taking in a deep breath, he savoured the intensity of his feelings. His body tingled with anticipation at the thought of holding her in his arms again. Yes, this was what he wanted and needed.

The Cathedral towers came into view and very soon, the car stopped alongside the wall of the city. In comparison with New York, everything appeared to be in miniature, which took him by surprise. It had not occurred to him that he had grown very comfortable with the giant city. After saying a happy goodbye to the driver, he hurried to the Square, immediately observing the large amount of unemployed men dejectedly leaving the City with their boards and banners. He presumed they had been on a protest march and realised how little had changed since he was last there.

He stopped and looked around him. Now where would she have waited for the past two hours? A sudden bout of anxiety delivered a blow to his stomach. It really was bad that he should be so late. Then he saw what he thought the answer could be. Of course, somewhere like a Lyons Corner House that is where she will be. With a sigh of relief and a broad grin on his face, he made his way across the square hardly able to wait to see her face light up at the sight of him. He would make up for being so late.

Impulsively he rushed into the florist and bought the largest bouquet of flowers he could see. She deserved beautiful flowers.

After an exhaustive search of the eating-places, and the flowers drooping slightly on his arm, John desolately concluded she had given up on him. Unable to contemplate the awfulness of whether she had indeed even turned up to meet him, a dull thudding pain filled his being. He would have to find her, but where to start. Consoling himself that she did have his London office telephone number, he made his way back to the train station.

chapter 21

Catherine and Robert Dalgleish

"JOHN, WE'VE GOT A story here. Get yourself on a train and check out what happened in the Cathedral yesterday. There are all sorts of rumours floating around and I want a true account as soon as possible. Nothing like getting back into the swing of things my son."

The two men sat facing each other across the editor's cluttered desk, both knowing that they had a possible scoop on their hands. It was not every day of the week that a Bishop found himself fighting for his life amongst the pews in his own church.

John wished he had stayed in the area. No sooner had he got into London and he was on his way back. He nodded and jumped to his feet.

"I'll pack a bag and get the first train out to Durham."

"And not first class travel you cheeky sod. I'm on a budget here."

John grinned, knowingly. "Then why choose me boss?"

"You know why" the editor snarled. You know the ins and outs of church life, which in this case might be of some help." He added with a sarcastic tone to his hoarse voice, "Maybe you can say a prayer for the poor sod while you're there."

He was accustomed to his colleagues' jibes and taunts about his loyalty of attending church services whenever he could. It was like water off a duck's back – nothing had rocked his faith and the disciplines of the Church. His education and parents' influences remained profound. In fact, he stubbornly refused to question any of it. The discovery of his birth certificate, had temporarily caused some unrestrained behaviour. He had acted out with some flirtatious behaviour soon after and although sexually active with his first girl friend Alice prior to leaving Simon's Town for England he had waited to marry Molly. His relationship with Molly had quietened his anxiety about the facts of his birth. Since her death, he happily accepted God had his fate in His hands. It made for an easier life in his opinion.

"I'll see what I can find out. I'm presuming it wasn't the wrath of God that fell upon him." John said flippantly as he made for the door.

"Just make sure you get a headline story for me," the editor shouted "and while you're up there take some time to see your daughter, you make a lousy father you know."

"Thanks – it wouldn't have anything to do with the fact that I run around getting you headlines here there and everywhere would it?" he retorted.

Both men knew the score – a successful reporter put work first and family got what was left of their time if they were lucky. Neither would truly criticise the other when it came to career opportunities. John appreciated all this man had meant to him since he first joined the team. He could be abrupt and caustic when he was displeased; on the other hand, he was generous with his praise if he was impressed with a piece of work. He was the closest thing to a father as far as John was concerned.

꙰꙰꙰꙰꙰꙰꙰꙰

Matins ended and John looked around at the rest of the congregation. His knowledge of church-life came into its own; he knew there was nothing quite as informative as that of a regular and long-serving parishioner. The elderly silver haired woman collecting the prayer books seemed a likely candidate.

He put on his boyish smile and thanked her as he handed her his book. Then giving an impression of a deeply troubled member of the church said softly.

"What a terrible thing happened here. I can't believe such a thing could take place in the House of God. Do you know how the Bishop is?"

She nodded, her eyes glistening with tears as she deftly produced a handkerchief from her coat pocket.

"I still can't believe anyone would do such a thing. He is such a good man."

She sniffed loudly, but seeing his concern continued to tell him as dramatically as possible what she knew.

"He lost a lot of blood. The police think whomever did it must have aimed deliberately for his head. I guess it was something very heavy and hard." She lowered her voice as if drawing him into some conspiracy.

"I do believe they have found the weapon, but what it was I don't know. It seems that by the time the Church Warden found him he was hardly breathing."

She took a deep breath.

"Poor Mr Anderson, he must have thought the Bishop was dead. Fancy coming to church and finding an attempted murder!"

She waited for John to show his sign of agreement before moving on.

"Then an ambulance took him to hospital, and as far as I know the poor man is still unconscious."

She gave a deep sigh. "Why would the good Lord let such a thing happen?"

John shook his head as though as bewildered as she.

"Yes it is past all human understanding." He held back on his next question as they stood contemplating God's greater plan. Hoping his timing was right he asked

"Is he in the local hospital do you know?"

"Yes, I wanted to visit, but I was told only family is allowed," she paused, enjoying John's attention before adding unhappily, "but since his wife died and his daughter left home there is no one."

"How very sad. Is it possible that he has brothers and sisters that you have no knowledge of, possibly parents somewhere? You never know, they could be with him."

John tried to console her with his reasoning, at the same time wondering if there was any point in spending any further time with her. He gazed around and noticed most people had left so there was little point staying in the church.

The woman gained his attention again with her next comment. He could hear an angry undertone to her voice.

"I never understood how Victoria could leave home so shortly after her mother's death. You would think she would want to stay and take care of her father wouldn't you? It's a very selfish act for a Christian person if you ask me."

"And Victoria? ... She is the Bishop's daughter?" John asked questioningly.

The woman nodded, again tears welling up as she recalled her memories.

"I thought she was a lovely girl, so caring and well-mannered. I missed her dreadfully when she first left."

She drifted into her own thoughts saying quietly "I wonder how long it will be before she receives the news. It might bring her back to us."

There was some obvious hope in these last words.

"Why ... do you know where she went?"

"No. There was a rumour that she left to visit relatives. That is several years ago now and I haven't heard anything since. Father Dalgleish has been heard to say that she is fine, but rarely speaks about his family."

John nodded thoughtfully. How strange to hear the name Dalgleish and Victoria. He shrugged off a peculiar feeling of de ja vu, and let it go while he spent a few minutes more with the woman before deciding he was going to get no further useful information from her. He politely said his goodbyes, left the church and made his way to the local hospital.

Catherine Dalgleish sat at Robert's bedside praying fervently that he would regain consciousness. The thought of being without him was unbearable, wasn't he her firstborn. If she was to be honest, not her greatest strength by far, she would admit that if he had been her only child, a more contented woman could not be found. She based her understanding of love on this son. When asked to leave his bedside, she fought tenaciously with the Sister of the ward. No one, but no one could separate her from her son and the Sister was left in no doubt that this mother had no respect for rules.

Anyone not known to this family would find it hard to believe that the porcelain-skinned woman sitting by the side of the bed was this man's mother. Her face was free of any deep lines and her make-up impeccable. She still had a good body shape and the vitality of a woman half her age.

Stupefied and dazed, Catherine was at a loss of what to do. She had relied on Robert her husband and then in later years upon Robert her son. What she would do without him was beyond her comprehension. He made her life worth living. His prestigious ranking in the Church gave credence to her having to suffer childbirth. She had done something worthwhile albeit not by choice.

As time passed, she let her mind wander, not a common pursuit for her. Memories of her children flooded in, and as much as she tried to push them to one side, they insisted on dancing before her eyes. As much as she protested, her husband refused to accept her unwillingness to be a mother to more than one child.

When their second son John arrived she did all in her power to keep her husband from her bed, but to her dismay, there was to be another. After Ellen was born, she remained distant and aloof to the child, blaming her for her existence. Her attitude to Ellen created a rift in the marriage and much to Catherine's delight Robert never came to her bed again.

It did not worry her as to how her husband fulfilled his male desires. She was adamant there would be no more children and found ways of arranging time away from home. She travelled, with the children and a trained nurse, until they grew old enough to stay at home with Lizzy. Proud of how well behaved and attractive the children turned out she gloried in the compliments she received and was satisfied she was a good mother.

Catherine resented her daughter's adoration of her father, and their special bond. She found Ellen simplistic and uninteresting, eventually to become a liability to the family. The deceit and suffering she had caused to them was unforgivable. Ellen, so demure and beguiling yet with the ability to tantalise and tempt him to fill her sordid desires. Thankfully, there were no further consequences. As far as she knew, the baby had gone to a good, decent Christian couple. Once she had escorted Ellen to New York and settled her with relatives she returned home. Ellen ceased to exist for her.

Robert had first married the Church and then found a devoted Christian woman to become his wife. There had been two very premature births and then Victoria had arrived. Robert had been a model father and husband. She could not have asked for more from her son.

She wondered if she would see John again. He had tried to fulfil his father's dreams by going into the shipyard, but had preferred the idea of the priesthood, she guessed to emulate his brother. Without discussion, he left prior to his ordination. The last time he contacted her was to let her know he had joined the Navy and was sailing overseas. It was hard to believe that was nearly ten years ago. A faint smile hovered on her lips. At least one of her children had inherited something from her. She supposed that if she had been male, she herself might have chosen something similar. Life quickly became boring except when she travelled.

She roused herself from her reverie, conscious that someone had entered the ward and was walking towards her.

John observed the way in which the woman put her hand to her throat and stared hard at him as he approached the bed occupied by the victim. He thanked the nurse accompanying him and smiled charmingly at Catherine as he held out his hand.

"Good morning Madam. I'm John Smith from the Times Newspaper. I am here to report on the vicious attack made on your son, the Bishop. This must be very painful for you. I understand he is still unconscious?"

Catherine, lost for words, nodded.

John felt a genuine concern for this attractive older woman who seemed too upset to speak.

"I don't mean to intrude upon your privacy, but have you any idea who would want to harm your son?"

With a shake of her head she managed a quiet "No, I can't imagine anyone wanting to hurt Robert."

John nodded his head in sympathy. "Will the rest of your family be here to see him later? "

Without hesitation, she said, "There is only me, but his brother might be here soon."

"I understand you have a granddaughter. I imagine she will want to get here to see her father?"

Catherine's back stiffened. "I don't think that is any of your business Mr Smith. If you are probing into our family affairs, you are wasting your time. I know nothing about the attack so I suggest anything you want to know you learn from the police. What are you hoping for an exclusive story with some ugly revelations?"

Taken aback by the bitter tone in her voice John wanted to question her reason for the stinging remark. Instead, he smiled benignly and concentrated on the man in the bed, his head heavily bandaged and his face bruised. His curiosity aroused John wondered what this man could have done to incur another's wrath, or was it more the case of a mad man at work. He would go to the police, but it was possible there was nothing more to it than a crazy outburst.

He turned his attention back to the woman. "Thank you for your time Mrs. Dalgleish I do hope your son is soon back in good health" and walked briskly back along the ward, thanked the nurse for admitting him into the ward and left.

Catherine watched his upright, strong young body walk away from her and although she had the feeling that she had seen him before, her immediate attention went back to her son and her thought faded into nothingness.

chapter 22

John and Kate

A KNOCK AT THE door roused Kate from her drowsiness. The anxiety of the Telegram Boy arriving with bad news uppermost in her mind made her tremble. She worried constantly about John. The thought of a telegram informing her of his death was her greatest fear.

With relief, she heard a deep voice calling through the letterbox. "It's only me Mama."

A gasp of delight and surprise shook her from her tiredness. Painfully she rose from her chair and made her way to the front door. "I'm coming John" she called out.

He stood there, the familiar wide grin on his face, the tuft of hair making its usual gesture of defiance not to mix with the rest of his hair, and the presentation of a bouquet of flowers, made the many weeks of worry and waiting to hear from him worthwhile.

Her eyes shone with her love for him. He held her to his broad chest, so she protested that he held her too tightly, and pleaded with him to let her go.

With feigned displeasure, she limped back inside and let John close the door behind him.

"I suppose you will want a cup of tea and something to eat now that you are here?" Her question, more of a statement, covered the embarrassment she felt by the display of affection shown to her.

John, colluding with her, agreed that it was exactly what he wanted.

John stirred the sugar into his tea carefully; respectful of the best bone china Kate had placed on a crisp white lace-edged tablecloth, in honour of his visit. He laid his hand on top of hers, feeling the deterioration of bone structure and paper-thin skin that covered it.

"Are you in much pain Mama?"

Shrugging her shoulders Kate gave a wry smile.

"Nothing I can't cope with. Now tell me all your news before Helen wakes from her afternoon sleep."

"To be honest Mama, I am working in the area for a few days and I have the Editor's permission to spend some of that time with you and Helen. Is it alright for me to stay here?"

Kate gave him a stern look. "As long as you keep to the routine, I don't want Helen over excited. The last time you were here, your Aunt Amelia and I had a dreadful time at bedtime. She wanted us to play, the same games as you had, all that throwing her into bed and tickling her tummy!"

With a false look of shame, John promised he would keep the rules.

"Is it very difficult without Aunt Amelia here to help?"

With lips sucked in and her eyes lowered Kate composed her thoughts.

"We miss her dreadfully John. Me for her help and companionship and Helen … she loved her very much. Amelia could comfort and cajole her in a way I have never mastered. Amelia was a very special person."

The tear that fell on her cheek was not unnoticed by John. Once again, he placed his hand over hers. "I was very saddened when I received your letter Mama. I could hardly believe it, and coming here today, I fully expected her to fling the door open and pull me into her arms. I do understand how much more painful it has to be for you and Helen."

Pulling her hand away from his Kate sighed, "I know you do John. Now drink your tea before it gets cold."

John did as he was bid and then poured them both a second cup. As usual, he ate Kate's newly baked shortbread with gusto and appreciation. He wiped his mouth with his serviette before telling her that no one could make such delicious shortbread as she. Not even in New York.

"Do you like New York John?" Kate asked.

"Very much. I have met many good people there and I like their way of life. People are less inhibited, less worried about others' opinions. They like to enjoy themselves and they are mostly friendly. So many are settled and established English and Irish people. Which reminds me, did a young woman, she originates from the Durham area, come to visit you Mama?"

Kate nodded. "She did. Victoria Delaney you mean. Yes a very pleasant young lady, she had tea with us and Helen was charmed by her."

"I'm so glad you have met her. She and I have been good companions and we hope to meet when I am next in New York."

Breathing deeply and speaking in a calm and off-hand way Kate said.

"Really, I was under the impression from what she was saying that she and her uncle would be touring many parts of the world in the next few years, but maybe I misunderstood."

Rather than show his dismay, John laughed "More than likely. There's plenty of money in that family, so anything is possible." He wondered if this was the reason why Ria had not met him.

His next request truly surprised Kate.

"Mama, I am ready to own my Birth Certificate and the paperwork that was given to you when I was handed over. Sometimes I think I might like to find my birth mother. On the other hand, if she had wanted to know me, surely she would have contacted me don't you think?"

A kind of fear gripped at Kate's heart. "I honestly do not know John. Your Papa was offered work in Simon's Town, which we always suspected was arranged specially by Mr Robert Dalgleish, who was, to my knowledge, related to your mother. Of course we were out of the country for all those years so it would have been impossible for her to trace you even if she had wanted to do so."

Earnestly John leaned forward; he tried hard to ask his questions in a way that he believed they could both cope with.

"Can you tell me as much as you know about that time Mama?"

"It's very little John. Some of it I have surmised, because it seemed to fit somehow." She smiled apologetically. John returned her smile and nodded that he understood.

"You were just two days old when the wet nurse brought you to us. You were a tiny mite, but so beautiful." She sighed deeply as she wondered where the years had gone. She forced herself to get back to the matter in hand.

"I think it had become known to most of our neighbours and friends that I and your Papa had lost hope of becoming parents, so when your Papa was approached by Mr Dalgleish, who owned the shipyard, saying, he knew that a baby would need adoptive parents, and would we be interested, we were delighted. Apparently, the only stipulation was that the baby would go to a solid married couple with strong Christian beliefs.

I never met him myself and there were no more dealings with him until he told your Papa that we should be prepared to accept the baby, along with a wet nurse, who was to remain with us for the first year, during the month of November. He added that there was a sum of money to help with the baby's needs. The most difficult thing to accept was to have a complete stranger living with us … but we wanted the baby … so there was no choice. October was an exciting time … wondering if we would have a girl or a boy."

The memories etched in her mind forever put a glow on her face that John could not remember ever seeing on his mother. He was able to glimpse the younger woman who had desired a child with a passion only known by women who are in love with their unborn child. He recalled seeing this look in his dear Molly's face shortly before Helen was born. "And then what?" he said wanting to hear the rest of the story.

"It was early evening and bitterly cold on the 27th November when we heard the horses clip clopping in our road. Your Papa opened the front door to see Mrs. McCullen, with you in her arms, stepping out of a smart carriage. He called me to come quickly. I tell you John I could hardly breathe for my heart pounded so fast with excitement. I watched as if in a dream as she moved closer to us. We parted to let her through into the front parlour and then followed impatient to see and touch you. She handed you into my outstretched hands and told me to welcome John Dalgleish Smith into our home; our son was finally with us."

John frowned. "You mean I was already named."

"Well yes … I was surprised too … I would have named you after your grandfather, my father, but the deed was done, and I liked the name, so did your Papa. We never put the name Dalgleish on any paperwork. Of course, I have always secretly thought you were born into the Dalgleish family, and when your Papa discovered that Mr Dalgleish's daughter Ellen had gone to America within months of your birth, I concluded she could have been your mother. As far as I know she never returned to England."

"Makes sense to me." John agreed. "And Mrs. McCullen … how did she work out?"

Kate laughed. "Your Papa never liked it, he liked us to be on our own, but he understood the necessity of it, and of course it was part of the agreement. I grew quite fond of her, although she was very strict about your feeding times and showed no flexibility all the time she remained with us. She left on your first birthday. I was relieved that we could have an ordinary family life, on the other hand I felt sorry for her because she was very sad to leave. That was the last time I ever saw her."

"Did you have any contact at all with the family? John asked as he mulled over what Kate had told him.

"No I didn't, but your Papa sometimes took you to the shipyard and he told me that Mr Dalgleish was always interested to see you and on several occasions asked for photographs. I do not know what happened to them; I never had sight of any so I presume he had kept them. Mr Dalgleish did visit Simon's Town from time to time, and I know he asked after you, but there was no indication that he wanted to see you. I found it very satisfactory. I suppose I always worried that one day he would ask for your return. Does that disappoint you John?"

His top teeth biting lightly into his bottom lip John shook his head. He could not say; he felt ambivalent.

Proceeding cautiously Kate said, "I was only keeping to our agreement that we would take full responsibility for your upbringing, ask no questions, and hand over a bank account given in trust to you, on your thirtieth birthday. As that is only a week away John I am sure I could give it to you now if you wish."

John looked at Kate in pure amazement. "I can hardly believe that you have kept this to yourself all these years; you have known all this time and never a word!"

Her head dropped into her hands, Kate rubbed at her eyes. Her voice sounded muffled to John as the words escaped through her hands. "I wanted to say something before we left Simon's Town, but you were so angry with me John … and after that there didn't ever seem to be an appropriate time."

Minutes ticked by. They held the silence between them as if worried that their next words would shatter some delicate piece of porcelain that had been a precious keepsake locked up in a china cabinet for safekeeping.

Like a trickle of ice-cold water offering relief to a parched throat Helen's excited entrance into the room brought them both back to the present.

"Da" she shrieked and scrambled up on to John's lap, promptly followed by Fluffy whose tail stood straight up as he purposely pushed himself into the gap between Helen and her Da.

That night once John had tucked Helen into bed and promised he would still be there in the morning when she woke up, he was concerned about how Kate was managing such a lively little girl. He knew she would always do her best, and against all odds at that, but her arthritis had worsened and he was mindful of the extra liveliness and energy his small daughter exuded now she was of school age.

He realised that there were delicate issues to be discussed before he took his leave.

Kate listened to Helen's whoops of laughter and shook her head at the futility of hoping John would ever take notice of the bedtime routine she recommended each time he visited. She despaired at his lack of parental skills. She descended the stairs with the leather wallet from thirty years ago held tightly in her free hand wondering how this evening would pan out. Helen's intervention during the afternoon had served as a valuable time for both she and John to prepare for a conversation the like of which neither relished. Little shrills of delight filled the upstairs rooms as Helen scampered around endeavouring to avoid the inevitable moment when her young body became one with the bed waiting to receive her from her father's arms.

Opening the door to the front room a wave of tiredness surged through her. Sitting in her armchair Kate thought over the past few months without Amelia and recognised acutely how unchildlike her granddaughter had become with her. No such thing as giggling and screams of laughter for them; no wonder Helen was so delighted and excited to see her father again. It reminded her of the relationship between Bill and John as a young boy. Bill only had to be walking home from work and John would be straining at the leash to run and meet his Papa when they would act out a repetitious greeting; Bill would throw his bag to the ground and hold out his arms and John would trustingly catapult himself into them. Deftly lifted high in the air and placed on Bill's shoulders a trot around the front garden would proceed with Bill constantly pretending to drop John. Between them, they created enough noise to alert the whole neighbourhood of Bill's return whilst she told them to make less noise in the sternest voice she could summon up. Ah, they were good times.

She pondered on the sadness of any child denied of their natural inclinations to be silly, have fun and get into scrapes. She and her sisters had had their childhoods cut short and forced into adulthood due to their parents' life threatening illnesses. With a deep breath, she released her thoughts and was surprised at the strength of her emotions. She was lonely and truly missed her favourite sister. It had happened in the wrong order, surely she as the eldest of the sisters should not have outlived them.

Expecting the usual reprimand for his behaviour with Helen, John noted the careworn look upon Kate's face, and felt tenderness towards her. He knew what it was like to lose loved ones, but he was young and the future stretched way out in front of him. How was he going to express his concerns without causing any further pain to her? He sat opposite her quickly apologising for over exciting Helen, his face etched with an appropriate sorry look.

Lips pursed Kate shook her head wearily. "John you have no intention of changing so why do you apologise? " She paused before saying "I'm glad you're here … it's what Helen needs. Life is far too quiet for her in this house, but she's making friends at school so that is good."

John nodded in agreement, hardly able to believe Kate seemed ready to talk as much as he, and settled back in his chair. Without further ado, he cheerfully put his question to her. "St. Hilda's take Boarders I believe. Would it help you if we made enquiries about Helen becoming a Boarder there?"

Seeing her face change, he knew immediately he had made a mistake.

Pulling her body into an upright position, Kate looked him squarely in the eye.

"No grandchild of mine is going to be boarded out at the young age of five … no John she has to have a secure base … how on earth could you consider such a thing. Imagine how she would feel!"

Jumping to his own defence he said emphatically .

"Come on Mama, I'm thinking of you. I know it can't be easy for you now you have no help."

"So you think it would help both of us to be separated do you?"

She took a deep breath before quietly coming out with,

"John you have a lot to learn. We don't all deal with things the way you do."

Taken aback John felt confused. "What do you mean, the way I do?"

"I don't like saying this and I prefer not to upset you, but you seem quite unaware of the fact that you give little thought to the consequences of your actions and you are old enough to have learned. I feel certain that nothing you do is malicious … on the other hand … so it seems to me … as long as you have done what you think is your duty, and you have a clear conscience, that is the end of the matter. You do not consider what others are going through. Not everyone is able to cut off their feelings the way you do."

"That's not fair Mama" John retorted hotly. "I do care. I try to do the right things and not showing my feelings is my way of coping."

"And I am not criticising the way you deal with yourself, only that I wish you could try to discover what the other person might need or want before deciding you have the answer."

With his arms crossed tightly across his thumping chest, John crossed his legs. He cast a hostile eye towards Kate desperately wanting to stop this going any further. Knowing he could always beguile women with his special smile, he nudged himself to use this as his next line of defence.

Acutely aware of the prolonged silence Kate looked up to see her son's charming smile. A sense of guilt suffused her being. She questioned how often had she in fact been open about her feelings in front of John. She had charged him with a failing that she also possessed. She wondered what had come over her, but the thought of little Helen in the care of strangers was too painful to contemplate. An awkward smile played on her lips. She was unsure of how to proceed and her reluctance to say more resulted in an uncomfortable silence, neither knowing what to do to ease the situation.

John jumped to his feet and with his back turned on Kate he stared through the front window and across the street. The urge for a stiff whisky was strong and he contemplated stepping out before the public house called 'time'. On the other hand, it was not much fun drinking without the company of friends or colleagues. The silence was intolerable and without more thought he almost groaned –

"Mama let's start again. This is awful. We both want the best for Helen."

Relief swept over him to hear Kate agree.

For the rest of the evening they concluded that, for the immediate future at least, nothing would change, although Kate promised to tell him the moment she wanted more help. Between them, they kept their conversation light and made no mention of their earlier heated altercation.

Engulfed in a massive yawn and eyelids that felt as heavy as lead Kate decided it was bedtime whilst John laughed and gently helped her from her chair.

"You need your sleep more than ever with me around." He said jokingly.

"Don't worry I'll give you a break and take Helen out for the day tomorrow. The following day I have to get back onto the story I'm researching and then back to London."

Fondly patting his hand Kate smiled up at him.

"You need to work to further your career John. You always have my support you know that."

A further large yawn made her eyes water and like a stern parent John opened the door and pointed to the stairs.

"Go. Sleep well."

With her foot on the first stair, Kate turned.

"I will see you in the morning John. You will find the original leather wallet and its contents that came with you, in the top drawer of the bureau. I would like you to take it so that everything is as it should be."

John nodded his acceptance and went back into the parlour.

The large wallet was where Kate said it would be. John grasped hold of it as if it was a living thing and might jump out of his hand. It was hard to understand why he felt anxious over such a material object. He who had shrugged off any suggestion that his origins could be of any importance to him; so why did he feel this churning in his stomach and the strong reluctance to look inside it.

chapter 23

Robert Dalgleish

ACCORDING TO MATRON, BISHOP Robert Dalgleish had another comfortable night. This was the standard answer given to all enquiries, of which there had been many throughout the time of his semi-conscious state.

Young student nurse Edith Bronley worked quickly and deftly as she drew a soapy razor across two days of stubble to return a healthier look to the once handsome face, now deeply etched with frown lines. The wiry hair that grew thick and furious from his nostrils and ears fascinated her. She noticed that even his eyebrows grew like weeds and she mischievously imagined plucking the rogue hairs and giving him back shaped eyebrows. She had bathed and shaved him, brushed his unruly deep brown hair, which insisted on falling over his forehead no matter what she did.

She carefully patted his face and neck dry, then gathered up the toiletries and returned them to the bedside cabinet. Edith loved her work knowing it was important that she carry out her duties carefully, with no mistakes, if she was to pass her fast approaching examination. Patients and beds must be tidy at all times Matron constantly told her when she did her rounds. Accordingly, she smoothed away a crease that had annoyingly appeared in the top sheet by slightly leaning across her patient. The last thing she expected was to feel a hand lightly brushing across her bosom.

Alarmed, Edith studied his face. His eyes fully closed gave no sign of consciousness. Yet there was something different, could it be there was a glimpse of the slightest smile on those lips. In all her seventeen years, she had never attended Church, and was now uncertain of how to address her eminent patient.

She spoke quietly and hesitantly.

"Hm … Bishop Robert …." she lightly stroked the top of his hand "can you hear me?"

Waiting anxiously for some response, she looked urgently around for Staff Nurse or Sister. She was out of her depth and scared. Completely unprepared for any movement she let out a squeal of terror as his hand gripped hold of her wrist. Swallowing deeply, she prised his fingers from her wrist, whilst assuring him he was safe. His lips were moving. Lowering her face closer trying to catch any words, she felt his hot breath on her cheek. He was delirious and imagined her name was Victoria, and although she told him she was a nurse, he continued with a tirade of sexual threats towards this person. Edith's naivety could not protect her completely and she involuntarily jerked away, her face hot and flushed.

Enormous relief swept through her as the sound of footsteps drew close. She spun round.

"Oh Sister … I do believe that the Bishop is rousing." Her voice sounded breathless and slightly wobbly.

"Thank you Student Nurse Bronley." The Sister's clear voice rang out as she looked at her quizzically.

"So did he say something?"

"Mm … no … he kind of moved his lips … and then caught hold of my hand."

"Really Student Nurse Bronley, well we had better call the doctor down here to take a look."

Together they walked along the ward to the Sister's desk, with Edith feeling very unsure and confused about the whole episode. How could she verbalise what she had heard without enormous embarrassment, and how believable was it that a Bishop revered and respected, could or would utter such loathsome language. Better to stop dwelling on it she decided.

While they waited for the doctor, Edith stole a furtive glance at Sister wondering how she would deal with the tall, good-looking reporter who had been waiting outside the entrance doors for the past two hours. She knew categorically he understood he could not interview the Bishop until the police gave permission, which made her marvel at his stubborn refusal to leave.

She blushed furiously upon receiving a flirtatious wink from him not realising he had noticed her looking at him. Not wanting to incur Sister's disapproval, she returned a scanty smile and once again, she received another playful wink.

❧❧❧❧❧❧❧❧

Keeping a careful eye on the comings and goings of the ward John adopted a resigned and persistent standing position in the hospital corridor. It would not be the first time he had doggedly held his own while waiting for a story and on this occasion he was even more determined to see the patient. His curiosity had multiplied tenfold since he had learned the name of his benefactor. Not only had he opened the wallet, he now had a conundrum. Should he leave things alone or find answers? He felt crazed by this continual and rotating question. He drew from his pocket a small hip flask and took a long swig of its contents. He did not have to shake it to know it was empty.

The young neat nurse was a nice deviation. It would be good to know when she was on her break. His thought was to suggest they go to the canteen together when he found an opportunity to speak to her. In the meantime, it was his priority to get his story and head back to London.

Footsteps echoed in the long clinical corridor. He turned and inwardly grinned. This was his lucky day.

"Inspector Harry McGregor" His cheerful greeting brought a smile to the face of his drinking companion.

"I might have known it was you making a nuisance of yourself.

God I hate the smell of these places" he finished blowing his bulbous nose into a white handkerchief.

"Look, make yourself scarce for a while and I will meet you at the Castle in a couple of hours."

Shaking hands John agreed. "Thanks, but before I go I have a little something to do."

"This something … doesn't wear a nurse's uniform by any chance?"

Harry's sarcasm brought a wide grin to John's face.

Putting a friendly arm round Harry's shoulders, he laughed.

"All in the name of work … we all have to make sacrifices at some time or another don't we?"

Harry shrugged John's arm free and pushed the door open to the ward saying under his breath.

"Bloody sacrifices my foot, you're a randy sod"

A few minutes later Edith pushed the ward doors open, gasping slightly because John was pulling the door from the other side.

"I hoped it would be you" he gave a broad smile, his eyes twinkling as he closed the door behind her.

"I am famished … and it would give me great pleasure to have such a pretty girl as you join me … I guess you must need nourishment too?"

He questioningly cocked his eyebrows in a fun loving way as if he had known her before today.

Noting that she was flustered he masterfully guided her by her elbow along the corridor.

"Show me to the canteen and let's get to know each other. I'm John Smith and you are?"

"Edith Bronley."

She could feel her cheeks burning and hated that she could not control it. Still she enjoyed the flutter in her stomach and the excitement of this tall, good-looking man walking by her side. He was obviously a lot older than she was and she was flattered that he should want her company. She was not the kind of girl to have many boyfriends. In fact, the only boy she had been out with was Jeffrey Adams, and that was as platonic as a male, female, relationship could be.

Happily, she showed John to the canteen, slightly fearful of Sister's caustic comments if she should see them. Mixing work and pleasure, often frowned upon within the hospital fraternity could cause problems, but on this occasion, she was willing to take the risk. She considered he was the kind of man she would risk a lot for, although just that thought brought a deep blush back into her cheeks.

He was charming and easy to talk with. She had no qualms in telling him about the patient's progress, and the fact that he had very recently recovered consciousness.

So enlivened by John's obvious interest in her work and the patient, she chatted without caution.

"I think his memory has been affected he was very confused about who I was."

She physically shuddered as she recounted the fact that she had been at his bedside when he first showed signs of recovery. Slightly embarrassed she confided how creepy she thought the Bishop was.

John raised his eyebrows.

"In what way do you mean?"

"Oh I don't know … a bit … well if he wasn't a Bishop I would describe him as … not quite a pervert … but shall we say improper."

"Really," John nodded interestedly. "Well don't you take any nonsense from him Edith, Bishop or no Bishop?"

She practically preened under his scrupulous concern for her welfare, her cheeks showing a pink glow. What an interesting man. She was immensely disappointed when he stood up to take his leave. Accepting his apology that he had to leave, she bravely gave a cheerful farewell and watched him briskly walk away. She nursed a secret hope that she would see him again.

The Castle Public House known to be the place where journalists, police and informers congregated was noisy and crowded. It was dark and dingy and the smell of mild and bitter hung in the air together with spirals of cigarette smoke wafting and wrapping itself around the patrons. Waiting for his eyes to adjust to the gloom, John peered around him, his ears alert for Harry's sonorous laughter, which would guide him to wherever he sat. Within seconds, he honed in to the giveaway laugh. Pleased with his powers of observation John made for the far end of the bar, ordered two pints of bitter and took them to the table crammed in the corner.

Pushing through Harry's cronies, he added his pint to the other three already lined up in front of the Inspector. No one batted an eyelid as John wheedled his way into the group to wait his turn. He surreptitiously glanced at his watch, it was now six thirty and he had to be on the nine fifteen train if he was to get back to London today. He drank his pint with relish, accepting another put in his hand by someone he hardly knew. He acknowledged it with a nod of the head and happily swigged a quarter of it before placing it on the table.

He passed away the next hour with small talk to those around him and consumed another two pints before Harry indicated he was ready to talk with him. There was an unspoken agreement with the men that they waited their turn for an invite to Harry's table where he would consider the request put forward to him.

"So, what do you need to know John?" Harry motioned for John to take a seat next to him. "I guess it is to do with the Bishop eh?"

With a grimace, John nodded. Was it that obvious? He pulled a notebook from his inside pocket then with pen poised, he reeled out a list of questions.

Harry swigged back more of his beer. "You've got the cheek of the devil, you lazy little bugger. You could have found most of this out for yourself … with a bit of research."

A broad smile spread across John's face.

"I know, but I find it much more interesting this way. It's good to meet up with a buddy from time to time."

"You're all flannel John Smith."

Harry's mouth quivered with a suppressed grin, he was fond of this young reporter. He had a way about him.

He leaned forward elbows on the table.

"Well I sure haven't made head or tail of the attack. Who other than an idiot would imagine a prayer book an appropriate murder weapon? It was just unfortunate that it struck him at an angle that proved to be near fatal."

I'm inclined to agree. Could it be an angry parishioner?" queried John.

"Could be, but I doubt it somehow. The Bishop told me to drop the investigation when I returned this afternoon. He maintains he can't remember anything. I suggested we wait a day or two to see if his memory returns."

"Bit suspicious don't you think. I mean a Bishop … why would anyone want to harm him. … Has he been up to no good?"

Harry raised his eyebrows.

"Trouble with you journalists is you all have over-imaginative minds. He's a Bishop for goodness sake."

"So … I often think it is easy for men of the cloth to cover their indiscretions … you know … under the guise of a trusted position."

"Mm possibly … but not easy to crack hard nuts like him without any evidence or charges made against him. As far as I can fathom, everyone thinks he is wonderful … Jesus Christ himself! I don't believe that for one moment, so, unless anything comes to light I have no option than to drop the case."

"So all I have for a story is conjecture," John said dully.

"'Fraid so my friend." Harry finished his pint and pulled the next glass towards him.

"I find him boring … a nonentity. Since he was widowed some years ago, his mother is his only regular family visitor. Nothing like his father, or his brother comes to that … now they were gentlemen."

"You knew them?"

"Mm … weird how the father went missing … apparently he was lost at sea … but his body was never found … he was eventually presumed dead."

"How long ago was this?"

"If I remember correctly it was about 1927.

"And the brother, is he still around?" John asked.

Staring into his beer Harry shook his head. "I really don't know. I liked John. He went down South years ago … I think he joined a holy order or something of the like, but even that is only hearsay."

Drawing in his breath John paused before letting it out.

"Sounds like a fragmented family to me."

"Possibly, but a pretty affluent family, my friend. The father owned a shipyard in North Shields … his Company gave good jobs to the workers that went to South Africa … a very popular employer."

"What a disappointment to have two sons and neither in the family business. Strange … I wonder why they both chose to enter the Church."

John lit a cigarette and took a gulp of beer.

"I wonder what happened to his business …"

He looked at Harry who shrugged his shoulders.

"As far as I know it was sold and the money distributed according to his will. I know a lot of good men lost their jobs around that time."

"So the Bishop and brother are probably wealthy men?"

"I guess so," Harry agreed. "Are you intimating that might have something to do with the attack?"

"No such thing, just musing."

John closed his notebook and replaced it in his pocket.

"Well thanks Harry, it's been good to see you again. I'd best be off, I've got a train to catch."

With a nod, Harry pocketed the note that came with the handshake and wished him well. He abruptly turned to beckon the next punter to join him.

The London bound train pulled out from the railway station on time. Sinking back into his seat John lit a cigarette and began putting his article together. The story he had recently heard made him wonder. Did this family link up with his in any way? He could no longer deny his curiosity and yet the only common denominator appeared to be the man who was lost as sea.

chapter 24

Helen - June 1943

HELEN OPENED THE FRONT door, and called out to let her grandmother know she had arrived. With a large smile, she approached the old woman's chair and kissed her.

"I'm going to put these roses into a vase and then I will be back."

Putting the small bouquet of pink roses into a cut crystal vase she returned to the parlour, placed the vase onto the table, and then sat beside Kate and caressed her arthritic hands.

"There, flowers to brighten your day Grandma."

She spoke lovingly, hoping to pacify and settle Kate's anxieties Entreatingly Kate took Helen's hands in hers.

"Please Helen think about what you are doing. You'll be amongst girls and women from all different lifestyles."

A delightful laugh slipped from Helen's mouth.

"Grandma, I went through all of that at boarding school. I'm a big girl now. Don't worry so."

She was to join the Women's Royal Naval Service, and would be reporting to Mill Hill University in London in two days.

Kate shook her head forlornly. "You'll miss all the nice things you have become accustomed to."

She knew she had little chance of changing Helen's stubborn mind.

"And you know your Da won't be happy with you."

"He'll come round. He always does," she said chuckling flippantly.

"And he's not going to find out until after I have joined up is he?"

After a short pause, she added wryly.

"Knowing how his mind works he will presume I will resign within a few weeks … but, he will be wrong.

"He really doesn't know me Grandma" she finished triumphantly.

Knowing Helen's determination, Kate laughed and kissed her charming granddaughter's cheek

"You're probably right; all I want is for you to be safe. I will miss your sunny nature but I won't ask you to change your mind anymore."

Smiling she said. "I think we had better have a nice cup of tea."

Helen was quick to see the effort her Grandmother made to hide the chronic arthritic pain that plagued her as she moved across the room. It worried her to know that she was alone except for her church friends.

As always, she fought back the guilt that stirred within her whenever she contemplated a life outside the village of Tynemouth. Her conscience had been less troubled while she was at boarding school, because she knew it was with her Grandmother's approval. Kate had never made a secret that Helen's education and welfare had remained her main priority.

"I'll make the tea Grandma" she insisted, guiding her back to the high backed armchair. The only chair that was suitable for Kate nowadays.

Gratefully, Kate sank into the chair.

"We're very fortunate to have enough tea Helen. I have no idea how large families must be managing in these awful times."

As Helen left the room, smiling tenderly, Kate took in how feminine, graceful and elegant she had become in the past year. Her memory nudged her; yes, she was a lot like Molly, fine manners and a pleasant nature. There was also an uncanny likeness to Victoria, or at least as far as she could remember, so she presumed her looks came from the Dalgleish side of the family. She had certainly inherited John's desire to be in the thick of things. She sighed. How long it was since she last saw him.

She tried hard these days not to imagine his life in war torn London or wherever else he was working. Nearly thirteen years had gone by since she had explained to him the existence of his legacy. To her knowledge, he had not touched it and she no longer wished to ask questions.

She frequently questioned the wisdom of the decision she and James Delaney had made in the Grand Hotel. Neither James nor Victoria ever made any further contact with her after their momentous meetings.

It had been heart-breaking for her to see John's dejection, although cleverly disguised, when he returned from America. Although there was no mention of Victoria, she guessed, the girl's decision to travel with her uncle had caused him a lot of distress.

She roused from her reminiscences and dragged her mind into the here and now when Helen came back with the tea tray.

"Are you alright Grandma?" Helen quizzed.

"I'm fine. Shall we look through the photo album?" she suggested brightly.

"Why not; and when I have joined up and completed my first six months I'll get a photograph taken of me in my uniform for it" Helen promised.

Kate nodded her head happily. What more could she ask for?

A little hesitantly, she asked, "Will you see your Da when you get to London?"

"I will if he is around. I'll try to get in touch with his office. The last letter I got from him was about two weeks ago, but as usual it was mainly to let me know he was safe. Like you Grandma I do miss his visits."

"Yes, I know you do Helen. How much longer will this war go

on? That awful man Adolf Hitler, keeping our men away from their homes and families."

She sighed unhappily and patted Helen's hand.

"But we have to remember we are more fortunate than some and have to be grateful that your Da's career gave him permission not to join the armed forces."

"You're right. Don't fret Grandma all will be well."

Kate smiled, grateful for Helen's optimism and naivety about life. Goodness knows how lonely life was to become without her.

chapter 25

Two Days Later

S LOWLY THE TRAIN CHUGGED into the station and stopped its
funnel belching out clouds of steam, and seeming to sigh in relief
at reaching its destination once again.

Carriage doors began slamming the length of the train and Helen
placed her foot, encased in a high quality leather shoe, onto the step
as she looked down the platform trying to establish that she was
indeed at Kings Cross Station. The bustle and the noise convinced
her it must be. The whole of London seemed to have converged on
the platform, either to meet friends or take a train.

She put her 'I know what I am doing look' on her face and
stepped down from the carriage. There were men and women in
uniforms everywhere. Helen felt a tingle of excitement to know that
soon she could be one of them.

She gaped in surprise as a Scots Piper Band started playing
a welcome to a detachment of troops just getting off from the far
end of the train. She felt small and of little consequence here; at
home she knew about how others lived and was comfortable with
her surroundings. As she looked around feeling somewhat lost, she
noticed how many young men in uniforms were on crutches, or

had bandaged heads. Most surprising was the fact that they seemed happy and wore big smiles on their faces especially when loved ones greeted them.

With so many people thronging around and no signs or directions, it was difficult for her to distinguish how to find her way to the Northern Line. With a sinking heart, she stood still while others dodged around her or tried to push her along. She would have to decide which way to go she could not stand here all day. With a hope and a prayer she moved towards a group of confident looking WAAFS, her fingers crossed that they might be going where she wanted to go, and so she began to follow as inconspicuously as possible which wasn't too hard to do with so many people huddled together. She wished she had brought a smaller case, each time it hit into her own or someone else's legs. Why had she not found out such things before she made the journey? She should have asked her father, but then she had not wanted him to know what she was doing for fear he would try to stop her. She bumped into the person in front of her as they came to an abrupt stop at some stairs.

"I'm so sorry" she apologised profusely to one of the women of the group who had been laughing loudly prior to this.

"No problem happens all the time." She answered with a grin.

A bit further on and it happened again. This time the woman seemed to notice that Helen was sticking close to them. "Are you lost ducks?"

With a nod, Helen embarrassingly told her she was new to London and wanted to get to the Northern Line.

"I would walk, if I was you," exclaimed another in the group. "It will be jammed pack and the platforms crowded. They'll be queuing to take shelter for the night by two or three o'clock."

Helen's face visibly drained of colour. "But" she stuttered, "I have to keep an appointment, I don't want to be late."

The crowd lurched forward again with Helen being forcibly taken along with them.

The woman who had spoken first asked where she needed to be and she would do her best to give directions.

"It's Mill Hill University. I was told to get to Mill Hill East and walk up the hill from there" Her worried tone carried in her voice.

"Look, you come with us. We're gonna have a cuppa somewhere and between us we'll draw you a map" another woman said kindly. Without further ado, she put her arm around Helen's shoulders and they all shoved themselves towards the exit.

The smell of smoke from firebombs wafted around in the air as they entered Euston Road. Smoking buildings were visible in the distance and rubble thrown from afar was still in the road and along the pavements.

Helen drew in her breath this was awful. Her thoughts went instantly to her father. She should have contacted him. Was he safe? None of his letters had mentioned bombing and destruction. For a moment, she felt a wave of frustration. He was always protecting her from life, as if reality was never going to affect her.

She was jolted out of this line of thought as she felt herself pulled across the road, zigzagging between the traffic, until they got to the other side. Everything seemed to be one big laugh to this group of women and very quickly, they had her feeling the same. She found it contagious and very new for her. Laughingly they rushed towards an eating-house.

Sitting in the crowded, smoky, tearooms, with the five WAAFS, her laughter subsided. Helen felt unsure and out of her depth. She had not given a thought to how she would manage this major city during a blackout. Her memories from her last visit with her father were of exciting shops and theatres. Little more than a child at the time, she was oblivious to the everyday life of adults. Leaving home without contemplating these things now seemed foolish and foolhardy.

Not giving her father any warning of her plans and trusting that she would see him, when in fact it was more than likely he would be working away, now seemed particularly naive. Again, the frustration welled up. She knew very little about journalism, or exactly what her father's job entailed and this filled her with dismay. The reality was that she knew so little, except he sometimes had to be out of the country. For the first time Helen felt perplexed by her lack of knowledge about him.

An arm nudged her back into the room.

"Penny for them" they said in chorus.

She smiled bravely as the women all contributed their knowledge of London and drew a map for her. They concluded a bus would be preferable and pointed out the bus stop that she would need. She put the paper into her coat pocket and sipped her tea, watching and envying the women's obvious camaraderie.

"There's a bus coming along now; if you hurry you might catch it," piped up one of the women closest to the window.

Helen scraped her chair back and thanked her. She grabbed her case and headed for the door, at the same time wishing them goodbye and good luck.

The bus came to a stop a few yards away from where she was. She waved through the window and sprinted to the bus. She caught the pole on the platform and asked the conductor if this was the correct bus for Mill Hill.

"It is" he told her curtly "but you will have to go to the back of the queue you can't push in."

"I'm so sorry."

She apologised to the passengers closest to her and with her face flaming with embarrassment she made her way to the end of the queue. Once on the bus, there was standing room only, but the relief of having got this far reduced her discomfort, especially as the bus conductor had put her at ease when he jested with her about being a newcomer to the city and promised to let her know when she reached her stop.

Slowly a black cab drew up outside the Dorchester Hotel. Inside the driver looked over his shoulder and told Helen, they had arrived. Thanking him, she handed him the fare and apprehensively alighted the cab.

The impulsive decision to come here, after the driver had taken her to her father's house at the other end of Park Lane, arose because she discovered from a neighbour that he had been away from home for the past week and had no idea of when he would be back. Tears of overwhelming disappointment had sprung to her eyes as she thanked the neighbour for his help. Feeling helpless and lost, she blindly returned to the safety of the cab and asked the driver to take her to the closest hotel.

"That would be the Dorchester, Miss, you sure that's what you want … a might expensive if I may be so bold."

Nodding her head she assured him as confidently as she could that it was fine. Without further delay, the cab pulled smoothly away while Helen wiped away the tears.

The Doorman walked towards her with a welcome, took her case and escorted her to the reception desk.

Silently thanking her father for his very generous and regular allowance, she booked a room and a supper with room service, hoping fervently that the receptionist could not detect her nervousness.

With the events of the last few hours whizzing around in her head, Helen kicked off her shoes and lay on the bed. She was uncertain whether it was fear or excitement, she felt. It was not often she admitted to disappointment when it came to her father, but today his absence felt far stronger than normal. She had imagined telling him her news and his being startled by her capacity to have done so much without him. It was her dream that he would have taken her for a meal and talked through any problems she might have. Then he would have congratulated her on her initiative to do something for her country. She bit her lip and swallowed hard, this was her secret dream.

She wondered. Did he ever miss her? It was hard to imagine he no longer considered her his special little girl anymore.

Hands behind her head she looked around the room and a wave of loneliness swept over her. To fill the empty void within her she switched the wireless on. A scratchy voice was hardly audible. Eventually she tuned it in and heard "This is the BBC Home Service." She sighed, it was better than the silence.

Only two days and she would be going to Portsmouth and a new life. She drew in a sharp breath of near panic. Portsmouth was unknown to her like so many other things.

Again, she bit her lip and squeezed her closed eyes to stop the tears of frustration escaping. Da was not there to reassure her that she would be fine when that was all she wanted. She asked so little of him. She had no idea where he might be. Lost in thought it became clear that she hardly knew him, or anything about his job. What was he like with his friends? Who were his friends? It dawned on her; she truly did not know her own Da.

The next time they met Helen decided she wanted to ask many questions, it was time for them to become acquainted. She unpacked the three photographs that went everywhere with her, her mother, father and grandmother, and placed them by the side of her bed.

chapter 26

Helen and New Friends

THE TRANSFER TO PORTSMOUTH was probably the most uncomfortable ride Helen had ever experienced.

The lorry had a canvas roof that rattled and the two benches to either side were hard and unforgiving There were eighteen girls in all. Some were with a friend and chatted the whole way and others like she were quiet and kept their heads down.

She constantly fingered her new short haircut. The hairdresser had called it a Liberty Cut. Helen liked it well enough, but it felt strange not to have hair way past her shoulders. She felt conspicuous in her well cut suit and was sure the other girls had decided she was different to them. It made her reflect on her Grandmother's words. At the time, Helen had thought they were said in the hope that it would deter her from joining up, yet upon reflection, she could see it might have been said to protect her from experiencing this feeling of being an outsider.

The girl next to her coughed and cleared her throat.

"Do you think we are nearly there?"

Looking up Helen realised she was speaking to her.

"I do hope so." Then with a quiet laugh, she added. "These are not the most comfortable of seats are they?"

The girl returned the laugh.

"They certainly are not. My name is Peggy Jameson. I come from Enfield."

"Helen Smith. I'm from Tynemouth." Then added hastily, "but I also have a temporary home with my father in Bayswater."

She could have kicked herself. It was unnecessary. Her father's home had not featured in her life. She had suddenly felt ashamed to be in the south without being domicile in London, and the lie had slipped out so easily.

"Gosh you lucky thing. Two Homes! We only have two bedrooms. I'm the eldest of six and I can tell you it's great to have a good reason to get away from all the bickering … 'cos you can imagine we are always in each other's way. My mum's forever telling us how lucky we are to have each other."

She shrugged and pulled a face. "But then of course she would say that wouldn't she?"

"I suppose so," Helen agreed. I've never had to share a bedroom being the only child, although I did share with four girls at boarding school."

She wished she could disappear, as Peggy said with awe.

"Boarding school! Ooh, what was that like? Only posh kids go to boarding school, don't they? Did you miss your mum and dad?"

"I've not got a mother." Helen confided. My goodness what is wrong with me she thought, I seem unable to keep my mouth closed. Confused by her own behaviour, and the ease with which she could talk to this girl amazed her.

"She died when I was born. I grew up with my Grandma, and my Da visited at often as he could. It was hard work for my Gran having a lively toddler, she being somewhat disabled with arthritis. When my Aunt Amelia was alive it was easier for her, but she was on her own from when I was four. When I reached eight, she decided I would be happier in the company of other children, so she and Da found a School not too far away, and I was able to come home some weekends. I was lonely at first, especially at night but you do get used to it."

"Wow, I can't imagine life without my mum, or without brothers and sisters for that matter."

Peggy's large brown eyes danced with life and compassion.

"Shall we be friends?"

Helen's face lit up.

"I'd like that Peggy."

Slipping her arm through Helen's she laughed.

"Well that's that sorted then. I love your suit," she purred, her hand playing gently with the material.

"I wonder if living in barracks will be anything like boarding school Helen."

A loud cheerful voice broke into their conversation.

"Not if what I've heard about life in the WRENS is like."

Both Helen and Peggy looked over at the attractive blonde-haired woman opposite. She obviously wanted to join in. Before they could say anything, she continued.

"My cousin tells me you can expect to be sleeping with at least twenty other girls in the sort of huts they provide for the likes of us."

"Really?" Peggy said wide-eyed.

"Yeah, and apparently it's like sleeping in a corridor"

The blonde was obviously enjoying the attention and said in an overly confident manner.

"And, only the Corporal gets a separate room you know."

"Where is your cousin based?" enquired Helen.

"Oh I don't know. They can move you on whenever they like, so you never know where you might be from one week to the next."

"Wow." Peggy turned to Helen "I was hoping we would be able to stay together weren't you?"

Trying to remain unruffled, Helen spoke quietly.

"Well we don't know for sure what will happen do we, so there's no point worrying."

She was somewhat unsettled by the possibility of too much change as was Peggy. However, she was a master of disguise. She hid her feelings well. Perhaps she should have listened to her Grandmother.

Sensing she might have said too much to the two younger girls, the blonde smiled broadly.

"Don't fret; it could be my cousin teasing me. It wouldn't be a first, she likes to make me feel the baby of the family. My name's Rita."

Helen found it difficult not to be charmed by Rita's obvious gregarious personality and Peggy was visibly in awe of someone who knew more than she did. They could all be more like sisters than friends Helen thought excitedly and leaned forward.

"I'm Helen, and this is Peggy."

Her well-manicured hand on Peggy's shoulder indicated a sense of intimacy. They would be friends no matter what happened.

"What more can you tell us Rita?" Peggy asked with a childlike eagerness.

"Well young trainees have to wear navy blue overalls, and they get all the menial jobs. The wilting spam salads are no fun either," she said with obvious delight at having caught their imaginations.

Peggy giggled.

"I think I can cope with that. As long as we get permission to go dancing so, we can keep our boys happy before they are drafted abroad. I can't wait." She hugged herself in mock anticipation and turned.

"What about you Helen?"

"I'd not given it much thought, but like you I guess I could be quite happy to go dancing."

With a big grin, Rita responded.

"Right, let's have a pact, when there's a dance we all three go together and keep an eye on each other."

All three slapped palms in agreement.

Thirty minutes later the three girls entered the double doors of the Nissan hut and peered at the fifteen metal beds to either side. A strong odour of floor polish and a pungent smell of burning coke from two stoves reached their nostrils. They looked at each other and roared with laughter as Rita proudly curtsied.

"Told you so."

chapter 27

Early Days

SUDDENLY LIFE WAS GREAT fun. Not that it was easy for Helen being away from all her home comforts, but the company of the other girls made her feel alive and ready for anything.

She greatly enjoyed the drill and marching, much to her surprise. The midshipmen she was assigned to were very pleasant. Not that she saw a great deal of them, she took their morning tea in at six thirty and cleaned their shoes and that was it. She chuckled to herself as she walked briskly to the Mess to see if she could catch up with Peggy. She was sure her Grandmother would frown and insist it was demeaning for her to clean shoes, lay out their clothes after pressing their suits and carry out any other jobs they wanted done. Yes, she could have gone for plotting ships and aircrafts, she had the intellect and capacity for such work, but for her it was far more important to have the opportunity to form relationships. Never had she been as happy as she was right now in her life.

The Mess was an enormous shell of a building, full of long trestle tables and benches. Her eyes scanned the bottom table to see if Peggy was there. Over the first few days of their training this was the table they had chosen and it had now become their regular meeting place.

The sound of chatter was deafening. This she still found uncomfortable. Rita who enjoyed the control she had over how much food went on to the plates greeted her with a wide smile from behind the serving counter. She was the life and soul of this place, although the girls had discovered to their cost it was in their best interest not to upset her if they were particularly hungry.

Chatting as she poured tea into a mug, she handed a plate of scrambled egg, tomatoes and toast, to the next in line, then excitedly imparted her new bit of information to Helen. She had heard about a type of club and restaurant where they could get cheap meals, a cup of tea, and best of all where dances took place.

Easily excited, Helen felt entrapped by Rita's eager vibrancy to socialise and happily agreed that all three of them must go there very soon.

As she walked over to Peggy now seated in their familiar place, she questioned why she had been quite so enthusiastic about Rita's proposal. She had never been to a dance. She had learnt how to dance at school because it was the done thing, but the very thought of going to a club sent a shiver of disquiet through her. She was not sure she knew how to have **good fun** as Rita described it.

Peggy grinned with a knowing look.

"Rita obviously let you know about her new found club then?"

Smiling back Helen nodded.

"Will you be going?"

"Of course. Let's see if we can get some others together, and then there will be enough of us to keep an eye on each other."

Helen frowned. "Do you think there will problems Peggy?"

"No, it's just being careful. Anyway, I'll stay with you and we can learn the ropes together. There's a dance in here on Saturday. If we are free we could come and have a little practice. What do you say to that?"

"Hm hm. That's if we feel like it after we have had our vaccinations."

"Oh don't remind me. I hate the very thought of it." Peggy wailed.

It was Helen's time to grin as she joked.

"Not to worry the pain doesn't last too long. Well so I've been told."

The colour visibly drained from Peggy's face.

"Oh Peggy, don't worry so." Helen put an arm around her shoulders.

"It will be fine."

"I know. I am such a baby. The quicker it's over the better."

Changing the subject Peggy asked her friend if she was going to join her for lunch. With a guilty look Helen told her she had already eaten. She was well aware that the food she was having was far nicer than what was on offer in the Mess.

"You knew what you were doing when you asked to be a Steward." Peggy said pulling a face as she finished her meal.

"Eating the same food as the Officers." She chuckled. "You knew which side your bread was buttered on you clever girl."

"I know. Who would have thought it? And I've learned how to carry four plates on one arm!" Helen proclaimed proudly.

"Then you will make a good Nippy at Lyons Corner House, if for some reason you change your mind and decide you want out."

"No way. I love it here."

Helen looked closely at her friend and said with some consternation.

"You are happy here aren't you Peggy?"

"Course I am. Come on let's get out of this commotion. I'll walk back your way."

Arms linked they left the Mess, as if they had known each other all their lives.

Helen caressed her arm gingerly as she pulled the red ribbon over her sleeve. She prayed the ribbon would work. The thought of someone knocking into her arm made her shudder. She admonished her cowardly thoughts and reminded herself that all the girls were in the same situation and they had not complained; not even Peggy who had fainted as soon as she had seen the needle. She hoped it would feel easier tomorrow so she could go to the dance.

Gritting her teeth, she pushed her shoulders back, straightened her back and swung her arms back and forward. She grimaced as she recalled the words of her Officer advising that they all keep those arms moving if they knew what was good for them. It had sounded easy, but it now seemed the worst possible advice. With a determined effort, she put her best foot forward and made for the parade ground. She needed to hurry; she was the last out of the hut.

The frosty look she got from the Petty Officer when she fell into line, made her wish the ground would open and swallow her up. She suppressed tears of hurt. To be late was one thing, except she was not late, only the last one out. Up until now she had liked and respected the Officer and stood up for her when any of the girls made derogatory remarks about her. She wasn't sure she would do it again.

The girl next to her said in a whisper.

"Take no notice she's in a foul mood this morning. Probably got thrown over last night."

Grateful for the support, Helen swallowed hard and smiled timidly as they waited for the order.

Thankful for the cool drizzle, she went through her paces in a daze. Every movement was an effort. Her limbs felt like lead. Her head no longer felt attached to the rest of her body and the Officer's commands sounded a million miles away.

Struggling to concentrate she was burning up and at the same time shivering. Second after second a queasy feeling built up inside, her head began to spin, she could no longer see clearly and without any further warning the ground came up to meet her. She fought to rise from a crumpled position before succumbing to the comfort of the ground.

Helen groaned. It was as if there was a hammer banging nails into the back of her eyes. Her head felt like a ton weight. She craved for someone to dampen the fire. To sooth her burning skin. As if her prayers were answered someone placed a cool flannel on her forehead and assured her she was safe. She licked her dry lips and murmured her appreciation as she felt them moistened with water. Exhausted she gave way to unconsciousness.

"How long has Helen been in the Sick Bay?" one of the girls asked Peggy.

"It's two weeks today. At long last she seems to be on the mend. Poor love has been so poorly. I'm going over to see her later."

"Well give her everybody's love. As soon as she's up to visitors I will pop in to see her. The others will as well I know. It must be rotten stuck in that place."

"She didn't know where she was for the first week, she was delirious and out of it, but she has been in good hands, those nurses are smashing really caring and gentle."

Chipping in, Rita said in her usual joking way.

"A sick bay in the top Fort! It's almost a first class hotel. Our Helen knows how to get the best."

Peggy smiled. "Shut up Rita. She's been so ill. She'll probably feel ultra-sensitive for a while so no jokes,"

"I know" Rita returned in a soothing voice. "I'll come with you later and we will cheer her up. Promise no jokes."

With plumped up pillows and her hair brushed neatly behind her ears, Peggy saw someone who was beginning to look more like her friend Helen. She had been so worried that now her relief showed as tears sprung into her eyes. She hugged Helen's fragile body to which Helen very weakly returned.

The nurse hovered for a while, letting them stay in this warm embrace before reminding them that Helen was only allowed visitors for fifteen minutes. She would give Peggy and Rita a call and they were not to expect any extras.

Rita chatted away, telling Helen all her up-to-date news, in the hope of bringing a smile to her friend's face. Not fooled by Helen's attempt to appear interested in what she had to say she hid the panic that welled up within her. Perturbed by the dull eyes and lethargy she now understood why the visit was limited to a short time.

Taking hold of her friend's hot hand, she felt Helen's forehead with the other hand. Surely, this was not right she thought. She is so hot and yet as white as a sheet. She had not heard of anyone suffering from vaccine fever for as long as this.

A kind of telepathy was at work when Peggy's concern coincided.

"Shall I telephone your Da or your grandmother Helen?" They would want to know you are this unwell of that I am sure."

"No" Helen whispered, "Give it another few days "

"Okay, but just another day or so. Are the numbers in your diary that you keep by the side of the bed?"

With the little energy she had, Helen nodded and closed her eyes, too tired to offer reassurance to her friends.

Peggy and Rita tiptoed out of the room both alarmed by Helen's appearance. Peggy hated to pester people, but she desperately wanted to speak to the nurse. She could not leave without being reassured that Helen was going to recover.

The nurse looked up from her paperwork as Peggy approached and smiled.

"Don't worry; your friend will be on the mend soon. The doctor is coming in later to see her again. He may send her to the hospital for a few extra tests, but it will be a precautionary action. She is weak and she will need to convalesce when she is able to get about again."

"She is so hot … it's as though she is still running a temperature. I think the doctor should be here now." Peggy blurted out, with tears running down her cheeks. She could hardly contain her frustration with the cool and calm nurse. Her friend was obviously very ill and as far as she was concerned, the nurse should be more worried.

The nurse stood up and came round to where Peggy stood, gently taking her hands into her own.

"I understand it is very upsetting to see your friend like this, but she really is in good hands. Doctor Jackson will be here shortly. If you wish, you can stay and wait to see him if it will put your mind to rest."

Mutely, Peggy nodded and the nurse directed her to a small sterile room. There were just two small armchairs and a table with a jug of water and two glass tumblers. Sitting on the edge of the chair, she closed her eyes and offered a prayer to God.

"Please make her better. I know I don't pray very often, but I promise I will if I can see Helen happy and healthy again. Please God I've never had a friend like Helen. She is kind and caring and she makes me laugh and I miss her company more than I can put into words."

Her mind went blank and she stared vacantly at the white wall opposite, unable to conjure up any clever words. She said an abrupt "Amen", slid back in the chair, and waited.

That night, two young sailors carried Helen to the ambulance. Doctor Jackson had arranged the transfer to Queen Alexandra Hospital for further investigations. She waved feebly to Peggy as they whisked her away wishing her friend would not be so worried.

The hospital lights were bright and the activity of admitting patients was noisy compared with the sick bay back at camp. Everybody was kind to her. The staff scooted around in an attempt to administer drugs, bandage limbs, supply sick bowls and speak calmly to hysterically frightened patients. They plied her with constant assurances that she would soon be on the ward while the minutes ticked away.

The pain in her stomach heightened. Helen had paid little attention to it until now. Gritting her teeth, she convinced herself it was nothing and that if she breathed deeply and slowly it would go away. Perspiration broke out on her forehead immediately prior to an overwhelming nausea accompanied by a further searing pain. She looked around wildly; convinced she was going to vomit. Struggling into a sitting position, she called out for help, but it was too late for a sick bowl and to her humiliation, she was retching, the pain causing her body to curl up. She sensed people coming to her aid amid the hustle and bustle and talking to each other in quiet, urgent tones. Very quickly, she felt movement as they pushed her trolley at great speed along the corridors. She was on her way to the operating theatre. She heard voices shouting instructions on the way and someone insisting that the Surgeon on duty was in the Ward Room. Confused and muddled Helen's anxiety rose. Would a surgeon who had consumed alcohol operate? Instantly, she started to murmur "Da where are you, I need you Da."

The doors of the operating theatre swung open as the trolley pushed straight through them. She could feel her heartbeat frantically pounding, smell antiseptic, hear voices giving instructions, and then she felt lifted from the trolley. A searing pain went through her stomach like a hot poker and a scream from somewhere in the distance reached her ears. A mask covered her nose and mouth. She struggled for a moment, and then submitted to the power of the gas.

chapter 28

Corporal John Field

FALTERINGLY, HELEN PUT HER feet to the ground. With help from two nurses she gradually raised her body from the bed her teeth clenched. She swallowed hard. The skin around the wound pulled, feeling tight and inflexible.

A sharp pain upon standing rendered her to grip her stomach and gasp. Perspiration broke out on her forehead causing her to falter and cling upon the nurse's arm.

"There, just another step and we will have you in your chair."

The younger nurse glanced at her colleague who was shaking her head with sympathy for their patient.

"You've had a bad time of it, but you are now on your way to recovery. We'll soon have you back to normal and before you know it you will be at home convalescing."

Together they lowered Helen into her chair by the side of the bed.

Smiling the older nurse handed knitting needles and wool to Helen.

"Here, you can contribute to the war effort and start knitting socks for our men.

She whispered in Helen's ear.

"Helps the time go by."

She elevated Helen's feet, gently patting her shoulders before leaving for her other duties.

"Is there a pattern, because I've never knitted socks?"

Helen looked up warily at the nurse; she hated to admit the only knitting she had attempted was a doll's blanket when she was about nine years old.

"Don't worry, we will send our helpers round to see you. They have everything on their trolleys … well that's what they always tell us."

The nurse giggled. "We call it boasting."

She then sprinted across to another patient who was calling for a sick bowl.

Looking around the ward Helen noted that the women were mostly older than she. Those who were on the way to recovery sat in chairs, knitting or reading. The bed next to her was empty so she had no neighbour.

Playfully, her mind conjured up a picture of all the patients knitting socks, nineteen to the dozen, trying to knit their way out of this place.

A grin played on her lips as she attempted to cast on a row of stitches to do a practice run before she received a pattern. She could imagine what Rita and Peggy might have to say when they found out about her new hospital job. They would never let her live it down. Knitting!

A short while later a cheerful male voice penetrated through to her semi-conscious condition. Lifting her woolly head and heavy eyelids she found her head dropping back on her chest.

"What a way to knit socks … in your sleep."

With a start, Helen struggled to see through her blurry eyes. The needles and wool were still safely on her lap. Rubbing her eyes to force them open, a cheerful smile and a pair of twinkling eyes met hers. He appeared tall and broad chested from where she sat. He was wearing an airman's uniform, but his accent puzzled her.

"Come on sleeping beauty, wakey, wakey."

Gingerly pushing herself into a more comfortable sitting position, she smiled up at him.

"And you are?"

"Corporal, John Field, Royal Air Force at your service" … then looking at the name over her bed … "Miss Helen Smith."

He pulled a trolley, piled high with books, magazines and all types of bric-a-brac, closer to her.

"I am told it is knitting patterns for socks that you require," With an open smile and a flourish he presented her with a full folder.

"Yes I have been told the same" she chortled. "It seems we must have no idle hands."

"Sizes nine and ten are most popular, especially in that very becoming navy blue wool that you have there."

Helen held her stomach.

"Please don't make me laugh."

An instant concern entered his eyes.

"I'm sorry. I have an awful habit of being flippant in the wrong situations."

"No, please don't apologise. I would love to laugh, but not quite yet"

She lowered her eyes.

"Where are you from, not England for sure?"

Struck by her boldness she hid her embarrassment by searching through the folder. Blushing she took the first sock pattern out, laid it on the bed, then offered the folder back.

Seemingly amused by her demeanour he took it from her with an air of generosity and replied.

"I started off in South Africa, then New Zealand and for my sins ended up here … but I appreciate the English roses," he smiled roguishly.

A nurse came up behind him.

"Don't we know it Corporal?"

Raising her eyebrows, she laughed.

"I think it's time you got back to your ward, lunch is about to be served."

"Right, I'm off. Bye for now Miss Smith. Hope to see a pair of socks when I see you next time."

He turned with a wave, slowly and painfully pushing the trolley in front of him.

"What happened to him?" Helen asked the nurse.

"He's one of our amputees. A nicer man you couldn't meet; a model patient and such a willing helper; he's making good progress and will soon be discharged."

"Oh really?" Helen disguised her disappointment with a cheerful smile. Odd, a strong mutual magnetism had passed between them she knew it had. For such a brief meeting it was hard to explain her wish to see him again.

"Well for someone who has suffered the loss of a limb he has certainly maintained a good nature."

Looking up at the nurse, she pulled the little knitting she had completed off the needle and picked up the pattern.

"Right I need to start getting some socks knitted if I want to impress Corporal John Field, don't you think?"

The nurse winked as she turned to leave her.

"You won't be the first to feel that way about him, believe me. Only he seems oblivious to the effect he has on the ladies. He's gorgeous. Oh my, looks like you have a neighbour Helen."

Hardly able to believe her eyes Helen's mouth fell open. Unrecognisable, so badly burnt, but there was no mistaking that voice. Although the speech was slurred it was unable to remove the pleasant lilt of Rita's vocal chords. Her beautiful blonde hair scorched and charred. The top half of her body completely covered with dressings, and still she managed to crack a joke.

"Just you make sure that when you've finished with me you send me out looking a hundred dollars. I've got a date on Sunday and I don't want him telling me I look like a lobster!"

The porter and the nurse assured her they would do their best colluding with her pretend joviality.

"Rita! You poor darling. What on earth happened?" With a tremor in her voice Helen tried to hide the horror she felt by the sight Rita's tragedy.

"Helen? Is that you?"

Rita was lifted onto the bed by the staff and laid flat on her back.

"It is …" to control her tears Helen took a gulp of air and said flippantly "Rita, you really are the last person I expected to do this to find a way in to keep me company!"

"Yea, well you know me … I'll take on any disguise to get where I want to be." Her laugh had an edge of despair to it.

"Sorry to be wearing the face mask, but apparently it draws out all the impurities in the skin leaving it soft and dewy." She struggled for breath before she added.

"Anyhow what about you … are you on the mend?"

"Yes, it's my first day out of bed. Apparently as soon as you can sit in a chair you are obliged to knit socks for our boys, so I've just been supplied with needles and wool to get me started."

"Huh, bit of luck my hands are bandaged then. I don't mind giving the boys some fun, but socks … I don't think so." She wheezed slightly.

"Be serious for a moment Rita, what on earth has happened to you?"

"Tea towel caught fire, … thought I was being clever, picked up a pan of boiling water to put it out, but the tea towel and the water got me before I got them. I've not asked what sort of a mess I'm really in … oh God Helen." She let out a moan. "I can't believe what I've done."

Looking down at her own manicured hands Helen was at a loss of how to comfort her friend without it sounding false. Before she could structure a sentence Rita pleaded,

"Please don't try to say something nice Helen, I would rather not talk at the moment."

With a nod of her head, Helen murmured, "of course, just remember I'm in the next bed." Perturbed she watched over her friend for the next few hours, waiting for Rita to show some sign of wanting to resume a conversation.

Although busy, the nurses took time to either cheer up or reassure their patients whenever they could. It was never too much bother fetching and carrying for the bed-bound. Helen watched them with admiration wondering why she had not contemplated nursing as a vocation. Caught up in this pensive mood, she mulled over one thought after another. She ought to write to grandma, but she would only worry. There was no word from Da.... not that he knew where she was ... Peggy fetched any mail so had no messages got through to him? What had the nurse said about going home for convalescence? The journey back to Tyneside held little appeal. She hankered after staying close by her new friends. If Da was around she could stay with him until she was ready to work again.

With a quiet sigh, she looked back at Rita. She had no right to complain suppose she was in her friend's position, then she would have something to moan about.

One day felt much like another for Helen. Without Corporal John Field's jokes and general banter she guessed she might easily have become downhearted with the laborious healing process. Within the short time they had known each other, they had forged an easy and comfortable bond. Able to converse on almost any subject, especially how they imagined life after the war, was stimulating and encouraging to those around them.

They visited Rita, who was in a specific ward for specialist treatment, every morning and afternoon. Helen's heart went out to her friend; it was clear that she might end up badly scarred even though the doctors held great hope for her to have moderate damage. Their concern was how she would survive the trauma and retain her happy disposition.

Rita and John Field had the mammoth task of living with disfigurement in common and in his easy way John instilled positive thoughts although not idealistic. Helen understood exactly the bond that grew between them and secretly harboured the desire for something similar with him.

It was two weeks since her operation and she expected the doctor to discharge her for convalescence within the next few days. With a sigh, she cast off the last stitch of another completed sock. What could she expect from now on? To continue in the WRENS when she was one hundred per cent fit she would have to start her training again. Peggy visited when she had time away from the barracks and Helen appreciated she had made new friends and was well into her training, but she was sad to realise that the close friendship that had seemed so feasible when they first met now seemed improbable.

"Penny for them" John Field sat down next to her.

A pensive smile played on her lips.

"I was thinking how different things have turned out for me. I assumed I would sail through my training and play my part. I had hoped to have friends, with some fun thrown in. Instead of which I have to travel all the way back to North Shields until I am well again, and then I suppose start all over again."

He nodded his head slowly.

"Mm … so you don't class me as a friend. I'm the funny one legged man you met in hospital. Someone forgettable eh?"

"Oh no not at all! You know what I mean. We are not likely to meet again are we? Not once we leave here."

"That would be a shame. I've got used to your funny little nose now."

Standing up with the aid of his crutches, he jerked his head towards the door.

"Fancy walking round to see Rita for a while?"

Thankful for the diversion Helen accompanied him, her face burning with shame. Neither he nor Rita ever complained and they had reason to. Her frustrations were minimal in comparison to theirs.

Rita, her usual jovial self, happily greeted them.

"Doctor told me I will soon be able to join you on your walkabouts. We'll be like the Three Musketeers!"

"Good for you old thing."

John kissed her forehead through the bandages and took hold of her bandaged hand.

"It will have to be Two Musketeers, you and Helen, because I'm out of here tomorrow morning."

Helen reeled round and Rita moaned.

"I'll miss you."

"Don't worry, I have to come back and forwards for some time yet, so I will visit."

Rita turned towards Helen and whined.

"I suppose you will soon be on your way too."

Nodding apologetically, Helen sat by her side.

"I know I am sorry … and I will be too far away to visit … I had hoped my Da would be in touch, because then I could have stayed at his place … I have no choice but to go back to North Shields."

John cocked his head to one side giving her a sideways glance.

"My sister has a spare room; if you wish to lodge with her … it certainly is not as far away as North Shields."

Helen regarded him seriously, he was not laughing.

"Are you kidding me?"

Expressing shock, horror, John rested his hands against his chest.

"Would I? No, she really does have a room to let. She did have two evacuee children until a few weeks ago, but they've gone back home … so … voila one room!"

A tender, almost sisterly affection for him washed over her.

"John that would be fabulous … where does she live?"

Gratified to see how overjoyed Helen was with his suggestion he realised how young and naïve she was. With slight misgiving about his ulterior motive, he put his hand up as if to halt the process.

"She lives in Windsor … but before you become too jubilant … I must tell you … that I will also be lodging with her … this being the case, you might want to give it a little more thought… so don't rush into it … as I say give it some thought."

With a furrowed brow and slightly disconcerted Helen looked at him with consternation.

"Why should it make any difference to me, because you will be there? It will be excellent."

Then with acute discomfort, she added.

"You're not sure that your sister will like me, are you John? I understand that … she must meet me first and decide if she wants me in her house, of course she must. I would do the same in her position."

Very rarely rendered speechless John pondered ... she is a sweet girl ... she has a lot of growing up to do ... it might be a good thing for me to be around ... I'll have to ensure she comes to no harm ... not such a chore!

Without further thought he played along with her.

"You are so perceptive ... I will arrange for you two to meet as soon as possible ... she'll probably be here in the morning before I am discharged from the ward. That way you can sort it out between you ... I have no doubt that you and she will click immediately."

Helen's face shone with glee

"I do hope so ... I really do."

Bringing them both back to earth with a mock chuckle Rita broke into their reverie.

"Well that's you two sorted for the time being, so does that mean I can expect both of you to visit me. One at time if you please ... well it will give me more visits ... or at least now and again."

Looking at the clock John frowned.

"Sorry, but I have other patients who have need of my services young ladies ... so I will wish you goodbye and hopefully see you before I leave."

Rita and Helen watched as he wobbled slightly before leaving them.

"He is such a delightful man, isn't he Helen? You are so lucky, to live under the same roof as him ... it's just so unfair ... you have all the luck."

There was a touch of irony in Helen's reply.

"Mm ... but don't forget I have to pass the test with his sister first."

Then she added with dismay. "Oh and I never even asked for her name!"

Rita's chuckles, so well performed, now expressed themselves flawlessly, having traded places with her facial expressions.

"Ha Ha, but guess what, I know it. He has mentioned her to me in our conversations. She's a lot older than him, seems he was a big surprise to his mum and dad. Makes you wonder don't it, people of that age ... downright disgusting if you ask me."

"Less about his ma and pa, what's his sister's name?"

"You may well plead young Helen. Don't forget you'll owe me one for this."

"Whatever just tell me her name."

Helen made as if she was going to strangle her friend, laughing as she made the threat.

"Alright I submit" Rita chortled. "It's Alice. Her name is Alice."

chapter 29

Alice

SLOWLY, HELEN FOLLOWED ALICE up the stairs to the room she was to rent for the near future. Excitement bubbled up within her when Alice threw the door open to reveal a window opposite dressed in chintz style curtains, spoilt slightly by the dark blind for the night time blackout. She squeezed past Alice and looked around the room. A bedroom suite in polished oak and bed to match draped with the same chintz style bedspread, astounded her. A fresh bouquet of burnt orange chrysanthemums placed in front of the mirror ordained the dressing table adding a special touch to the room. Walking to the window, she was able to see open fields and the river. Turning towards Alice, a wide smile on her face she held her arms out wide.

"Alice this is a beautiful room. Are you quite certain I am a suitable lodger, because if you are, I would love it?"

Delighted by her lodger's response to the room, Alice laughed aloud.

"Then it's yours. So long as you keep it clean and tidy, no young men allowed, and you make sure the front door is locked by ten thirty, you are a most welcome guest."

"I can't believe my luck."

Helen held her hand out to Alice and they shook on their deal.

"Then I shall make a cup of tea before you leave to make your arrangements and collect your belongings from the camp. The room is yours as from now. I will have your rent book ready for you when you return. Can you manage half a crown a week and I will want your food coupons?"

Helen nodded eagerly. "That will be fine. I am so grateful to you."

Alice waved away the compliment.

"It's my pleasure. It isn't always easy to find likeable people you know. When my brother told me about you, I liked the way he described you to me and that clinched it as far as I was concerned. I trust Johnnie's judgement of character, even when it is a pretty young woman who obviously caught his eye" she ended with a carefree laugh.

Helen was careful not to jar her body as she followed Alice down the stairs praying for the day she could run up and down without any effort. Surely, Alice had only been joking about John taking a shine to her. He had never been improper in any way. She had heard him teasing Rita in a flirtatious way, but not with herself. No, Alice had that wrong.

It was an interesting house. The room they sat in was homely and comfortable. The walls were covered with framed photographs of people and places. The cooking range kept it warm, and a spicy aroma filled the air. Alice opened its door and took out a tray of fruit buns, placing the hot tray onto a large well-scrubbed wooden table. Easing the buns out with a narrow spatula onto a large china plate she turned to Helen to reveal her playful warm brown eyes.

"Do you like butter?"

Not waiting for an answer she promptly put a bun onto a side plate

"Ooh do I like butter? What a treat. It seems an age since I tasted butter."

Sitting comfortably they enjoyed the mid-morning break while they shared a little about themselves.

"You are lucky to live in a house like this," Helen said as she licked the butter from her fingers.

"I guess I am, but sadly it isn't the way I planned. My husband should be coming back here to be with me. His family have owned the house for many years. We pictured ourselves living our lives out here. When he was killed in action, I inherited it.

She paused for a moment.

When this wretched war is over, I shall make a huge effort to try to discover whether his stepson is still alive. He held a great affection for him. He joined the army at a young age and after his mother died I believe their contact lapsed. To my knowledge he is still in the Army, but I have very little to go on."

"Oh dear, did you ever meet him?"

Alice placed her cup on to the saucer.

"No. I wish I had had the opportunity in the short time I was with Reggie. Life is complicated and even more so during war time."

Helen agreed.

"I wish I knew where my father is. He's a Journalist," she explained to Alice.

"The last time I saw him the most he could say was that he was off to Europe."

Scraping her chair away from the table Alice smiled kindly.

"For as long as you are here you can make believe I'm a mother that you can turn to whenever you need to."

Touched by her generosity Helen thanked her.

"Have you any children Alice?"

"No, never got around to it, had enough to do looking after Johnnie and my teaching job. When I met Reggie, who was an English Pilot, he was widowed and ten years older than me. His step-son lived with his mother-in-law and by the time we married in 1936, that was in New Zealand, it was too late for motherhood. Reggie wanted me to come to England, so here I am living in another country hardly knowing anyone. That is why I agreed to look after evacuees, made my life more bearable. Of course Johnnie came with us, but he eventually joined the RAF and I have lived with my heart in my mouth ever since. It's awful to say such a thing I know, but because of his injuries I have loved having him back where he belongs."

"I understand what you mean I think my Grandma would have similar feelings if she could have me back. John is very lucky to have a sister who cares so much."

A loud blast of a car horn interrupted their contemplations. Alice glanced through the window and smiled.

"I do believe you have a chauffeur to take you back to barracks, better hurry and put your coat on. I'll see you later."

Opening the window she called out. "She's coming Johnnie."

Grateful for the lift Helen walked to the car. She did not recognise the driver who introduced himself as Pip. He ushered her into the back seat to join John.

"Thank you Pip." Smoothing her skirt around her knees, she said a little shyly.

"John this is really so kind of you."

As the car moved, she turned and waved goodbye to Alice, who appeared smaller as she stood waving from the large wooden porch to the house. Enchanted by both Alice and her home, Helen glanced round at John a large smile on her face.

"Your sister is lovely ... thank you so much for helping me. I suddenly feel convalescence will not be a chore after all."

John laughed.

"I think I have just made two very lovely people happy ... it wasn't hard you know. By the way, if we are going to be seeing each other every day, could you call me Johnnie? John always sounds so formal."

Surprised, Helen concentrated on his face. She hadn't imagined him as a 'Johnnie', although now he had said it she could see it suited him. It would have been unacceptable to Grandma where Da was concerned, so she found the informality rather charming.

"Of course I can. Will you forgive me though if I forget from time to time? My father's name is John, so that is far more familiar to me. I think Johnnie suits you, whereas I could never in a million years think of my father as Johnnie."

She chuckled as she imagined Grandma's face should she ever have done so.

Settling back in her seat she enjoyed the companionable silence and let her mind wander. Peggy had contacted her Grandma to tell her about the appendectomy, and again to reassure her that it had been successful. As soon as she could unpack and settle in, she would write Grandma a letter to let her know all the news and put her mind at rest. If only she could say, she had heard from Da, which would be the best news of all.

She wondered why after all this time she continued to expect her Da to fulfil her expectations. Over the years the disappointments had been many and yet time after time she desperately hoped for the wished for outcome. Perturbed by the persistent voice, echoing how little she knew of her father, her body quivered involuntarily. Wistfully she longed for the mother she never had and valued the offer from Alice just a short while ago. She obviously had a flair for adopting orphans, had she not taken Johnnie on as if he was her own when her parents died.

Conscious of her hand held in his she roused herself and looking up suddenly, was aware of the solicitous look on Johnnie's face before withdrawing her hand from his.

"You seemed troubled," he said ruefully.

Lowering her eyes, she murmured "No just a little sad. It will pass."

Nodding his head Johnnie smiled compassionately.

"It happens."

chapter 30

New York — January 1944

JOHN'S HEART THUDDED AS he unlocked the solid wood door of his apartment. Would she be there?

The smell of freshly baked bread filled his nostrils and a sensation of relief swept through him. After two years, he continued to suffer the same anguish each time he returned. Suppose she had decided to leave. He swallowed deeply, his throat parched with anxiety. Her name came out as a hoarse whisper. "Ria?"

Her back turned, she was oblivious to the fact that he had entered the apartment. His eyes caressed the tresses of hair that nestled in the nape of her neck, her porcelain coloured shoulders snuggled into a leaf green blouse, and her tiny waist. How he loved this woman.

Fearing he would startle her he called her name gently before moving towards her.

Ria swivelled round and their eyes met. Tears welled up as they moved into the others arms their bodies moulding into one.

John held her away from him, his eyes appreciating everything about her and then pulled her back into his arms.

"It's seems so long since I was last here. How have you been?"

"I have done well, I really have." Ria smiled up at him.

"I have missed you dreadfully, but I knew that would be the case before you even left … and how about you?"

"Me, I'm doing well. I've had plenty of work. Done a lot of travelling … always living in hope for an assignment to get me back here in New York … Oh God it's wonderful to see you again Ria."

Smiling with pleasure Ria took his hand. Without further words, they made for the bedroom. Undressing they admired each other's bodies hardly able to wait to satisfy and be satisfied. Embraced and moaning with pleasure they gravitated towards the bed their longings heightened to such an extent their lust overtook their desire for lingering moments of lovemaking. Within minutes, completely spent, they rolled over onto their backs laughing, much amused by their mutual urgency. John leant on his elbow and grinned down at her.

"You really are a bad girl, I didn't stand a chance."

Ria grinned back.

"Well you might have to leave without delay and I can't afford to waste a moment."

More seriously, she asked, "How long have we got John?"

"Don't you worry, long enough to eat some of your delicious cooking and at least one overnight stay. I've got to check in to the office tomorrow and then I will have a better idea."

Throwing their dressing gowns on, they returned to the kitchen.

They laid the table up quickly with warm bread, butter, jam, cake and a large pot of tea. This had become a ritual that John and Ria performed to ease their way back into each other's lives. He cut a slice of the bread and she sat down with him.

"Mmm, this is delicious" he said as he pushed half a slice of bread and jam into his mouth.

"Really John, anyone would think you had not eaten in days" Ria mocked him good humouredly.

Playfully John ignored her and lavishly buttered another two slices of bread.

"There … one for you and one for me … eat and enjoy it Ria. Seriously, though, food rationing at home has meant great deprivation for the working class. As usual those with money still manage to avoid enduring the indignities of the less fortunate."

He shook his head in disbelief.

Ria nodded her agreement.

"I know it seems to happen everywhere. I am one of the lucky ones, living here. I hope the parcels I send to the Red Cross help in some small way."

"I'm sure they do" John reassured her.

"You don't have to apologise for your own good fortune though. It's just the way of life. Take me for instance; I received an inheritance that has remained in the bank for over ten years. It fell into my lap ... more money than I ever envisioned owning ... a mystery ... why me ... what for? I was given away so I conclude the money was some gesture of regret. It probably eased someone's conscience. Whatever, my parents provided the best they could and loved me as if I was their own."

He paused to take a breath.

"Believe it or not my home in London is mortgaged and paid for from my salary and I intend to continue to live comfortably by earning my own living"

He paused as an idea came to him.

"I'm sure I can put my inheritance to good use in the future ... I need to give it some serious thought."

Surprised by his reference to adoption Ria murmured.

"We've never talked about our families and childhoods have we? Why do you suppose that is?"

Shrugging his shoulders John looked thoughtful.

"Something to do with trust ... or fear of being judged?"

Ria detected a slight tremor in his voice. Her own voice was particularly quiet.

"I suppose it could be that ... but does that mean we haven't built up enough trust ... or ... that we are two insecure people?"

With a wry grin, John shrugged again.

"All I know is I don't want to lose you Ria."

Ria looked down into her lap and kept her eyes lowered.

"Why should you? There's nothing that would part me from you. I love you more than you will ever know."

She raised her head as John took her hands in his.

"I love you Ria. We are meant for each other …it's just the way it is with us."

Their eyes looked into the deepest recesses of the other as he leaned forward to kiss her and asked passionately.

"Why do we need to keep our relationship secret now that James is no longer alive Ria? Remind me why you thought it was necessary in the first place."

"Instinct that's all I can say. Ever since that trip to England, when Uncle James went to find his in-laws, my grandparents that is, and I met your mother, something happened. Uncle James changed his mind about staying in England, insisting it was his duty to take me travelling to expand my knowledge of the world as Aunt Ellen intended. I didn't question that, but whenever I spoke of you he would change the subject. That used to upset me, especially as it was he who offered you the hand of friendship in the first place. Without his saying anything in particular I got the impression he did not approve of you so rather than be upset I let him think I had no undue interest in you."

Shrugging her shoulders she fought back the memories of that time; she smiled sadly and stroked his face.

"I'm not proud of myself, I betrayed you, but I felt unsure and unhappy. Remember you did not show up for our meeting as arranged and I was convinced you had had second thoughts about us. It may sound illogical to you John, but did it never occur to you that I would naturally conform to family expectations?"

There was a pause. John looked past her and stared out of the window at the sky.

"You would think so … but true to form I was more wrapped up in my own misery and guilt … I could only think about what I had lost … I had let you down and as far as I was concerned, ruined any possibility of our relationship developing. The months went by and I heard from Irving that you were happy and having a wonderful time. I tried to put you out of my mind … with great difficulty I might add."

He smiled ruefully at her.

"It's awful to admit, my heart jumped with joy when I received your letter informing me of James' death. Not because he had died, but to know you still remembered me … and I had an address so I could make contact … I will never forget that feeling."

Ria's heart beat faster and a blush spread into her cheek bones.

"I wish I could have found the courage to write to you earlier … leaving England was rushed and I was running away."

Hesitantly she gave voice to her thoughts.

"You and I are very similar John. We both seem to think that things not talked about will miraculously go away and never show up in the future. I think we avoid facing our demons because we fear something will happen to us."

With a timid smile, she added.

"Or on the other hand, is it that we fear those we love cannot bear to know the truth about us?"

An involuntary shiver went through her body; she desperately wanted him to take her in his arms and make love to her again. The soft lingering deeply satisfying love making they had discovered together.

Slightly confused John quizzed her with his eyes.

"There is nothing you could say that would stop me from loving you Ria."

Breathing deeply Ria pursed her lips.

"I'm not so sure John. Why we are so diffident about learning more of each other's past? We should know if we intend to share our lives indefinitely."

"Let's stop this silly talk."

Rising to his feet, John held his hand out to her and guided her to the sofa. Holding her close he cuddled her as much to comfort himself as her. He spoke in earnest as he held her.

"We have to trust each other Ria. It's the way I want it to be, no matter what has gone on in the past. It's time to get things off our chests. I agree with you it's as if we have conspired to stay reserved, hesitant of an honest open relationship. It's obviously not good for you, and if I'm truthful it's not good for me. I want us to have an ordinary life."

Ria murmured. "Me to. No more hiding away."

John kissed the back of her neck.

"Exactly. I love you. You are too special to stay unseen."

"It will be scary, and yet exciting, especially with your mother and Helen."

John gave a chuckle.

"Helen is no longer a child, but a lovely grown woman. Difficult to believe, but true. If you two were to become friends my life would be complete. Mama will be fine once she knows how happy you make me. Whatever, the problems, we will overcome them, I promise."

Ria wrapped her arms around his neck. I'll take the chance if you will."

Jumping onto his feet John crossed his arms.

"Well there's no better time than the present, so I'll put the coffee pot on to help us tell all."

His calm exterior instilled a confidence in Ria that only James had been capable of. Her long-held doubts slipped away, he had offered her the opportunity to open up. It was now or never.

Meantime, John made coffee, knowing he was dreading what was to come. Kate's words came back to him that he should try to understand how others felt, and although he would try, he was more concerned that Ria would reject him once she knew his status. He calmed himself with the thought that anything was possible.

Placing their coffee cups onto the occasional table John's infectious grin triggered the little girl in Ria to giggle. John laughed at her response and proclaimed in a theatrical way.

"The time has come for us to bear our souls. Shall we toss a coin to decide who goes first?"

Sprawled on the sofa with Ria at his feet, her knees bent and drawn up to her chest, John began with the story of his life as he understood it, including his mother's scanty knowledge. He omitted his mother's speculations, deciding it held little substance.

"So you see, other than this benefactor, Dalgleish, I have nothing to connect me to another family. It is obvious I was not meant to know about my parents, even though I received a small inheritance. Someone cared enough to ensure I was safely ensconced with an upright Christian couple. My adoption saved me from the fact that I was indeed a bastard child. Even so, it is clearly obvious from my Birth Certificate. Molly knew of course, but it remained our secret."

Slightly agitated John sat up and with his arm around her shoulders twirled a strand of Ria's hair, waiting for her reaction. It was out, she now knew. Unaware of how onerous this was to admit to, he felt the energy literally drain from him leaving him empty and deflated.

Her silence puzzled him. He felt keyed up by her lack of response and tickled the back of her neck. She appeared immobilised.

"Ria?" he questioned with a note of alarm in his voice.

He noticed her face was ashen which increased his anxiety.

"Ria, please talk to me" he urged.

Turning towards him her eyes wide open and a look of puzzlement she said quietly.

"Oh John I feel so strange. My surname is Dalgleish."

A look of astonishment crossed John's face.

"What are you talking about, you are a Delaney."

"No ... no ... I just prefer to be known as Delaney. It was easier to fit in with the family when I came to New York and Uncle James was very happy for me to use their name. In fact my Aunt Ellen was a Dalgleish and obviously her name changed when she married."

With an incredulous look, John shook his head.

"How strange ... I had not heard the name Dalgleish until I was twenty years old, and then I had to do an article some years back on a Bishop Dalgleish and now this ... it feels somewhat odd."

For a brief moment, they stared at each other, tongue-tied as they individually speculated on what this could mean. Ria broke the silence.

"Let me tell you my story before we begin to conjecture ... sit down John … it is a strange coincidence I must admit … but that is probably all it is."

Contemplating the other, they agreed it was indeed weird, but that they should put it to one side while Ria told her story. As she explained she would happily avoid talking about her life, but they had a pact.

Huddled within John's arms, Ria struggled to tell him about the shameful things she'd endured from her father whilst her mother occupied another room in the house. Tearfully she described how she would pray with all her heart as she lay in bed each evening for her father to stop coming into her room. Her voice barely rose from a whisper as she told John how her father would warn her not to make a noise while his hand slid under her nightdress. She feared she would suffocate from his weight upon her, at the same time death would be a welcome release from his despicable behaviour.

Certain from her mother's behaviour, Ria strongly believed if she had known what was happening, if Ria had said something, she would have rescued her and stood up to her husband. Whenever Ria had attempted to stammer some words, she would be overcome by shame and guilt, and know how awkward she would make life for her mother, so never explained.

Her mother discussed the feasibility of Ria spending time with her Aunt Ellen and Uncle James in New York almost as if she detected Ria needed a safe place. She had written to Ellen who had sent an invite by return. Ria dearly wanted to go, but declined the offer. Her dear mother, so ill and obviously dying, how could she leave?

Nearer the time of her mother's death Ria promised, albeit tearfully, that she would do as bid and go to her Aunt Ellen as soon after the funeral as possible. Between painful gasps, her mother apologised for not being strong enough to keep her safe from her father, but that her Will substantially provided for Ria. She could then be independent of her father. The letter she handed to her daughter contained her husband's consent for Ria to leave England and go to New York whenever she chose to leave.

Even to this day Ria told John, it still amazed her, that her father let her go so easily.

John looked at Ria quizzically.

"And you have not seen him since that day?"

Lowering her head Ria mumbled.

"Just once. Please John let me finish my story."

Shuffling to make herself more comfortable, she continued.

"The day you were late, I swiftly regressed to my old insecure self, and was awash with grief. I decided to go and visit my mother's grave and foolishly retraced my steps to our place of worship where we sat each Sunday for most of my young life. That was when I saw him again ... I ... I find it hard to put into words my feelings at that moment. He chided me, was sarcastic about Aunt Ellen and insinuated that he had treated her in the same way as he had me. I became incensed with anger. I was at a loss for words. I picked up a hymnbook and threw it at him with all my strength. He fell to the ground ... and ... oh John ... I fear I could have killed him ... and all I did was run away."

With her head in her hands, she spoke through her fingers.

"That's why I complied so easily with Uncle James to go travelling ... how could I stay? I still do not know whether I am a murderess ... now you know the truth John. Really, I will understand if you want to leave this minute. All I ask is that you give me enough time to find somewhere else to live ... I would rather not impose on William and Geraldine, especially as they have just added another son to their growing family. I'm sorry John" she ended lamely.

They sat quietly, not moving. Both exhausted.

chapter 31

———✦✧✦———

Ria's Discovery

GENTLY CLOSING THE FRONT door behind John as he left for the office, Ria felt an unknown contentment. If unburdening oneself of hurts and fears could instil this stillness, engendering such tranquillity she wished it could have happened a long time ago.

Wandering back to the kitchen she felt an impulsive desire to do some more unpacking of memories. If only Uncle James and Aunt Ellen could see her now. See how happy she was. Her body was alive and her eyes sparkled in anticipation of what the box containing items of James' memorabilia held for her. William and Irvin had thought she might like to have some keepsakes and yet until now the box had sat in the corner waiting for her curiosity to be aroused. Her grief eased and her spirit lifted, furnished her with renewed energy and optimism.

Mulling over the previous day, Ria felt an extra closeness to John. It was as though she was fulfilled and they were even more suited to each other. Strange that they shared the same surname. Without their revelations they could not have known. And the question remained unasked, was there any family connection? Whom could they ask without divulging their situation? As much as she hated the thought, there really was only one person. Her father. Then again he was the last person she would talk to. It was interesting and a great relief, to hear from John that she had not killed her father. At least she was not a murderess. That alone provided some inner peace.

Feeling this happy was strange, unnatural. Hugging herself with glee, she danced into the other room, a future without fear and doubt, how wonderful.

For the first time since James died a new freedom to rummage through the box and see what little treasures it held pulsed through her veins as she lifted the lid and put it to one side. Like a child at Christmas, she could hardly control her eagerness to discover its contents.

Lovingly she handled the two gold bracelets, the cameo brooch, and the stunning emerald and diamond dress ring. Exquisite, personal treasures, bequeathed to her. She could not have asked for more. Uncle James had known the pleasure she would get from these trinkets. As much as Aunt Ellen had.

There was a layer of silk and satin evening stoles, which, even after all this time, had retained Ellen's favourite fragrance. Ria raised them to her face and deeply inhaled the familiar perfume. Dear, dear Ellen, unselfish, loving Ellen, always in my heart.

Returning them to the tissue paper wrap, she spied through her tear-filled eyes one last item. A satin lined box containing a mother of pearl pen and pencil set. These were more precious than the jewellery to Ria. Ellen's writing, so elegant and neat. She removed them from their box and handled them tenderly. As she did so, a definite charge of energy shot through her hands. Taken aback, she hastily let them drop back into their box staring at them wide-eyed. Pulling herself together, she laughed at her rapid heartbeat. Of course, it was some sort of static, nothing else. Lifting the box, she could see that part of the satin casing was rucked and tried to uncrease it. She could feel something underneath making it pucker. With her slim forefinger, she worked her nail to prise a flimsy paper from its hiding place.

The paper had begun to yellow with age adding to its fragility. Ria unfolded it meticulously, before revealing Ellen's delicate writing. She hesitated to read the words. It felt as if she was spying, on the other hand the paper was in the gift box that she now owned. Reading slowly, she sat at the table by the window.

I cannot leave this world without leaving a true record of my life before I came to live in New York. It is calming for my soul to make a clean breast of my one hidden secret. I did not come to this decision lightly, I have fretted daily since knowing my life is soon to come to an end. I will never know if this will be read and by whom, but it seems the right and proper thing to do. If it is not read no one will be any the wiser and my secret will follow me to my grave. On the other hand I will have conveyed my remorse onto paper.

I gave birth to a baby boy in a picturesque Manor House, a true haven, away from my family home. This was my mother's preferred answer to my shameful pregnancy. I spent four months there with dear Lizzy my nanny and housekeeper, without whom I would have suffered enormous loneliness.

Although it was only for a very short time, little more than an hour I believe, the baby lay close to me. I have lived with a permanent image of his tiny face, and hands. When I recovered from an awful infection he was gone.

I have never spoken of this with anyone, not even my wonderful husband. How could I? I had to protect the family from the shame I would have brought upon them. My brothers were oblivious to my predicament and believed my absence from home was for me to attend finishing school; although in truth they were responsible for my condition. Only one forced himself upon me, the other was his accomplice because he did not stop it from happening.

My father consoled me upon the loss of my son and was compassionate considering the situation, but my mother never uttered a word. In her eyes, her sons could do no wrong; it was far easier for her to believe I was to blame.

She happily accompanied me to New York as if nothing had occurred and expected me to do the same. Fortunately, I soon met a lovely man who was happy to marry me and became the solution to my mother's quandary. My parents came to my wedding, but I never saw my mother again.

I received a cleverly disguised message from my father to let me know my son was healthy and well looked after by a good family. My mind became a little less troubled and I pray to God that he has indeed had a happy life.

I have truly loved and been loved. I have two wonderful sons from my marriage. I have tried to be a good and caring mother to them in a way I could not be for my first.

I am content to put pen to paper to acknowledge the son I never knew.

I beg whoever may read this confession will have compassion and pray that I receive forgiveness from my Maker.

If you know me, I am sorry that I am a disappointment, but I trust anything you do with this information will be done with love.

Ellen Delaney, nee Dalgleish.
     Easter 1927

Stunned, Ria carefully folded the letter into its original shape and nudged it back where she had found it. Alarmed she needed to think. The gravity of the contents had thrown her thoughts into chaos and a kind of numbness spread through her body.

Several hours later John returned to the apartment. It was obvious to Ria that something important had occurred since he left home. She could smell alcohol on his breath and feared what it meant. She had learned from experience that he drank either when he was celebrating something good or when he was facing a trauma. She had to determine whether to talk about her discovery would best be left until he was completely sober.

With little time to assess the situation, Ria accepted his warm hug eagerly.

Looking into his face, she saw his eyes sparkled. That together with his charming grin gave her every indication that he must be happy.

"Ria, I have to stay here for at least another week, but then I must return to England to see Helen. Although it seems she is fully recovered she has been through a bad time with her health. In fact, I can't believe she almost lost her life. Apparently her appendix burst and the doctors had to do an emergency operation on her."

Not expecting to hear that he had this worry Ria was mystified by his happy demeanour.

"Poor Helen … and Kate … how has it affected her?"

"Well that's another thing. The young minx has joined the WRENS and is based a long way from home. Peggy a friend from her barracks did the communicating so I guess I'm lucky to even know about it. As far as Kate is concerned I have no information so you can see it is important we go to England as soon as possible."

"We? You want me to come with you?"

John kissed her fully on the lips.

"Yes I do. In fact I want you to come back with me as my wife."

He took some paperwork from his jacket pocket and waved it in the air.

"This, my darling Ria, is a Special Licence to be married here in New York."

Ria put her hand to her mouth.

"But we can't … "

"There's nothing to stop us. You love me, I love you … we have no secrets anymore … the war will soon be over and we can plan how to spend our future. It will be great, just imagine you and I growing old together."

He stopped in his tracks and looked at her earnestly.

"You do love me enough to marry me Ria? I couldn't bear it if you turn me down … say you love me … tell me you want to be my wife."

Inwardly Ria felt torn apart. If only she had not opened the box today and found that letter.

She held her arms out to him and sobbed into his chest.

"Oh John I love you more than words can say. Of course I want to be your wife … but we don't have to rush into marriage … I can come to England anyway."

Stroking the back of her head John laughed.

"Are you crying with joy or sorrow? Whatever, we will be married before this week is through."

Smiling through her tears, Ria kissed him. She loved him to distraction, she could not, would not, spoil what they had together. A hidden letter did not prove they were related. It was Ellen's story, and if John was indeed her son, he was oblivious to it. What right had she to cause him further heartache and pain? There was no reason for him to know about the letter. Had not Ellen said she wanted its contents dealt with love. As far as she was concerned, disclosing those details would not be a loving gesture.

She kissed him again.

"Our wedding day will be the proudest and happiest day of my life … have I time to invite some friends and of course my cousins … let's have a small celebration for our special day John … do you think that would be possible?"

John laughed again.

"Ria you are so easy to please. Anything is possible. I know how much you like to organise, so get organising this minute … oh and Ria I want to be known as John Smith only, I intend to drop my middle name of Dalgleish."

With a kind of rapture, Ria nodded in agreement.

"Me too. I have my change of name certificate so want to be Victoria Delaney. The name Dalgleish means nothing to us any more … this is our new beginning."

Heightened with exhilaration their eyes sparkled with joy. Hardly able to contain their emotions, they snuggled into the corner of the sofa happily exchanging ideas about how they envisaged their wedding day.

chapter 32

Tynemouth Village -- March 1944

L EANING AGAINST JOHNNIE'S CHEST, Helen silently offered a prayer of thanks to her God for his friendship. Without his love and support, she would have fallen apart. Johnnie's lips brushed her forehead and she raised her face. Through her moist eyes, she saw the compassion he had for her etched on his ruggedly handsome face. She offered him a feeble smile. It seemed wonderful to her that they could communicate without words, so easily attuned, and her hand in his was enough from which to draw comfort.

The highly polished black coach drawn by four black horses came to a standstill in front of their coach, which also came to a gentle halt. Anxiously Helen peered through the rain-splattered window. Amidst the grey damp mist, she recognised some of Kate's friends and neighbours, waiting respectfully for the coffin to be lifted from the coach. Johnnie squeezed her shoulder as one of the undertakers opened the door to their coach and offered her his hand for her to step down onto the soggy ground beneath them. With a slight tremor in her voice, she thanked him for his kindness and waited until Johnnie was by her side before moving towards the Lych-gate.

She had walked this gravelled path a hundred times before, but never had the tombstones appeared so mossy, hostile and cold as they did now. Gripping Johnnie's hand tightly she remembered to hold her head high as they approached the Church and Rev. Dunbar, who was nearly the same age as her Grandmother, waiting with a Bible in his hand. He shook Helen's hand gently and encouraged her to enter the church and make her way to the front pew. She and Johnnie did as instructed, neither familiar with funerals and very much out of their depth. They passed the three pews before the front one and noted it was all regular parishioners, offering their last respects. How kind of them thought Helen as she settled down to pray.

Preceding the coffin the Reverend's voice rang loud and clear.

"Jesus said, I am the resurrection, and I am the life, he who believeth in me, though he die, yet shall he live, and whoever lives and believeth in me shall never die."

Helen and Johnnie both rose quickly from their knees and stood up to behave in the same way as those behind them. Through her tears Helen watched, her heart heavy with pain, as her grandmother's coffin came to rest upon the trestles in front of the Altar. Life would never be the same again. Kate the only constant person in her life had gone. Unbelievably gone. She could not imagine a world without her Grandmother. Her shoulders shook and her tears flowed uncontrollably. Valiantly, she tried to stop as her mind firmly reminded her to be strong. Her grandmother would expect if of her. "I'm sorry, Grandma. I can't be tough, I love you too much … I already miss you. How can I possibly not cry, my life is empty without you. What will I do without you Grandma?" Her tears flowed unheeded.

Hugging her close into his chest Johnnie comforted her, whispering that he would always be around for her. Helen calmed down enough to hear the vicar's words, although none of them seemed to relate to the Grandmother she knew. How upset her Grandmother would be to know that her only son was not present. Tears of disappointment also flowed. Where she wondered was her Da.

"And now we will sing the twenty-third Psalm" announced the Reverend looking directly at Helen. Johnnie kept his arm around her waist willing her to join in. Keeping her eyes steadfastly upon the coffin, she sang,

"The Lord's My Shepherd I'll not Want" with as much courage as she could summon until the end and then silently said goodbye.

She conjured up warm and happy memories of her life as a child with Kate and came to the realisation that nothing could take them away from her. This thought comforted her. Abruptly, Helen was jolted into the present. The Undertakers had returned to remove her grandmother's coffin from the trestles. The time had arrived. Finally she would be placed to rest beside her dearest sister Amelia.

The music from the large organ sounded particularly loud and drowned all sights, sounds and thoughts from her head as she followed the coffin. Johnnie's hand remained clasped in hers. She felt the rise and fall of his wooden leg, and sensed the effort he put in to keep up with her. She squeezed his hand to let him know she understood.

The cold damp ground gave way under their feet and clogged itself onto their shoes. The walk turned into a trek. Helen shuddered at the thought of what lie ahead. The deep hole loomed to the front of her mind. Could she bear to see her grandmother lowered into it? Numb with the cold she moved slowly towards the grave. Drizzly rain penetrated the mourners causing them to rub their hands and stamp their feet once at the spot. The dismal weather hastened their desire to escape the misery of such an occasion, and sought comfort in the knowledge that they would soon feel the warmth of the church hall, where steaming cups of tea awaited them

Helen's eyes followed the Reverend's hands as he took a clump of soil ready to throw into the grave. It landed on the coffin with a thump. The whole cemetery seemed to resound with the noise and thundered in her ears. Her knees buckled, she felt faint. She whispered. "No … I can't do this" and blackness came. A pair of strong arms caught hold of her.

Muffled voices, reached her ears. She groaned. The voices became clearer. Johnnie's voice was the first she identified followed by another familiar voice. She thought she must have been dreaming. It was her Da's voice. She shook her head and wearily opened her eyes.

"Helen, sweetheart, are you alright?"

It was her Da. It really was her Da. Her mind went into a frenzy wondering when and how he had managed to get there. Overcome by emotion she fought against showing him the relief of having him nearby speaking to Johnnie who was hovering above them.

"Johnnie I'm sorry. I don't know what happened. Can you get me to the hall I am so cold."

Johnnie nodded and with the help of John helped her to steady herself. He put his arm around her shivering body and cuddled her close to him.

"Of course," he said looking dubiously from Helen to John, "but you might want to walk with your father."

Shaking her head, she said softly. "I've waited a long time to see Da, so a little longer will make no difference. No I'll walk with you Johnnie."

She smiled wanly at her father and his beautiful female companion.

"You wouldn't want Johnnie to walk on his own would you Da? We'll talk later, yes?"

Surprised and slightly disappointed John nodded.

"Of course sweetheart."

He and Ria watched Helen and Johnnie walk ahead of them and hung back until they were out of hearing.

"Why oh why did it have to be like this? I feel as if my whole life has revolved around not being in the right place at the right time."

Gratefully John took a lighted cigarette from Ria and inhaled deeply.

Slipping her arm through his Ria started to follow the others. "I know, but you have to get this as right as you can. Helen is obviously grieving deeply and needs you; we have all the time in the world to catch up now we are in England."

In the draughty church hall, the ladies from the church poured teas and offered small delicate sandwiches for refreshment. Helen and John gave their attention to Kate's friends and neighbours and thanked them for their condolences. It was very noticeable that there were no family members, just themselves, which made it even more poignant that John had managed to get there. He held back his tears and swallowed hard. Kate always showed courage, even when life was at its most difficult. Unselfish to the end. He had so much to thank her for, but he had arrived too late to tell her. He wondered if she had received his last letter telling of his marriage to Ria. He glanced across to Helen. Had Kate passed on his news to her? His little girl was a grown woman, and a very attractive one at that. He returned her generous smile aware that he had done so little to deserve the unconditional love she bestowed upon him.

The mourners drifted away in ones and twos; they had fulfilled their duty and wanted to return to their homes. The weather was not conducive to standing around keeping up the obligatory small talk. John and Helen both understood this and were secretly relieved that the gathering would soon end.

Helen thankfully accepted a cup of hot tea from Johnnie, to replace the cold one she had held onto for some time, as he rescued her from a particularly demanding neighbour.

"What would I do without you? You are so kind."

"Rubbish, it's only what you deserve." He smothered a laugh. "Lucky you, here comes another one for a little talk," smiling he limped away with the cold cup of tea and placed it on the serving hatch. He turned and found himself face to face with John who had obviously made his way over to the hatch to speak to him

"I just want to thank you for taking care of Helen when she fainted out there. He held his hand out to Johnnie. I did appreciate your calmness." As they shook hands, he continued … "have you known my daughter long?"

Johnnie grinned. "Not really Sir. We met while we were in the same hospital and have stayed friends ever since. Being here with her is the least I could do in the circumstances."

He hesitated before continuing. "She was devastated, both by her Grandmother's death and your absence Sir, so of course she needed support and company to help her with the arrangements."

Johnnie's tone was somewhat apologetic as he studied John's sombre face.

Of course she did," John responded "and once again I appreciate your care and thoughtfulness."

Interrupted by one of the mourners wanting to say her goodbyes their conversation ended.

With some unease, Helen observed her two favourite men from across the small hall and wondered whether they would like each other. Strange that even though her friendship with John had been for a relatively short time she found him easy and comfortable to be with, whereas her Da, he seemed distant, more so than ever before She loved him, of course she did, but now they appeared to have so little in common.

He knew nothing about her life, how could he, his visits were few and short lived; and she, she had no idea of who he really was. Did he have many friends? How many women had he loved since her mother died? Obviously, the woman with him, Ria, thought the world of him. Did he feel the same about her? Nervously, she wandered towards him. The last two mourners were leaving. What now?

John closed the door behind the two women and took a deep breath. It was imperative that he handle this reunion with care and sensitivity if he was to have a meaningful father – daughter relationship. He was painfully aware that she had no family other than him and questioning thoughts flitted through his mind. Has she many friends? Is she a happy person? On the other hand, could she be as insecure as Ria was at this age; he recalled he had thought Ria's father was a beast and didn't deserve to be a parent. So how was he different to Ria's father. Certainly, he had never had improper thoughts about his daughter, but he knew he had been neglectful in many ways. Didn't Kate constantly encourage him to visit more often? Was it too late to make amends? No time like the present he thought.

They walked toward each other, John with his contagious smile and Helen smiling wistfully. He caught her up in his arms and held her close to him while she cried softly into his camel hair coat.

"Oh sweetheart, I'm sorry I was delayed. I'll explain later."

Ria and Johnnie glanced at each other, finding their situation rather awkward. Ria took the initiative and asked Johnnie whether he thought Helen would like to go to the hotel with them and share dinner together.

"You so obviously understand her in a way that neither John or I can, and it would be so much nicer if we could do something pleasing."

She looked earnestly into his eyes hoping she had not offended him in any way.

"She's a very easy person to please; I can't imagine her not wanting to spend as much time as she can with her father. I think", he said hesitantly, "that she probably idolises him which must make it a piece of cake."

He cocked his head to one side, a slight smile and a sparkle of fun in his eyes.

Nodding with approval Ria returned his smile.

"Mmm he is indeed a very fortunate father. Some daughters would have overturned the pedestal by now, but let's hope we can all get to know each other better and enjoy a fresh start."

Waiting for an appropriate moment, Ria and Johnnie encroached upon the father and daughter's reunion.

"It's freezing in here, and I'm sure we could all do with something warm inside us."

Ria crossed her arms and rubbed her hands up and down them in an attempt to get her blood moving.

"I'd like to suggest we go back to the hotel John where we can sit in the warmth of a fire, and order lunch. I'm sure Helen would find that far more comfortable than standing here."

Compassionately she looked at Helen and smiled.

Gratefully, Helen returned her smile, and nodded.

"It would be nice Da. How long are you here for this time?"

John hugged her.

"I want it to be for a very long time. I've gone freelance so I can choose where and when I work."

He turned to Ria.

"That's a great idea. What do you say Johnnie, you up for it?"

"Fine by me, if it's what Helen wants."

Helen left John's side and took hold of Johnnie's arm.

"You bet it's what I want. Let's go."

She surveyed the hall and realised the ladies had quietly and efficiently cleared the crockery away and were ready to leave.

A last farewell followed and together they vacated the hall greeted by a blast of icy air as they walked along the church path. Helen glanced over her shoulder, and saw that soil now covered her grandmother's grave. With a shudder she knew there was no denying her life with Kate had truly ended. Sliding her arm into Johnnie's she pulled him closer.

"You'll be fine," he said with a reassuring squeeze.

The biting wind whipped around the four of them as they trudged along in silence to avoid breathing down the freezing air. A sigh of relief ran through all of them as they turned onto the promenade where the Grand Hotel stood waiting to welcome them. They hurried eager to dispose of their outer garments to settle by the fireside in the reception lounge.

The two men had rum and Ria and Helen had sherry. It trickled down the back of their throats, spreading its warmth as it travelled through their bodies bringing life and flexibility back to their faces.

While they waited to be summoned to the dining room John gave a lively explanation of the eventful journey, he and Ria had undergone endeavouring to reach England from New York. He was an accomplished storyteller, mimicking voices and actions as he went along, and eliciting smiles and laughter from his audience. Helen enraptured by him as always, knew it would appear peevish to remain cross by his late appearance in the church. It was obvious it had not been deliberate and she recalled the many times she had waited for him in the past, anxiously watching the clock and listening for his footsteps. He was more often than not late, but he did eventually turn up. She should have known he wouldn't let her down. A little voice inside piped up, *yes, but how much better if he had arrived earlier and managed the funeral arrangements.* Pushing the voice aside Helen smiled and assured her Da that it had not been a problem; that with Johnnie's help and support she had coped well.

Ria watched, fascinated by how easily John had convinced Helen of his helplessness in the situation. She had accepted what he said without question. Like father like daughter. Isn't that exactly the way John dealt with life?

At the same time Johnnie, bemused by Helen's response, could identify the pain and upset in her eyes, and yet here she was showing nothing but adoration for her father. Surely her father was sensitive enough to realise his daughter was putting on a front. A strange relationship he thought seeing they were both desperate to hide their emotions. Not wanting to interfere he physically bit his lip.

Throughout the meal that followed Johnnie continued to watch with pure amazement as John informed Helen that he and Ria had married in New York and that he hoped they could all get to know each other better in the next few months. Could he not tell that it had come like a bombshell to Helen? Johnnie detected a little tic in her eyelid. Something he noticed happened when she was anxious.

Relieved that Ria appeared far more sensitive to Helen's situation he listened with interest as she reminded Helen that they had in fact met many years ago. Helen unable to remember shook her head with consternation, while Ria told her it had been for a very short time and that she was barely four years old then so of course she was hardly likely to remember the occasion.

At this point Helen's face lit up, as if it made all the difference to know Ria had indeed met her Grandmother.

"Yes" Ria confirmed. "It was not long after your Aunt Emily passed on. Oh and you were a charming and beautiful little girl. Truly happy and so in love with Fluffy your cat."

Smiling with affection Helen murmured "Ah yes … Fluffy … Da brought him home for me on one of his visits … he was my nicest ever present … I must have been very young then." She looked at John questioningly.

John grunted with a grin on his face.

"You loved the present, but Grandma was not impressed. She told me I was irresponsible bringing you a pet while you were still so young. She was right of course, but I never gave it a thought, and seeing the delight on your face when I let that kitten out of the bag, she succumbed without further protest."

He chuckled, "I could always get around her, a hug and a smile of persuasion was all it took."

"Mm" interjected Ria, "much like he continues to do with me and you Helen, but he is so charming and loving with it don't you agree?"

Helen started. "I ... I have never thought of it in that way. You just like to make people happy don't you Da?"

"Exactly sweetheart ... but it often ends up that as I make one person happy, someone else is unhappy because of my actions. It never seems straightforward. Like I have made Ria happy to become my wife, but I'm not so sure I have made you happy by presenting you with a step-mother?"

The blood rushed to Helen's face in embarrassment.

"No Da, I don't think you understand ... it has all come out of the blue ... and on top of losing Grandma ... I ..." tears filled her eyes ... " just feel ..." she searched for words to explain and feebly finished ... "lost."

The silence was palpable around the table. Helen pushed her chair back and spoke directly to Johnnie.

"Can we go back to Percy Square now, I feel so tired?"

Johnnie rose from the table and addressed John and Ria.

"It's been a long day. Will you excuse us?"

John also stood.

"Of course. When shall we come and see you Helen. Tomorrow afternoon?"

Mutely she nodded and took Johnnie's arm for support.

chapter 33

———⟨⊘⊘⊘⟩———

The Next Day

THE OVERCAST SKY SHOWED signs of an impending snow storm. John and Ria strode briskly away from the Hotel in the hope they could avoid the snow for the ten minutes that it took to get to Percy Square.

Ria pulled her fur collar closer to her neck to cover the gap between that and her matching hat. She now recognised the folly of her hair-cut; she should have waited for the warmer weather. At the time, it had not occurred to her that she would miss the warmth of her mane of hair to such an extent. Although she loved her new look, a fashionable bob, she also missed her long hair. She wanted to make a physical change to signify she had a new life, and was ready to face new challenges. A smile hovered as she recalled how John had laughed at her new abandoned attitude.

"England here she comes" he had whooped, which filled her with pleasurable anticipation and excitement and had remained with her until yesterday, when it had dawned upon her that John's relationship with Helen held signs of fragility, signs to which John appeared oblivious, which worried her. She hoped she was mistaken and she would witness a difference when they met up with Helen today.

While keeping in step with Ria, John was also considering how little he knew about Helen's life, her foibles, hobbies and friends. She had seemed unreceptive, almost unwelcoming yesterday which had left him feeling uneasy. She was almost a stranger.

Secretly troubled he wondered how to rekindle the warmth and love they had once shared. And what about her companion? He was obviously a pleasant young man, but Helen was far too young to be caught up with a cripple. He and Ria would have to introduce her into their world of friends and colleagues to broaden her lifestyle before she settled for this relationship. Some shopping trips with Ria and other sorts of things women like to do would give Helen opportunities to acquaint herself with fashion and etiquette. Johnnie staying at the house with her overnight, which he imagined had happened, was far from acceptable. He considered it his duty to enlighten her of this; he was after all her father.

His stomach churned as he recalled his little girl was no longer so little and indeed, if he was honest with himself, her enforced maturity had shaken him. He had unwittingly presumed she and Kate would jog along quite happily until he was ready to return to England to step in. This present situation had not been in his plan. No the sooner they could settle down together the better. England was under less threat from the Germans and according to one of his colleagues, his house had escaped bomb damage, so with a good spring clean it would be perfect for the three of them. It was almost as it would have been with Molly. His wife, daughter and him, living as a family in London with no financial worries. He had fulfilled Kate's dream at last although unhappily she would never know.

Startled, that they had nearly reached the house, and not a word had passed between them, John squeezed Ria's gloved hand and smiled.

"A penny for them," and daringly kissed her cheek.

"Not in the street John, we're no longer in New York," she gasped, exaggerating her shock-horror at his boldness. She hesitated slightly before confiding her thoughts.

"I guess I'm a little uneasy ... I wonder if it was fair of us to marry before you and Helen were re-united. I think it was too much for her to take in yesterday." She sighed, "Our timing could not have been worse."

Smarting, John pursed his lips.

"And you think I planned it this way? I wasn't to know that her Grandmother would die at this particular time." She could hear the exasperation in his voice.

Putting a conciliatory hand on his arm Ria shook her head sadly.

"Of course I know that, it's just ... I think we should be ... well ... be sensitive to her perception of things. She's still young and naïve John."

Pausing for a moment, she added,

"Maybe the two of you would find it helpful to have some time together without me or Johnnie getting in the way."

John grimaced. "I think it might be too late for that."

He opened the gate to the small front garden.

"Let's play it by ear for the moment shall we?"

They had no time to knock at the door. It was opened and Helen her face flushed with pleasure was eagerly encouraging them to step inside and out of the bitter cold.

"You poor things you must be frozen come in and get warm."

Relief flooded through John. His darling girl was not going to be difficult.

"I'm so glad you're here. I don't enjoy being alone. I'm missing Johnnie already."

Ria looked around as if expecting Johnnie to jump from behind the sofa. "Is he not here then?"

"No he has to report back to base. The air force is in his blood and if he can resume flying, he will. His Commanding Officer has encouraged him all the way through his recovery to remain positive about his career. Apparently, having a false leg can be overcome. He has shown such strength of character with his battle to get back on his feet. I am so proud of him Da."

Her voice burst with pride as she continued.

"I am so grateful for him ... I have no idea how I would have managed without him. You'll find out how generous and loving he is when you get to know him."

"It sounds as if you're smitten with him," John said jokingly. "I hope he comes from a good wealthy family."

"It's not like that Da" Helen retorted, her cheeks flushing. "We're just really good friends, and even if it was more than that, I couldn't give a fig about wealth."

"It's easy to feel that way in the first flushes of love, but when reality knocks in, it's not always so simple my sweetheart," he said waving his first finger mockingly at her.

"And you know that do you Da?" Helen poured three cups of tea, raising her eyes with a smile in Ria's direction.

"Yes I do" John returned with resolve. "Your dear mother suffered an austere beginning with me because we had so little money which meant I had to work long hours to get our home together. She didn't deserve that, although she never complained even at the end of her short life."

There was a hint of nostalgia in his voice which his daughter had not heard before.

Helen sat next to Ria. "You have never told me that before Da."

Looking across at the two women in his life John said wryly.

"It's a long time ago, and I suppose I'd never experienced a lack of finance until then. Your Grandma and Grandpa managed money well and I had no idea how different it would be once I was a married man, and responsible for another's wellbeing. Your mother's family were ordinary working people, and she was one of many siblings. They managed the best they could so she was familiar with making ends meet, especially after her mother died. Her father was a drinker and often spent his wages the same day as he got them.

I wanted her to have a better life so I worked all the hours I could get. She never complained even though she was away from her family and friends. I know she found the days long and lonely in London, but I didn't really give it that much thought. When we knew, she was expecting our baby it seemed so right and natural. She could do what she did best, she loved children, and she blossomed knowing she was to become a mother." He shrugged his shoulders, "but, life can be a bitch sometimes. She did not have a good pregnancy, and I could see then how much better it would have been if I had had money for her to see a doctor in the early stages. Instead we convinced ourselves that once the baby was born she would improve." His expression was sad as he finished. "And she gave birth to a beautiful daughter, who sadly she was never to see grow up."

Instinctively, Helen pushed her head into the back of the sofa and shook her head.

"Do you truly believe that money would have changed that Da?

"Possibly not, but I would have preferred to have had the chance to know. It spoilt your life that I do know."

"I only knew the way it was. Grandma loved me and so did you what more could I have asked for?"

"I gave you the occasional visit, which you settled for whereas if I had had money I could have employed a nanny and kept you with me in London."

He glanced over at Ria and smiled.

"If only we two had fought harder for each other all those years ago … things might have been so different."

Stirred by her father's willingness to talk, Helen seized the opportunity to hear more.

"So what stopped you and Ria … oh how sad that it took you all this time … I could have had brothers and sisters … I would have loved that. Don't tell me … you still thought money was the answer to happiness?"

"Not just that sweetheart. Ironically Ria was much loved by her adopted family and very financially sound. I was out of her league. Our different social standing meant it was complicated. The family were particularly helpful with my career, but marriage was a no go area. That's how it was then. But as they say the path to true love is never smooth and here we are."

Turning to Ria, Helen met her eyes.

"So how did you meet again?"

Searching John's eyes before answering, Ria trusted he was happy for her to respond.

"What your Da omitted to tell you was that he met a very mixed up young woman all those years ago. One who mistrusted men and did not encourage relationships, who was afraid of her own shadow. He was persistent, and I was very attracted to him, but I would not let him get close. When I did have some courage to try, he was called back to England; of course, he had his job and had to do what his paper demanded of him, so we arranged to meet in Durham, but, on the day, we missed each other. I concluded he was no longer interested in me and foolishly decided I would visit my mother's grave, followed by a time of prayer in the Cathedral. My real father found me there, which turned into an altercation, that's another long story, which set me back years. I wanted to go home, and escape, but instead travelled to many foreign countries with my stepfather for the next two years.

Your Da caught up with me in New York a few years later and we realised it would be easier to keep our relationship a secret for a while. Each time your Da came to New York we would meet up in the apartment he rented there."

Helen looked over at her father and shook her head.

"I had no idea you had rented property in New York"

Halting his interjection she laughed.

"Please Ria go on."

"There really is not a lot left to say. My stepfather sadly died last year, my stepbrothers continued to run the business and had no objections to our marriage, so there was no longer any reason for us to keep our love a secret. The war seemed to be coming to an end, everything was quietening down. Your Da arranged for a licence, which was a complete surprise to me, although a lovely one, and here we are, married. The plan was to return to England immediately after, but there were so many hitches we had to wait longer than anticipated." She spread her hands "so we can only implore you to forgive us for not being here for you when you most needed your Da."

A lull settled in the room as they sipped their tea, conscious that although family, they were strangers.

Helen felt obliged to ease the situation and handed some papers to John.

"Grandma told me to keep these until we were together. I promised to live here, until you came back and we could read them at the same time."

John flinched. Had she not given him all the paperwork that concerned him? He felt the thickness of the envelope and decided it must contain the deeds to the house. Strange that he felt a rise of anxiety when he was certain that Kate would never disclose his history in such a way.

He smiled at Helen and placed the paperwork on the table.

"Another cup of tea and we'll take a look at them, yes?"

With a cheeky grin, Helen rummaged in the sideboard and brought out a bottle of whisky, kept for medicinal purposes.

"Would you not prefer this?"

John looked sceptical before taking the bottle from her.

"Why did Grandma dislike you having a drink so much Da?"

"Ah now that is a question for which I can only hazard a guess. Apparently my uncles, your Grandfather's brothers, enjoyed their alcohol a little too much for her liking, especially when they encouraged my father to join them down at the pub. My Pa was a very responsible and kind man, but Friday night was his night for a trip to the pub with his mates and he would not budge, no matter how silent my Mama became. I felt the atmosphere change on Fridays."

John laughed and smacked his lips as the whisky slipped down the back of his throat.

"She repeatedly warned me of what she called 'the demon drink' … and came to sleep in my room on Fridays when I was young … as I grew older I found Pa really amusing after he had his night out … Mama would go off to bed in a huff and me and Pa would sit and have supper together. That was when I got to understand my Pa, we called it our special time."

"Really?" queried Ria, while Helen observed John pour another drink.

Feeling relaxed he smiled nonchantly.

"Enough about me. Let's open this envelope and find out what it is about."

He slit the parchment envelope open with a knife and drew out its contents.

The two women kept quiet as he shuffled through the papers rapidly taking note of their contents. Eventually he put one sheet aside, handed one to Helen and the others he laid on the table.

"It all looks pretty straight forward. The Deeds to the house are with the solicitor and all personal effects are here in the house. Your Grandma has left the house to you Helen and the Solicitor will assist you to sell it, if that is your wish."

Picking up the paper, he put aside, and reading it, his expression softened as fond memories flooded his mind. Striving to stultify his deep seated and conflicting emotions, he took a deep breath before looking up.

"We both have personal letters Helen. I will read mine properly later, you might like to do the same?"

Lightly fingering the paper as if it might disintegrate in front of her eyes, Helen nodded. Seeing her Grandmother's fine handwriting brought tears to her eyes. She stood up and placed it under a large glass paperweight on the bureau trying very hard to keep control of her emotions. It somehow did not feel comfortable to show her feelings in front of the two people with her. Pulling herself together, she turned with a smile on her face in the hope that neither her Da nor Ria could detect her distress.

"So … what are you both going to do … now that Grandma is no longer with us. Will you be going back to New York?"

"Are you trying to see the back of us already?" John said jokingly. "I told you I can choose what I do from now on, so we thought it was a good time to live in London. We hoped you might want to come with us sweetheart."

He and Ria smiled in unison and joined hands.

Helen choked back her tears. She should be glad they wanted her with them and yet it highlighted her sense of exclusion from their life. She had wished for years that he would want her with him. Instead, a sense of deflation overwhelmed her. It could never be as she dreamed, she and her Da together, because now there was another.

"I had planned to go back to Windsor and continue my work

with the WRVS," she faltered before adding, "I want to be useful in this war. Knitting and making tea may seem mediocre, but it really is important for women to do their bit. I'm fortunate not to be working in a munitions factory after I failed my medical to return to the WRENS."

*Nodding gravely John gave her a pensive look.

"You're right of course, on the other hand the WRVS must be crying out for women in London, so you could still be useful."

Receptive to John's sympathetic response Helen realised that it was possible and reproached her immediate reaction to his proposal.

"Yes I agree, but I want to keep in touch with my friends. They are very important to me now and it would be easier if I was based in Windsor with Alice and Johnnie."

She kept her eyes lowered, not wishing to see disappointment on her Da's face.

John had not considered she would oppose his idea and struggled to stay good-tempered. Did she not appreciate he was endeavouring to make up for his years of absence. It was as if he was meeting his daughter for the first time. Not quite as meek and retiring as she had appeared the last time they met he sensed an invisible barrier between them. Dumb-founded he searched for words to express himself. He had always been a smooth talker, polite and plausible, never lost for words.

An uncomfortable silence filled the room, until Ria broke it with her warm compassionate voice.

"I think you both need a little more time together before Helen can decide. I guess you want to talk to your friends don't you Helen? See what they think and how you will stay in touch. We haven't sorted the house out yet John. It would be nice to have Helen's input if it is to become her home as well as ours don't you think?"

Ria's voice faded out as she apprehensively left her question in the air.

Appreciatively John nodded. "I think Ria has a point Helen, what do you say?"

Relieved by Ria's intervention Helen happily agreed.

"It would be better if I could look into my options."

Out of his depth John could only nod his acceptance.

"I'm looking forward to seeing more of you Da of course I am, but until this war ends I feel unable to make any definite plans My life has proven very different to my expectations. These past months have opened my eyes to how I see others and how kind Alice and Johnnie are."

She threw him a fearful look "I'm sorry Da."

Drawing in a deep breath John swallowed his grudge.

"Don't be sweetheart; I got carried away with the situation. It's me being selfish and expecting everything to be the way I want it. We will take it slowly and with Ria's help I'm pretty certain we will work things out."

"Thank you Da, thank you Ria, I can't wait to tell Johnnie how wonderful it is all going to be from now on."

chapter 34

July 1944

ALICE JUMPED. THE KNOCK on the door seemed extraordinarily loud. Not expecting visitors that day, she speculated on who it could be and cautiously opened the front door. A woman, oblivious to her rap having received a speedy response, was taking in her surroundings, and stood waiting her back to the door.

"Can I help you?"

Startled the woman turned to face her.

"I'm terribly sorry to bother you, but I believe you have a lodger called Helen Smith? I am trying to locate her."

Alice studied the tall, elegant, but weary looking woman who was quite obviously nervous.

"Can I ask who wants to know?"

"Oh … I do apologise." She held her hand out to Alice. "My name is Victoria Smith; I am Helen's step-mother."

Alice relaxed and took her hand. "Please come in, she has spoken warmly of you these past months."

Ria stepped into the restful hall and smiled gratefully at Alice.

"I didn't want to disturb your day like this … Alice … you are Alice aren't you?"

With a cheerful uplifting smile, Alice guided her along the hall and into the homely kitchen, where as always, the smell of baking lingered in the air.

"I certainly am. Let me make you a cup of tea Victoria. Helen is out. She's helping out at the Red Cross today I believe, but she is usually back here by five-ish."

"Oh goodness I can't put you out for that long," Ria gasped as she looked at her watch. "It's only three now."

"Nonsense, of course you can." Glancing across at her visitor Alice noticed Ria's stress etched face.

"Forgive me for asking Victoria, but is there a problem?"

Ria placed her hand over her trembling lips determined not to cry. Gulping, she took a deep breath and then removed her hand.

"Please call me Ria. Why on earth do I introduce myself as Victoria when I dislike it so much," she said laughing nervously. "How strange does that make me?"

She twiddled her fingers as she chewed her bottom lip before answering.

"Yes, I do have a problem, I feel foolish now I am here, because it is no worse than anyone else's, but I … I …" she swallowed deeply, "I want to speak to Helen before I take any action, for her to know my thinking around how I can solve my quandary."

"Oh dear" said Alice.

Not wishing to probe, she busied herself with the cups and saucers and poured boiling water into the teapot. Ria seemed rooted to the chair as if mesmerised by Alice's movements.

Alice recognised it could be a sign that Ria was reliving some trauma and decided not to break into whatever reverie she was engaged in. She placed a few shortbreads on a plate, poured the tea, and carried the tray over to the table.

For the next five minutes, they sipped their tea without a word passing between them. Alice, usually a non-stop talker, began to fidget, and pushed the shortbread closer to Ria.

"Do have a shortbread Ria" she almost pleaded, the silence becoming unbearable.

Slowly a glimmer of a smile reached Ria's lips and a spark of life reached her eyes.

"Thank you."

She nibbled the edges with pleasure.

"It's very nice, is it your own baking?"

"Mm" nodded Alice thankful to get a response from her visitor.

"I bake every day, some of it is for the baker in the main street and some goes to the WRVS. I'm fortunate enough to have chickens and the garden yields vegetables and the fruit trees give a good crop of apples and plums. Enough to fill plenty of fruit pies and the eggs are so much nicer than the dried egg for cooking cakes."

Leaning back into her chair Alice grinned. "Keeps me out of trouble, makes me feel needed,"

"You sound a very busy and practical lady. I can understand why Helen finds you an inspiration."

"She's a lovely caring girl; she is very easy to get on with and is delightful company. She is like a breath of fresh air in the house."

"I'm sure she is," Ria said wistfully. "John and I are looking forward to the time when she will feel at home with us. If only this awful war would come to an end. With things as they are there might be no home to return to."

She put her head in her hands and massaged her temples. Glancing up she confided in Alice.

"I have been so scared in the house during this last week. The floorboards shudder and the window frames shake every time one of those things … doodlebugs I hear people call them … come over … they just drop from the sky with no warning. They've blasted so many peoples' homes and lives apart. I see families wandering along with the few possessions they've managed to retrieve looking for somewhere else to live. London is reduced to rubble in so many areas, and I don't know how I will get on if John's house is hit."

Alice nodded sympathetically and took her hand.

Comforted by the gesture Ria told her more.

"This morning, we had yet another one of these awful summer storms but I decided to carry on and go shopping. I thought I would look around Marks and Spencer's, and Woolworths. It's lonely in the house on my own … and I thought it would cheer me up. I took the bus," she said proudly, "and had just alighted when I heard this strange, awful, horrible noise … I looked up and then I saw it, the engine had cut out and it was engulfed in flames."

She physically shuddered, her eyes betraying her fear.

"I didn't know what to do, but I heard someone shout, take cover, and without thinking I threw myself onto the ground and kept my arms over my head. The eerie silence seemed to go on forever, but I couldn't move, or look around me. I was absolutely frozen to the ground."

She laughed nervously.

"Never have I prayed so desperately Alice. I truly believed my end had come …and then there was this massive bang. It was as if all hell had been let loose with bricks and rubble whizzing about. I just lay there shaking until it stopped. I can still hear the sounds of glass shattering and people screaming."

Tears slowly trickled onto her cheeks.

"Obviously I was not hurt, although I'm sure I have gone partly deaf in my right ear, and neither were those around me thank God … I didn't know what to do with myself for a while then I made an impulsive decision to try to find Helen. I didn't want to stay in London. I was frightened and lonely and Helen is the only person I know in this area of the country."

Alice stood up and put her arm around Ria's shaking shoulders.

"Come on now. At least you are safe, and Helen will be delighted to see you. Where will you stay if not in London?"

Sighing deeply Ria shook her head.

"I wonder if Helen will let me stay in her house, at least until John returns. I know it's a lot to ask of her, but I have no other ideas."

Alice let her arm drop and said cheerfully. "Whatever, you are not travelling tonight so I will make you a bed up in the spare room. It is only a small room, but you are welcome to it, and then when Helen comes home you can discuss it with her."

Worn out and weary, Helen jiggled her key trying to locate the lock in the door. There was no moon so it was particularly dark causing her to feel particularly weepy and alone. She knew she absolutely had to go straight to bed to have some quiet time No staying up late with Alice, as much as she loved her company. She missed Johnnie immensely. His chance to fly again had become a reality, and although she was delighted for him, the loss of his friendship on a daily basis had affected her badly. Working long and hard hours to relieve the suffering of others was her way of dealing with her sadness. She like so many others had truly believed the war ended on June the sixth, only to discover Hitler was of a different mind. The blackout and gloom seemed to have permeated her very being in the past two weeks without Johnnie's optimism and good humour.

She stopped in her tracks once inside, her heart doing a double summersault. Could it be … was Johnnie here? Alice obviously had a visitor. She could hear them talking.

She listened closely before detecting it was a woman's voice. Refusing to acknowledge her disappointment, she told herself she was glad. That meant she would not feel mean leaving Alice alone for the evening.

Before she had removed her outer clothing, Alice called out a greeting and reassured her that she had a cup of tea ready for her, and a lovely surprise.

Unable as always to resist Alice's exuberance, Helen smiled broadly. It was lovely that she and Johnnie shared the same gift that lifted others out of the blues. How lucky she was to have them both in her life. She hung her coat on the hook and walked briskly into the sitting room knowing Alice would have her arms ready to give her a hug, then remembering there was another with her, she halted amazed to see Ria alongside Alice on the sofa. Something must have happened.

"Is Da with you?" She stammered, closely observing the two faces in front of her for signs of distress.

Alice jumped to her feet, quickly followed by Ria who was shaking her head vigorously and telling her there was nothing to worry about.

Hugging the two of them with relief she demanded to know what had brought Ria to Windsor.

Whilst sipping at the hot sweet cup of tea Alice had poured for her, she listened with compassion to Ria's story. She could well imagine how upsetting it must have been, especially for Ria, a comparative stranger to London.

Ria finished by saying how wonderful Alice had been welcoming her into her home and offering a bed for the night.

A wide smile appeared on Helen's face. "I told you she was one of the nicest people I have ever met didn't I? She made my life bearable when I was down and convalescing ... she was my rock ... and still is."

Holding her hands up Alice laughed. "Enough ... I only did what anyone would do ... and anyway look what a tonic you have been for Johnnie and me."

"So you say, but I know different," grinned Helen before returning to Ria. "So where is Da?"

"Oh Helen it didn't take long for your Da to feel restless. I could tell he was bored without his usual routine. Life for him is his reporting ... I don't know why I imagined, or he for that matter, that he could live a quiet life, just doing a little here and there. He needs to be in demand ... wants the excitement ... the deadlines ... wants to come up with that extra special story for the front page. What could I do ...?" She shrugged her shoulders. "I don't know when he will be back this time. He was following up a story about the little ships that left Sheerness and Ramsgate to help the troops get back home from Dunkirk. You know your Da, he is always interested in hearing the common people's side of things, the human element I think he calls it, and this event intrigued him so much I agreed he should follow it up."

With a downhearted nod of the head, Helen agreed. She had so hoped he could change for Ria.

"Are you regretting coming to England now?" She asked in a flat voice.

"I ... Ria cleared her throat "I'm a little confused ... he seemed so keen to re-establish a sense of family ... but ... I guess it's this war that's the real problem. How can anyone expect a normal family life? We failed to realise the true state of life here ... at least in the Cities near ports and of course we should have known the Capital city was always going to be under threat." Her tone was almost apologetic. "That's why I hoped you might agree to my living in Tynemouth Village for a while."

Stifling a yawn Helen said, "It sounds a good idea Ria, but can we talk about it in the morning, I feel so tired I just want to collapse. I don't have to report for duties until the afternoon tomorrow so we have time to mull it over."

With an enormous yawn, she rose to her feet. "So sorry about this, but I must get some sleep."

She kissed each of them on the forehead and wished them goodnight.

Alice and Ria returned her kisses and watched her leave the room.

Another cup of tea and several hours later, they both crept upstairs and fell into their beds. They were no longer strangers. Indeed, having unusually shared a great deal of personal details, a bond of friendship now existed. They both drifted to sleep with one thought in mind, if only they could have aired the one remaining secret kept harboured in their hearts. Only the most special friend could be trusted with such confidences.

chapter 35

John — August 1944

LISTENING INTENTLY TO THE group of men gathered around a table in the local Inn, John scribbled notes every now and then, encouraging them to tell him more.

He was now in Dover hoping to scoop some more true-life stories from seamen and boat owners who had put their lives at risk to cross the channel to save as many as possible of the British and French troops from the beaches of Dunkirk in 1940. They were an affable group, happy to give him first-hand accounts of the event. It was the most fired up he had felt since he returned to England. Buoyancy welled up within him, totally absent in his personal social life. Only his work provided this high. He hardly questioned the reason for this, merely accepting it as fact.

Some told him how their boats, blown to bits by the German dive-bombers, left them and survivors of the crew in the water gravely hoping to be rescued before they perished from either the onslaught of the Germans or the ice-cold sea.

Others recalled the sheer hell of turning their backs on injured and desperate soldiers, because their boats were full to capacity. They made for the large naval ships, in the deeper water, dropped off their load and immediately double backed, risking life and limb to evacuate more men.

Impressed by these brave civilians, who had volunteered in this early part of the war effort, he found himself embroiled in their enthusiasm to see an end to the war and a longing for peace and re-unions with families and friends. He ordered another round of drinks reluctant to take his leave of them until he had gleaned sufficient details to produce a riveting article. It would need to honour and pay tribute to their dauntless determination to bring back as many soldiers as was possible.

He knew that when this war ended, these stories could bring solace and pride, if only to make sense of what seemed to be a pointless loss of lives for ordinary families and communities within the British Isles. Having a fear of the sea aroused a greater zest in him to document the happenings of these heroes.

Glancing around confident that he could extract more if he tried harder, he noticed a man well into his sixties studying him. Slightly disturbed by the man's fixed gaze, John smiled over at him and raised his glass, as an invitation to come and join him. The man moseyed across a broad smile on his face.

"Sorry if I was staring at you young man, but you are the double of someone I knew a long time ago." He offered his hand and John politely shook it.

"Really, and who would that be?"

As soon as the words were out of his mouth, John regretted the question. Did he really want to know? It wasn't his style. Still this was a first to be someone's double. Recognising the man was determined to know more about him a hasty retreat seemed to be the only way to avoid this conversation. Unhappily, without appearing very rude, it was impossible. He listened courteously.

"Believe it or not, you are the image of my brother. At least, as he was when I last saw him. I haven't seen him for …" he paused to think … "must be thirty years now. I have a niece, his daughter, but as far as I know, no nephews. When I saw you, I had to ask, find out whether you could possibly be a son of Robert Dalgleish?"

With a look of consternation, John shook his head, deeply shocked that the name Dalgleish had arisen yet once again, and especially at this time and in this place. Confounded, he was at a loss for words.

Slapping John on the back the man smiled broadly and introduced himself.

"My name is John, obviously Dalgleish," he added with a wry smile. "I had to ask, I would have wondered for ever otherwise," he scratched his bearded chin," it really is an odd feeling to meet a complete stranger the image of one of your own family.

Finishing his drink in one gulp John agreed it must be weird. Tempted by the man's open, ready smile he was curious to know more.

"Thirty years is an awful long time not to have seen your brother, have you lost touch?"

"You could put it that way. It's no real loss, we had little in common. Being family is no guarantee of friendship and love. Be nice if it was, but that's life." He let out a husky laugh, "how about you young man, are you in contact with your siblings?"

"Don't have that problem" John answered light-heartedly "there was only me."

John Dalgleish caught the barman's eye and pushed his glass toward him and asked for another, and whatever his friend was drinking, whilst he continued his conversation.

"Best way if you ask me, no rivalry or entanglements, and of course you are always the favourite child. You married?"

Not familiar with this confrontational type of conversation, although he himself used it, took him aback. A complete stranger was interested in him. It felt strange and at the same time comfortable. It was he who asked questions not the other way around. Slightly inebriated his usual cautious nature was lessened and he answered without hesitation.

"Mm … second time around."

"Lucky you … oh sorry lad, didn't mean to sound insensitive."

John grinned, "Don't worry. I am lucky … unfortunately my first wife, my true love, died soon after giving birth to our daughter. I didn't believe I would ever recover from my loss of her, but then to meet another beautiful woman to love, well that is indeed lucky. I couldn't ask for more. How about you?"

"Me?" John Dalgleish let out a deep hoarse laugh, finished his drink and pushed his glass toward the bar attendant for a refill, motioning to John to drink up and indicating with a nod of his head for it to be replenished.

"I've spent a major part of my life at sea, never wanted to settle for one place so missed my chances where love was concerned. Started my life in the Church, convinced I was destined to spread the Word ..." his laugh was scathing at this point ... "discovered me and the Church didn't really see eye to eye ... bloody hypocrites most of them ... left that behind and fell in love with the sea. Now if anything is awesome it's the oceans ... believe me ... as unpredictable and erratic as any woman. On the other hand it can be tranquil, serene and soothing as a wife's soft hand. Ah yes ... but without the complications." Easing off he suddenly asked. "Did you tell me your name?"

Accepting the glass offered to him John's face lit up with a mischievous grin.

"Funnily enough I could be your namesake ... its John ... Smith is the surname" and then as if he was unable to stop himself added, "although there was a time when I was known as Dalgleish-Smith."

"By God I knew it," exclaimed his newfound drinking partner. "There is too much of a resemblance for you not to be who I took you for in the first place."

Bewilderment and fear ran through John's veins. He leaned heavily against the bar, trying his hardest to keep his panic at bay. It was too late to walk away. He knew in an instant of certainty he had to accept the time had come to end a lifetime of constant denial.

His new acquaintance took his arm.

"So how come you turned your back on the name Dalgleish. What did your parents think of that? It is not possible for you to look so like my brother and there be no connection." He regarded John's perplexed expression and was concerned.

"Come and sit down let us talk. Don't you see we are more than likely related and I for one will be delighted if that is the reality? Between us we can try to make some sense of our situation."

John Dalgleish motioned to the barman

"A bottle of the best you have, together with bread, cheese and some pickles. I will pay you well for your trouble" he urged before the man could explain the shortages of food and drink. "In fact I'll pay you more for the use of a room out the back my good man"

He surreptitiously pressed some notes into the barman's hand, his arm around John's shoulders and smiling broadly.

"Come John let's eat, drink and speculate."

chapter 36

September 1944

HELEN HARDLY RECOGNISED THE house of her childhood any more. A happy and buoyant atmosphere welcomed anyone who came through the door of number six Percy Square.

That was not to say that Kate had not been friendly, but few younger people ever stepped over the threshold, during her lifetime. As Helen had attended boarding school her friends had not been local girls, and because she constantly considered her Grandmother's health, she resisted asking friends to visit.

She and Ria were getting on famously together and had built up a close relationship. Having Rita with them was equally fulfilling. Helen had used persuasive and cajoling tactics where the very independent Rita was concerned. It would be a very long time before her poor body recovered from the trauma of the burns, although her face was much improved. The left side of her face hardly scarred, gave a false impression of no damage. However, even though the skin around her nose and mouth was not quite as tight looking, it was plainly obvious that she was a victim of fire.

Helen and Johnnie had maintained their friendship with Rita through thick and thin. She faced life with a tight upper lip, and rather than accept help, she endeavoured to push them away with her flippant and sometimes cynical remarks. Rita found it difficult to believe they offered friendship and not sympathy. She allowed no one to see beneath the surface and many of her friends now stayed away. Kindness was not something she accepted easily.

Johnnie was extra forceful about keeping in touch with Rita and Helen often wondered whether he had stronger feelings for her than plain friendship. It was Johnnie's sensitivity and understanding that she loved most about him, so when they visited Rita she felt envious of the undivided attention he bestowed upon her friend. Helen cringed at the thought that she could be jealous and fought to keep it hidden.

When she and Ria decided they would both return to Tynemouth Village it seemed an excellent way of proving true friendship by suggesting Rita go with them. She persuaded Rita that she would love to have her live with them. She could give her the care she needed and it would be so much better than hospital life. Together they could take walks along the beach, and when she was ready to face the world, they could go shopping, or go to see a film as friends do.

Helen was so excited she could not understand Rita's reluctance to join them. It seemed such a perfect plan to her. It had taken a visit from Johnnie to encourage Rita to leave the safety of the hospital and venture out. He knew about the glances people in their situations received from strangers, and yet he knew it had to come at some time. She could not remain invisible and hidden away. Rita could not be in better company than that of Helen and Ria.

Whatever he had said, Helen appreciated Johnnie's ability to persuade Rita to change her mind, and although curious, resisted asking questions of either of them.

Within a month the three women had settled into a comfortable relationship, which involved bringing the house up to date, sharing a morning cup of tea together, discussing the latest news and embracing a daily walk along the beach. The strong breeze and sea air brought roses to their cheeks and produced healthy appetites in each of them. The bomb damage and destruction of London life, was exchanged for the smell and sight of the sun on the sea.

They unanimously agreed it was unhelpful for them to be worried about things over which they had no control. There would be time enough to worry, of that they were sure.

Having become proficient at using Kate's old sewing machine Rita astonished them all with her new found creativity. Any old material she could lay her hands on was transformed into up-to-the-minute fashion, bed covers and cushion covers. Helen, eager to express her admiration of Rita's skills, proposed they all go to Durham where with any luck she could purchase new fabrics and patterns to promote her flair. It would give them a day out away from Tynemouth. Neither Rita nor Helen had visited Durham so it would be different and interesting.

Ria, was hesitant about the trip, Durham being her home town. It held nothing except unhappy memories, ones she preferred to keep buried so she urged the younger girls to take the opportunity to do it together, just the two of them for a change without a chaperone. The thought of anyone recognising her sent shivers down her spine. Had she not left her father for dead when she was last there?

Helen, unable to detect Ria's reluctance, would not hear of leaving her behind. Of course, she must go with them; it was to be a treat for all of them. Rita added her plea that of course they wanted her company and they would not accept no as an answer, and so Ria hesitantly conceded.

Cloudless blue skies and bright sunshine greeted the three women as their train pulled into the station. Their laughter and smiles brought a smile to the faces of those who passed by them, although the friends were oblivious of the effect they had on others. They decided they would have coffee before they began their shopping and gleefully made their way to the nearest tea and coffee shop.

It was difficult to find a vacant table in the popular eating place and they waited patiently for a waitress to clear a table by the window for them. Helen expressed her surprise at seeing it this way.

"It must be very popular here, I don't know why but I imagined Durham to be a somewhat quiet area; shows how wrong you can be."

She laughed at her misconception and looked around with

curiosity. Everybody appeared to be locked into deep conversation and unaware of his or her surroundings. It was the ideal place for Rita to be, no one was the least bit interested in other customers so she could relax. With a last look around, she followed the others to their table.

"Nice here isn't it?"

Ria and Rita nodded their heads in agreement, and examined the menu eager to order as soon as possible. Amused Helen motioned to the waitress coming away from a table to their left. Glancing through the tables she thought she recognised a man looking very much like her father sitting to the side of them.

Speechless she realised it was her Da. He was listening attentively to an older man. Was he working on an assignment she wondered? Before she could alert Ria to his presence, he raised his head and their eyes met. He was obviously as shocked as she was to meet in this way. He said something to his companion, waved and then came across to their table.

"How wonderful to see you here," he said whilst pecking Ria and Helen on the cheek.

"What brings you here?"

Not waiting for an answer he continued light-heartedly

"I was planning to make my way to Tynemouth later. I thought I would check that there was nothing wrong with the house while I was in the area."

He paused realising they would not be in Durham if they were living in London, and at the same time became aware they had a guest with them.

"I'm sorry; I don't believe I know this young lady."

He bestowed his charming smile on Rita before Helen had time to answer, and turned to the table he had occupied.

"You must join me and my acquaintance we have only been here a few minutes and are yet to be served. I would like you to meet him and he you."

Without further ado, he stood behind Ria's chair, waiting to pull it away for her, and not considering for one moment the women's wishes. Ria turned her attention to Helen.

"Do you want to join your father or would you prefer to stay here?"

John laughed, "Of course she wants to be with me don't you my precious girl?"

Helen automatically nodded.

"Of course, how often does this happen,"

She laughed aloud to cover her irritation at her Da's thoughtless ways, "and Ria, Da can foot the bill."

She grinned at her friend.

"You will have gathered by now Rita, that this is my impossible Da. Da, Rita is my friend from the WRENS, remember? I did write to you about my friends in some of my letters."

The reminder was almost a challenge.

Once again, John produced one of his appealing smiles.

"Of course I do … it's nice to meet you Rita."

Rita blushed and returned his smile. She found him very attractive.

Ushering them to his table he implored one of the waitresses for extra chairs. Obviously seduced by his tone she nodded happily and obliged.

John's acquaintance stood, solicitously waiting for the women to sit, before returning to his chair.

Ria and Helen curious to know who this rugged, bearded man was unanimously gave John a questioning look.

"Please meet my wife Ria, my daughter Helen, and their friend Rita. Helen and Ria this is John Dalgleish."

They all acknowledged each other with polite smiles and proffered hands. It did not show outwardly, but Ria's heart was pounding. Dalgleish, was he from her family? Trying to recall exactly whether there was a family tie, she bit on her lip in deep concentration, trying to dredge up an answer. She studied his face discreetly while they all settled themselves around the table. With her stomach knotted, she began to feel uneasy in his company.

His eyes, it was something to do with his eyes, if only he would stop gazing as her. Then it hit her. His eyes … that was it … it was his eyes … so like those of her father.

Acutely aware that this was an undesirable situation for her to be in she stared at him as if stupefied. Her body and mind went into slow motion when his next remark came from out of the blue.

"My goodness … I can hardly believe my eyes … you must be … it's Victoria, isn't it, such a sweet dear child … oh my goodness… I would recognise you anywhere … you are so like your mother … you could be her. I am astounded at the likeness."

He shook his head in disbelief.

"How is she these days, such a delightful person is your mother."

In a shaky soft voice Ria answered in a dreamlike state, "was … not is".

The moment was broken by the waitress requesting their order. Ria's trance ended with a rush of voices and every day sounds pouring into her head. She knew without doubt that her past was once again with her, although she could not imagine why and how John and this man could know each other.

With her eyes lowered, she placed her napkin on her lap while surreptitiously studying his features and noting how he regarded her. He knew her … but obviously, from a long time back, he had only recognised her because of the likeness to her mother. She swallowed, attempting to moisten the dryness of her mouth. She felt, rather than observed, those eyes burning into her. Her heart quickened and her head reeled. He must be her father's younger brother, her uncle John. To her knowledge, he had disappeared many years ago in a cloud of supposed disgrace, but that was as much as she knew. The question that reverberated within her, was, did he know about her Aunt Ellen's secret, because if he did he could deduce John's relationship to her and then what? … Terrified, she excused herself from the others.

She needed air, somewhere to breathe, to dissipate the nauseous feeling that she now had. Hurriedly making her way through the narrow gaps between the tables, she headed for the entrance door. Once outside she leaned against the wall and gasped in deep breaths of warm air desperately trying to stop the panic that threatened to overwhelm and destroy her.

Think … think, she told herself sharply. It was only that she had found the hidden letter that she had put two and two together. No one else knew anything so why was she acting this way. Feeling certain that this was a fact and as far as she was aware no other evidence existed, she took another deep breath. Her heart's normal rhythm returned.

A sense of calm gave her the courage to go back inside and take her place at the table again. Observing the worried looks she received she hastily reassured them that she was fine, and that for some unknown reason the heat had temporarily overcome her. Cheered by their unanimous acceptance that this had indeed been the case, she once again participated in some light-hearted banter with Helen and Rita whilst attempting to keep at bay the constant disquiet she felt nagging away in the back of her mind.

She smiled across at John wishing she could have him to herself, to be wrapped in his loving arms and sharing kisses. Instead, she reached out and touched his hand.

"It's so good to see you. Did you receive my letter about the house and why I left London?"

She noted the blank look on his face and hurriedly continued.

"Doesn't matter we can talk about it another time."

John nodded, obviously distracted by more important matters pertaining to her Uncle. Helen and Rita were happily engaged in conversation with him and she reluctantly admitted to herself that this man seemed relaxed and pleasant. So much so, that she doubted her first thoughts of him as an estranged uncle.

After the waitress had cleared their table of crockery, Helen suggested it was time to make their way to the shops, at the same time enquiring of her Da, of his plans.

"I'll come back to the house this evening and stay overnight."

Lifting his eyebrows in mock consternation he continued, "That is if there is room for me."

Helen and Ria laughed unanimously.

"Of course there is."

"See you later then."

John kissed his wife and daughter, gave Rita a charming smile and then he and his companion let the women, still oblivious as to the reason he was in Durham, continue with their day out.

chapter 37

Later the same day

THE TWO MEN WALKED briskly along the path past the church building and on to the Bishop's Court. As they approached the front door, John Dalgleish spoke aloud.

"Long time since I met any of my family ... not sure what to expect ..."

With a slight shrug of his shoulders he took the metal knocker and let it fall against its anvil. The door shuddered as the noise echoed inside.

It seemed an eternity before there was an answer. The two men strained their ears to detect any signs of life and just as they decided to give up, the door opened to reveal a rather dishevelled young woman, obviously interrupted from some chore. "Yes?" she enquired in a breathless tone.

John Dalgleish introduced himself and asked if he could see his brother Robert.

The woman had a stupefied look on her face and peered more closely at him.

"Didn't know he had a brother ... still if that's what you say you had better come in."

She led them along a wide dark brown wood panelled hallway and opened a door to what was apparently a kind of waiting room. The room had fitted bookshelves to three walls, three armchairs and a table covered in a dark green tapestry cloth. On the mantel of a fireplace sat a loud ticking clock reminding any visitor of the passage of time.

"Father Robert is in poor health and has taken to his bed this day. The doctor will be back shortly, he is worried and wants Father Robert to go to hospital, but if you wait here I will see if he can see you, being as you are his brother."

The young woman closed the door on them and hurried away.

The men passed the time away by silently flicking through some of the books, both looking up with relief when she returned some five minutes later to inform them that she was to show them up to Robert's bedroom.

Considering the heat outside, the darkened room was surprisingly cool. Robert half sat up with plumped pillows to support him in his bed. John was aghast that the man he last saw in a hospital had deteriorated to such a degree. The man here was skeletal, almost bald and seemed to bear no resemblance to his former self. Fascinated he watched the two brothers slowly eye each other up. In a feeble voice, Robert spoke first.

"My, my ... you have lived well brother ... obviously food and drink have been your constant companions ... you must have doubled in size!"

Reaching out to shake hands and attempting to laugh, he waited for his brother's hand.

John Dalgleish placed his hand into his brother's trembling one.

"You're right of course, but from the look of you the same can't be said. How long have you got?"

"Nice greeting brother, no diplomacy as usual."

Robert succumbed to a violent fit of coughing leaving him spent and exhausted. John had difficulty hearing the raspy and faint words that he uttered.

"Any time now brother ... any time now."

His head fell against the pillow as he gasped.

"I thought you must have died years ago. Mama presumed that you had met your end at sea."

"Mm well I guess that suited her fine, first Ellen and Papa, then me, all of us out of her life."

"Jealousy and resentment my brother, is not good."

Robert peered into the gloom through his half-closed eyes. "Who have you got with you?"

John Dalgleish beckoned John to come closer as he looked his brother fully in the eye.

"We hoped you might be able to shine some light on his identity. He is the image of you as a young man, and to assist you more, he has a document that names his mother as Ellen Dalgleish. Now I remember things I would prefer not to, but I am asking you outright is this your son?"

A further attack of coughing rendered Robert speechless. It was pitiful to hear and see him vomiting blood onto his nightshirt. John moved forward fearing the old man would choke himself to death, but his brother did not move a muscle. John looked at him in amazement.

"We've got to help," he exclaimed.

John Dalgleish shook his head.

"I'm sorry John; we are too late to help him. We want him to help us. Even to his dying breath he will avoid facing the truth."

His voice was hard and cynical.

"I should have known he would rather leave this world, his reputation still intact, than own up to his sin."

Shocked John turned on him.

"He can't help being ill. My God, what is wrong with you have you no compassion. He is your brother no matter what."

"No, why should I have compassion for a man who had no respect for his dear wife Mary, who always had a kind word for everyone, and yet, he humiliated and scorned her, until he had crushed her very spirit. She probably died of a broken heart, and in shame that she was unable to protect her precious daughter. God alone knows how he fathered young Victoria."

Stopping to draw breath, he put his hands on John's shoulders, their eyes level.

"There may be no proof, but I would swear he caused my sister great heartbreak and shame. You, John, could even be the result of his forcing himself upon her."

The men fell silent as they both turned towards Robert His shallow breathing prevented any sign of movement and without the slight gurgle in the back of his throat every few seconds they would have deemed him dead.

"How do you suppose you would feel if you were in my shoes? He could give you peace of mind and tell you the truth. That would be the only thing you will ever have asked of him."

Unable to answer John swallowed back the bile in the back of his throat. His mind in turmoil he shook his head gloomily, fearful of disgrace and reproach. To be an adopted child was one thing to be a known bastard quite another. This man, could be his uncle, and the man in the bed his father. Convinced he had discovered the truth, his heart beat faster by the realisation that he and Ria had the same father meaning they were half brother and sister. His anguished eyes sought guidance from John Dalgleish. What would happen if Ria and Helen were privy to this knowledge? It could be ruination.

The rattle of death drew their attention to the corpse-like figure in the bed. Tears running down his face John fell to his knees and beseeched the dying man to tell him the truth. At the same time, John Dalgleish was demanding his brother to take this opportunity of doing one last honest thing before it was too late.

Robert's attempt to utter some words was lost in blood and vomit oozing from his mouth. Shaking his head he spluttered

"Don't know."

The two Johns watched in horror as he fought for a last breath; his lungs filled. Slowly and painfully, he drowned in his own stench.

Retching John rose from his knees and stumbled from the room looking for the bathroom. The last person who could have answered his question had taken leave of this world. What the hell did he mean by "don't know?"

As he vomited into the toilet pan, he struggled with his conflicting thoughts. Relief that it was ended and need not be faced again or that he should tell Ria what he believed to be the truth?

Back in Percy Square, amongst Helen and Rita's laughter as they prepared the evening meal, Ria answered the telephone and listened. Without a word she replaced the receiver and quietly went to her bedroom. She dreaded what John had to tell her.

chapter 38

January 1945

ALICE HELD HER ARMS out wide for Helen who was running towards her tears streaming down her cheeks. Clinging like a lost child re-united with a mother she broke into sobs as if her heart was breaking.

Holding Helen close, Alice was unable to prevent her own tears from falling into the beautiful deep auburn hair that tumbled on her shoulder. No words fitted their emotions, and both took comfort from their closeness and the knowledge mutual understanding existed. Oblivious to their surroundings the two women stood merged in sorrow.

Eventually, heartened by Helen's retrieved self-control, Alice gently guided her to the car she had borrowed and tucked a blanket around her legs. Before driving away she smiled warmly and took hold of Helen's cold hand.

"I packed a picnic so we can sit and take in the loveliness of the river before we go back to the house. It might help to have countryside and natural surroundings to strengthen us. What do you think?"

"It's a lovely idea, thank you Alice."

During the drive to the river the silence was companionable, the low sun radiating its anemic warmth upon the windscreen offering some relief from the brisk frosty air outside. It was true what Alice had said; already both women felt life was worth living. The trees and plants now appearing lifeless, lingered patiently for the right time to burst forth into bud and toss their blossom along with the soft breezes. There in front of their eyes the cycle of life showed how it worked and they sensed how fortunate they were to be part of the natural world.

Sitting side by side on a wooden bench located in a sunny sheltered spot, blankets around their legs, sandwiches resting between them, Alice and Helen relaxed pleased to be together again.

"When you are ready, tell me what happened. I want to understand then I can appreciate how awful it has been for you in the last weeks. Remember Helen I am here for you and will do anything I can to make life more agreeable. I love you as if you were my own daughter. When you are grieving I am grieving. I can't take your sadness away but I can offer comfort."

Alice gave a weak smile, her eyes full of compassion for the younger woman, the most endearing person she knew. Being unsure of Helen's state of mind unnerved her. She was contemplating the wisdom of disclosing her own grief, and would only do so if appropriate. The last thing wanted was to worsen the situation.

"I will. I have to confide in someone and who better than you Alice."

She unwrapped her sandwich, more for something to do than because she wanted to eat. Alice followed suit believing it to be a prop for both of them.

"Have you heard from Johnnie?" Helen asked biting into the sandwich.

Shaking her head Alice looked sad, "Not a thing for the last couple of weeks." Then optimistically, "Which is better than receiving a telegram I guess."

"I wish he was here for you and me. He is the one person we can depend on to be cheerful and logical. He was even able to remain bright while he recovered from his amputation. Look how he helped

Rita, she is a new person. He has a wonderful gift and everyone loves him."

"You are also much admired and loved by your friends," said Alice softly.

With a big sigh Helen smiled gratefully.

"I feel so alone. It probably sounds foolish to say, after I have been without my mother all my life, but I do miss her so much. If only I could have known her. Do you know I have only one photograph of her?"

She paused as she wiped away an escapee tear.

"I sometimes pine for her, even more than I do my Da. How can that be? You must think I am crazy."

"Not at all my darling. Sometimes we crave for those precious moments denied us. It is often beyond understanding."

Helen looked intently into Alice's eyes.

"I have never asked, but I believe you really do understand. You have had your fair share of sadness, you are a widow and your parents died when you were quite young."

Alice nodded pensively unwilling to interrupt Helen's chain of thoughts.

"You know Da changed so much. Or at least he did where I was concerned, and I do believe for Ria also. The more I reflect on when the change came about the more I conclude it had something to do with that man John Dalgleish. I wrote telling you how my Da and his new friend turned up in Durham? But, how or why is a mystery."

Glancing down into her lap Helen felt a wave of guilt wash over her.

"Maybe I shouldn't say, but he became downhearted, almost melancholy. His lovely broad smile disappeared. He turned down work, and he was passionate about that for as long as I can remember. When he told me he and Ria had decided to go back to London to make a proper home of his house I imagined they would rejuvenate their relationship and his unhappiness would soon be replaced with his old positive, lively self."

Holding a hand over her forehead and covering her eyes she moaned.

"Why? Why did I not visit? It might have made a difference. He must have been so desolate and I wasn't there for him. I can hardly bear to imagine his misery."

"You have to remember Helen, your Da did have Ria with him and she could have contacted you. She was his wife and you have trusted her. Surely she would have urged you to see him if she was worried."

"But that's the point Alice; I'm never going to know am I? Was she protecting me from something, or was she in conspiracy with him? I am well aware that Da often consumed a lot of alcohol, but Ria? No she rarely drank."

"So are you saying you didn't see each other after the meeting with John Dalgleish?"

"Exactly. Well, a few days later when they left Percy Square. Rita and I were excited about setting up a dress-making service. I was dashing around buying materials and patterns, finding shop premises and setting up a window display, while Rita designed and made dresses so we had stock. It took over my life. I loved it and before I knew it time had flown past. I did telephone once or twice. Either they were going out or Ria was on her own. At least that is what she told me. You have to understand, and I know you do Alice, I am accustomed to considerable lulls where my Da is concerned, so I wasn't troubled."

"Have you any idea how to contact John Dalgleish? He may have some ideas or answers."

"None at all." Helen's eyes blazed with hurt and anger. "I shouldn't have to look for answers Alice. He could never have loved me, not truly, or he would be here now telling me the truth."

Alice spoke thoughtfully. "Some people are afraid of the truth; their idea of love is to protect those they care for from anything that will cause pain or disappointment. I don't believe they see it as a deliberate untruth, or intentional. Then out of the blue an instance arises when it is no longer possible to keep the truth hidden. It is a crisis. They have to choose whether to tell and disappoint, hurt and enrage, or do nothing and keep it hidden forever."

"What could be so terrible, to kill yourself and take another with you? I can't believe my Da has ever committed any mortal sin that deserves a sentence of death."

Alice snuggled up and took Helen in her arms. "Neither do I darling, neither do I."

Falling into contemplative positions they continued to sit in silence.

Something Helen had said was nudging at her stored memories. It had provoked instant contrition.

Alice made two promises as a young woman and had broken neither. How could she know that she would have to battle with one of them all of her life, and the other would regularly turn up in her dreams.

Her mind drifted back through the years to a sunny afternoon when she had happily given up her virginity. She still suffered no remorse, she had loved him and he her. If he had kept his promises to write to her she could never know. Her parents had moved on to Australia and then New Zealand. It was there that her gorgeous baby boy, named John after his father, and no longer to be known as her son, became her brother.

She often dreamed of the father and cried in her sleep. As the years passed he was etched upon her memory like a castle in the air, a fantasy that would not wane.

Her stomach turned. 'Dalgleish that was the name. He had told her that day that it was that name on his Birth Certificate. He named his daughter Helen so similar to Ellen. Was that a conscious decision? Did he ever find out the truth about his original family? Questions, one after another, tumbled around in her head.

She sat staring into space. Could it be possible? Was Helen's father the young lover of her youth? Did she want to know? Her Mother's voice rang out in her head – "Really Alice you have such a wild imagination, you must learn to curb it."

Dragged from her stunned daydream she felt her arm being rubbed. She turned, an automatic smile on her face, as she returned to reality.

"Oh sorry darling, I was lost in thought."

Helen whispered. "Can we go home, I'm tired and cold."